The Black Rose

The Adventures of John Grey
Book Two

Frederick A. Read

A *Guaranteed* Book

First Published in 2008 by
Guaranteed Books

an imprint of Pendragon Press, Po Box 12, Maesteg
Mid Glamorgan, South Wales, CF34 0XG, UK

Copyright © 1996, 2008 by Frederick A Read
Cover Illustration Copyright © 2008 by
Steve Upham (www.screamingdreams.com)
This Edition Copyright © 2008 by Pendragon Press

All Rights Reserved, in Accordance with the
Copyright, Designs & Patents Act 1988

No part of this publication shall be reproduced in any form
without the express written consent of the publisher.

Frederick A Read asserts his moral right to be identified
as the owner of this work

ISBN 978 09554452 7 9

Designed and typeset by Christopher Teague

Printed and Bound in Wales by
Print Evolution

www.guaranteedbooks.co.uk

Author's Note

The history books for WWII denotes a small chapter that records an incident that could well be an epic sea battle between an Australian light cruiser and a heavily-armed merchant ship of the German *Kreigsmarine*.

On 19th November 1941, this cruiser met up with the infamous **Kormoran**. They must have been evenly matched because the outcome resulted in that they sunk each other at the same time.

There were a few survivors that managed to escape in lifeboats, from the Kormoran but none from the cruiser.

Dedication

In memory of the **HMAS Sydney** and her gallant crew who laid down their lives to put a stop to such predators of the world's sea-lanes. Their ship and lives were given to save countless thousands of future sailors.

Foreword

This book is arguably the prequel to the 'Adventure' series, in that Captain Von Meir of the German Q ship the MV *Schelzwig*, bore a striking resemblance to the 'Adventure' series character John Grey.

The *Schlezwig* and the *Brooklea* are one, with the unfortunate link that certain crew-members who survived from the *Schezwig*, later became the the masters of the *Brooklea*.

When John Grey stepped on board the *Brooklea* for the first time, he was a spectre to his superiors on board, which was a catalyst for several incidents that was perpetrated agains him. John Grey experienced the backlash of Captain Von Meir's cruel treatment of Trewarthy, Cresswell and others whilst holding them captive.

The story related within, tells about a dashing and very daring young German Navy officer who turned out to be the scourge of the Allied Navies during WW 2, and proved to be a deadly predator and killer of any unsuspecting merchant ships that sailed into his waters.

His impeccable naval career was turned upside down when he was forced to pander to the dreaded martinets who latched onto him and blighted everything he touched.

Von Meir was forced to turn pirate to subsidise his clandestine operations, and in doing so became the worlds' public enemy No1. This meant that despite his honourable and heroic battles against his enemies, the Royal Navy and other allied navies, he was cast as a 'war criminal, with nowhere to hide or anybody to give him succour.

This was because his ship was turned into a surface raider called a Q ship, sailing under different flags, pretended to be what she was not. In fact she was packed with enough fire power to sink many a warship crossing her sealane.

When the tides and fortunes of the war turned against the German Nazi regime, and the British and Allies were beginning to get the upper hand, no so-called 'neutral' country that was an erstwhile friend of the German Nazi protocol, could be seen to help them any further, more so than the Itailans who not only defected to the Allies but also surrendered to them.

Thus Von Meir's war efforts for his homeland were short lived, and he was to suffer the consequences of 'acting on orders' as dictated by his ultimate predators, the worlds most hated outfit in anybodies war machine, Germany's **GESTAPO.**

Chapters

I	*Obey Orders*	1
II	*Loaded*	11
III	*Friends*	28
IV	*First Time*	44
V	*Calypso Queen*	67
VI	Jezebels	76
VII	*Corkscrews*	91
VIII	*Little Balls*	102
IX	*Spanish Drum*	113
X	*Pot People*	137
XI	*Tanned Skin*	147
XII	*Little Children*	160
XIII	*A New Dress*	181
XIV	*Chipolatas*	184
XV	*Crabs*	201
XVI	*In the Meantime*	208
XVII	*Single Again*	229
XVIII	*Confusion*	250
XIX	*Weaving*	257
XX	*Hands Up*	273
XXI	*Faces*	277

Chapter I
Obey Orders

Hans Otto Von Meir stood to attention as the admiral spoke harshly to him for several minutes.

"You have been chosen to undertake a special operation with myself as your exclusive contact and from whom your orders will come. You will obey only my orders from only my command centre, do you understand?" the admiral spoke in a guttural tone of voice.

"Just because you are a Von Meir, will not entitle you to any special privileges or treatment. In fact, because you are my son, you will be singled out even more. It is for this reason I have sent for you to prepare you for your special orders and the command you will be taking up."

"Admiral! You only have to command." Otto said quietly as he looked up at his craggy faced father, who wore several coloured rows of war medals and the regalia of a Grand Admiral of the German Kriegsmarine. The Admiral looked down on his youngest son, and although Otto was a fresh faced twenty-three years old, it belied his strength of character, and his expertise in maritime and tactical skills enabled him to command such a rank in the German Navy. His black hair swept back revealed the beginnings of a widows' peak, and his hooked nose gave him the look of a hawk.

"You have made an old admiral very happy, when he knows that his son will carry on the great tradition of the Von Meirs." the admiral said softly as he put a huge arm around his son and embraced him strongly.

"But father. What is it I'm about to do that has you so fearful, and dare I say so hush hush about?" Otto asked smoothing his long black hair back over his head again.

The admiral let go of his son and gave him a deep frown and a troubled look on his face.

The Black Rose

"Otto! What you are about to undertake with this new command of yours, will be out of normal, shall we say 'Naval protocol or Operations'.

This mission is so special that not even our Fuhrer and his high command even knows about it, and if they did they would not grant its resources. That is why you will be required to wear the Mercantile marine uniform and command a merchant vessel for the duration of your command." the admiral said quietly for fear of people listening. Then went on to explain in greater detail the rest of the secret plans that were to be carried out.

"From what I can deduce father, we would gain a tremendous advantage against our old traditional but fine sea enemy, the British Royal Navy." Otto replied incredulously.

"Indeed Otto! But that is for the future, and what we anticipate if it comes to such an outcome." the admiral rejoined, placing his arm around his son again.

"Let's go and see your new command. Even though she's gone through a major restructure, she's a ship you will no doubt be very familiar with." he added, as he ushered his son out of the building and into an awaiting black limousine.

The car made its way through the crowded dockyard and came to a barbed wire enclosed building, to be met by two burly men wielding rifles, and demanding to see their identity papers. Once the guards were happy, the limousine moved silently into a long building, to stop at a heavy chain linked fence that marked the end of the dock and a big drop into an enclosed dry dock.

"Here we are! Doesn't she look good Otto?" the admiral asked proudly.

"Your Uncle Heinz donated it to our cause. What do you think of her?"

Otto stood looking down at this much altered but still recognisable ship with amazement.

The Black Rose

"Why it's the old *Schlezwig*. I hadn't realised she was as long as that." Otto said in amazement as he took in several of her new features.

"No Otto! She's just been extended with two 15metre sections either end of her midships superstructure. You will understand the various alterations such as her false funnel and false hull later." the admiral said gleefully.

"But what are those bulges with large holes on both sides of her hull?"

"Those are 50 cm discharge ports for the torpedo tubes you can see. They've got closing outer doors on them when not in use, just like a submarine has. The false hull will maintain your streamlined shape and help with your speed. Also if you notice, we've put a twin 105mm gun turret fore and aft of your main superstructure. Both sets of masts can be unshipped at any time and be positioned to fit your current profile, but the guns will be on special lifts to take them up onto the deck when required, and lowered below decks again when not in use. Again we've mounted several heavy machine guns that will be disguised as stanchions that seem to prop up your promenade deck. And if you look at the overly large lifeboats, they disguise the multi barrel rocket launchers. You will have a 50mm armour belt around your bridge area and 100mm around your gun turrets, and your fuel tanks have been enlarged. Your cargo space will be adapted to take extra fuel, torpedoes and a small workshop for running repairs. Last but by no means least, you will be fitted with a special mine launcher rack on your poop deck, disguised as the after crews quarters. In other words dear Otto, you will have a floating fortress all of your own, which should be more than a match for anything, short of any cruiser, the British may send your way.

"Torpedoes and guns that look more at home on a destroyer. What do you intend me do with this armed merchantman admiral. Fight the entire British Navy with it?" Otto asked with surprise as he recognised the formidable shapes of the powerful guns being raised and lowered on their hoists.

"Not quite, but near enough Otto. Come aboard and take a good look around her. She's still got her good looks and her wonderfully powerful engines, that we've managed to refurbish."

"Has she indeed. Does she still have her top speed?"

"Otto! You had better believe it. She needs to be as swift as your reputation, but come and see for yourself, as this will be the ace up your sleeve, so to speak." The admiral insisted as he led the way down into the bowels of the ship.

The two officers roamed over the vessel, dodging the welders flying sparks of metal, and men moving things all around the place, with Otto asking questions about certain features he had noticed.

"If this was an ordinary merchant vessel, I can understand what level of crew you'll be giving me to man it. But from what I've seen, I'd expect at least a further 75 men, admiral."

"The officers you'll meet this evening, and the men in about two days. We were inundated with a flood of volunteers for your mission, but I have managed to select your crew of around 180."

"It looks like your impeccable organisation and planning skills have gone into full steam ahead this time Father. I wonder what the Furher would say about the wanton use of all the resources you have tapped into. Maybe I've learned a few tricks from you over the past few years, but this is one major tour de force."

The admiral scowled and whispered into his son's ear.

"I've told you Otto! This is strictly a covert operation with a special force of only three special ships to support our grey wolves already out at sea and on station. There are other special ships that will be sent out as surface raiders but they're

The Black Rose

not of our concern, so don't you dare go against your orders."

"And that is?"

"Keep shtum! Obey only my command unit orders, and the special documentation that I shall be issuing you with."

Otto sighed but acknowledged his father's wishes.

"I still await your command, admiral." Otto said quickly as he clicked his heels.

"That's another thing Otto! You will see to it that from now on, all of you will have to dispense with tradition and think civvy. As of tomorrow morning, you will be dressed as a merchant navy sea captain, and the rest of the crew dressed according to the role they will be needed for. So be very careful of instinctive mannerisms Otto."

"Admiral! It seems something dangerous is brewing. A disguised merchant ship with a pretend crew? Is this something to do with this phoney war with the British, or are we really at war with them? Better still, are you just playing one of your silly games again?"

The admiral looked at his son with a piercing glare.

"Otto! You of all people should know by know, I don't play games. Yes we are really at war against the might of the British Navy. But this is going to be a deadly but heroic operation that you have the privilege to take command of. So just be grateful for that. And besides its about time you earned your pay and promotion to Frigate Captain." he snorted indignantly.

"A Lieutenant Commander (Lt. Cdr) has only two and a half gold rings on his sleeve, whereas a sea captain has four gold rings. If I'm to become a four ring captain albeit four wavy rings, let's hope I get the Deutchmarks to match the rank, Admiral." Otto replied testily to see if his father took the bait.

"You've got a deal Otto, although God knows what you intend spending it all on! Now let's get back to my HQ to meet the rest of your officers. I have had them specially picked and billeted there for a few days now." The admiral grunted his acceptance, as the two returned to the insignificant looking office block that belied its contents and activities.

"Good afternoon gentlemen!" the admiral greeted the collection of officers breezily, with Otto by his side.

"No! Salute in the traditional manner! I'll have no silly 45 degree arm waving, and clicking of heels when I'm around. From now on, all of you are civilian merchant marine officers." the admiral rebuked the officers sharply, then introduced Otto to them as their new commanding officer.

"Good evening Captain von Meir!" the officers responded as they introduced themselves.

"Lt.Cdr Victor Schenk! We meet and sail together again! You'll be my 1st Lt, but will be called the First Mate." Otto greeted with a handshake.

"Yes Captain! Thank you for selecting me." Schenk said stiffly but was put at his ease with a smile from Meir.

"Not at all Victor! It will be just like old times together on the '*Hipper*'. Proud to have you aboard." He replied as another officer was recognised by him.

"Engineer Lt. Richard Emst! It's nice to meet you too. You'll be my Chief Engineer, like you were on the *Emsden*."

"Lt. Klinshoff. Glad you made it. You'll be my 2nd Mate, but as I know of your brilliant chart work, you'll also be my Navigator."

"Lt Kirkmiester. I haven't seen you for at least a year. As I know and can trust you, I'll make you my 3rd Mate." Otto said cheerfully as he accepted the pledged service offered by each and every one of them.

The admiral looked at his son in action with great satisfaction and a large smile greeted Otto's sideways look he gave his father.

"Well, it looks as if the party has started gentlemen. This old admiral will get out of your way for you all to get to know each other again. There's a double magnum of champagne on

The Black Rose

my desk and just shout for the steward if you need food as well. I must be off as I have some Admiral duties to see to." The admiral stated as he left but signalled Otto to follow him to the door.

"Tonight is party time. But there's a special pack of documentation for you to wade through with your officers before I see you all in my office again in the morning at 0800. Remember that everybody is to wear their new uniforms according to their rank and trade. You're new four gold ring uniform will be sent to your quarters by my steward." the admiral whispered then returned Otto's salute as he left.

Meir returned to his group of officers and proceeded to wade through the documentation all through the evening, as the champagne flowed and the food was eaten, before Otto called a halt for the night.

"Gentlemen! It is time to get organised for our meeting with Admiral Meir at 0800 sharp. Use your time carefully, and don't forget to wear your new Merchant Navy uniforms. But remember this, naval tradition prevails, not Nazi code. Be there!" Meir said tersely but with a smile on his face to sweeten the medicine the officers were about to swallow.

"Captain Meir!" came a whispered voice in the darkened cabin.

Meir woke immediately and went to grab his sword that was hanging up on the end of his bed.

"Who is there? Reveal yourself before I run you through with a yard of cold steel." Meir growled.

"It's me Captain! I'm the Admiral's steward, Petty Officer Winkler," the man said with alarm

"Winkler? I thought you retired from my fathers service a few years ago. It doesn't matter anyway, but what is it you want?"

"It's 0630 Captain. The admiral has sent me to look after

The Black Rose

you now, so I've brought you some breakfast and your new uniform."

"Very good steward. Put them on the table and come back in one hour!" Meir replied as he yawned and got out of his bunk to eat his meal and prepare himself for his day.

The steward knocked the door as ordered

"Captain I have the admirals staff car waiting for you."

"Well done as usual Winkler. You may live to regret taking on your new role, but in the meantime take my bags and put them in the back of the car and wait for me there."

"Aye aye captain. But the admiral has ordered me to clear your room and make sure all of your personal belongings remain behind in this suitcase he has given me."

"Very well steward, but you will to see it that all my officers share the same experience. Any quibbling from them report them to me, understand?"

"Perfectly, Captain!" Winkler replied with a nod of his head and started to go through the bags, fishing out items deemed as 'confiscated for the duration'.

Meir climbed out of the staff car and went towards the HQ building as Winkler carried a much-reduced collection of bags with him.

"Good morning Captain Meir! Meet Admiral Volginen." Admiral Meir announced as his son came through the office door and saw a collection of officers including his own, and this slight stature of the man standing before him looking at him behind a neatly trimmed beard.

"Admiral Volginen! Pleased to meet you! I'm one of your ardent followers of your naval tactics and strategic planning." Meir said cheerfully as he saluted the man.

"Yes indeed you are young Otto. You are also a chip off your old man's block; at least you show what we were like when we were your age. That is why we've decided that you would be the best man for the job and head our operations."

The Black Rose

Volginen said amiably and indicated him to sit down with them instead of in among the rest of the officers.

Admiral Meir commenced his conference but shortly handed it over to Volnigen who spoke for a while before announcing that everybody was to see a short film, in order to emphasise the role that the ship *Schlezwig* will undertake.

The half-hour film was followed by a refreshment break and a session of questions from the officers and elicited answers from the two admirals before the conference finally ended.

"What leave will we have before sailing sir?" Meir asked on behalf of his officers.

"None! Nobody is to step outside the perimeter of the HQ. Any person caught disobeying this order will be shot. The ship sails at 0700 the day after tomorrow." The admiral replied sharply and glowered at any officer who dared to give nazi salutes.

The two admirals left the hushed room as Otto took over the proceedings.

"We had better go over the ships drawings and individual job performances now, just so there can be no mistake as to who does what and when. I want each and every one of you to be fully conversant with your role on board, as you will be relaying it to your senior rates tomorrow. I will not tolerate any foul-ups, cock-ups, excuses or failure to perform your duties due to ignorance." Meir threatened as he looked fiercely at the upturned faces of the officers and paused for a moment, which seemed to silence the officers to a deathly hush.

"Just so that you fully understand what I'm saying. I wish to make it perfectly clear and with no doubt in any officers mind, that any officer, or anybody else on board, failing to perform his duty or obey orders that I have commanded him to carry out, will be instantly shot. That is a promise. Do I make myself clear?"

"Aye captain!" the officers replied promptly and eagerly, as each stood up and saluted their captain in a gesture of obedience.

"Very good gentlemen. Welcome aboard. Now lets get on with this strange craft of ours. It appears to have lots of tricks to perform." Meir said in a more conciliatory tone, as he led the way out of the room.

Chapter II
Loaded

"**O**fficers and men mustered Captain." Schenk reported as he saluted Meir, who stepped out of the staff car, with Winkler in attendance.

"Yes, I can see its pouring down, so stop fussing steward." Meir said angrily to the steward and returned Schenks salute.

"If the men are standing in the rain without overcoats, then so shall I." Meir scolded, as he rejected the proffered raincoat. Meir, at only 170 cm (5ft 6inches) tall was dwarfed alongside Schenk, and even smaller than most of the men standing in three rows, as he approached them.

"Ships company, Atten-shun!" a senior rate barked, which prompted a smart military movement from the body of men.

Meir walked slowly along the front rank of the men accompanied by Schenk, looking into their rain soaked faces, when somebody from the back moaned about getting soaking wet, but was instantly rebuked by the same senior rating.

"Silence that man! You're supposed to get wet, you've joined the bloody navy haven't you?"

Meir caught the reply and turned to Schenk

"That's what I want to hear first mate." he said gleefully, as he finished his inspection and turned to address the men.

"Right then men! Listen up, I shall say this only the one time. The Kriegsmarine is owned and run by the Grand Admirals, but this ship is mine, to run it as only I see fit. If any of you are not man enough to face our uncertain future and fate, then he may leave now. No discipline will be taken if he does!" Meir paused long enough to see if there were any takers to his offer.

"No takers? Good! Because from now on, you'll be expected to do the impossible, but leave the miracles to me. Any man not giving me his best will be swimming home, suffering from lead poisoning in his left ear-hole. Is that understood?" he challenged in a booming voice.

To a man, they all shouted loudly, "Yes sir!"

"Very good men! Get yourselves on board and be ready to sail in one hour." he announced then turned to Schenk.

"First Mate. Dismiss the crew and have the officers mustered in the passenger lounge. I'll be along in about ten minutes."

"Aye Aye captain!" Schenk replied automatically, then saluted and left to carry out his orders.

"Winkler! Take my bags aboard and get yourself dried off. I shall be wanting hot coffee for myself and the officers in ten minutes."

"Aye captain." Winkler grunted as he picked up an armful of baggage and staggered across the narrow gangway.

Meir walked along the dockside for the full length of the ship, looking closely at her before he was satisfied with himself, and crossed the gangway to be met by the quartermaster (QM).

"Don't you dare pipe me aboard QM. This is supposed to be a merchantman" Meirs growled.

The QM dropped his 'Bosun's Call' in amazement and replied meekly.

"Aye Aye captain!" he replied in a loud voice as he gave the customary salute, which Meir sighed at, but returned with equal smartness.

"Morning Gentlemen! I hope you've had your hot coffee?" Meir asked as he entered the old passengers lounge.

"Yes captain, much appreciated." the officers responded with smiles and lifted their cups as a mock toast to their captain.

Meir smiled back them and drank his own cup as offered by Schenk.

"As of now, we cease to exist, except through Admirals Meir, Volingen and Horstenitz and their HQ. They will visit me in about fifteen minutes time to give me my orders. First mate, you will accompany me. For the rest of you, I shall expect you all to have yourselves and your departments fully 'buttoned up' for when we sail.

After that it will be too late and you can look out for the consequences if you have failed to do so." he announced, and then took the time to speak with each officer with his immediate orders, obtaining nods or salutes as their acknowledgements.

"Very good then gentlemen! I wish you all a good voyage and good luck in our adventures now, as this will probably be our last time together for some time to come." he concluded, as he saluted his officers and left with Schenk to meet the admirals.

"Otto! You ready for sea then?" Admiral Meir asked gently as he returned his sons salute.

"Yes father. Just give me my charts and sealed orders and we're off!"

"That's the spirit Otto!" Volingen said softly as he handed a large sack over to Schenk.

"You are our best man by far, so don't let us down. Be just like a hawk, ruthless and fearless."

"We'll expect to see you back here in about 3 months, if all goes well. Other than that, there are special instructions in the bag for other occasions. Remember Otto. You will observe merchant ship protocol and behaviour at all times, but we expect you to protect our friends when you're with them. They are of paramount importance, not you." Admiral Meir added.

"I understand father. Just let our enemy come near me and I'll give him a bloody nose." Meir said eagerly."

"Once you've got clear of national territorial waters, we can't be seen to help you. You will be very much on your own." Volingen stated.

"It's all in your communications orders Otto! Be advised that there are other ships around you that have already been

The Black Rose

assigned for the type of duty you are about to perform. You will be given their profiles to help your recognition of them, as they will have of yours. Each of you will be operating independantly, and will be given separate operational instructions. As I've said, it's all in your orders anyway." Admiral Meir interrupted.

Meir took in the final briefings from the admirals then shook their hands before he left them on the dockside and followed Schenk back onto the ship again.

"First Mate! Remove the gangway. Get ready to slip." Meir ordered as he beckoned a sailor to grab the heavy bag and follow him to the bridge.

"Obey telegraphs! Obey the helm! Single up!" Meir ordered swiftly as he arrived onto the bridge, going onto the bridge wing.

He looked down the ships side and to the jetty and saw the two admirals waving to him.

Meir looked at the four new and shining gold rings on his sleeve, and grinned as he raised his arm to them, returning their wave.

"Good luck and good hunting Otto!" he heard them shout as he saluted back and continued to do what captains of all ships do.

"Let go aft! Starboard 15! Slow astern port. Fenders at the ready port bow!" Meir snapped as he saw his port bow almost meet the concrete and stone jetty.

The ship started to float away backwards and clear from the jetty.

"Let go for'ard! Midships. Stop port." he ordered, as the ship was now clear and free.

"Starboard 15. Half ahead port, full asterm starboard!" Which brought the ship almost right around to point towards the harbour entrance.

"Stop together. Midships. " he ordered agan, as he rattled them off.

The Black Rose

"Wheel midships!" the helmsman reported.

"Slow ahead together. Tell the engine room to set revs for 8 knots. Steer 020. Keep well to port of the middle channel buoys. I want to see a straight line of wake behind me, understand?"

"Aye aye Captain!" the Bosun answered.

The ship moved slowly and steadily out through the harbour entrance, as Meir navigated his ship out of the Hamburg dock complex and into the main river course.

Meir was not satisfied with this off-hand response from his bridge crew, and decided that it was time to impose his personal stamp on this voyage. He was renowned for his ruthless and abrupt manner, and made it quite clear from his orders or his actions that he was to be obeyed at all times.

"I want all my orders repeated back to me, then report them having carried out those orders." Meir said loudly to everybody on the bridge.

"Officer of the watch! Tell the engine room to reduce the smoke emissions by at least 50%. I can't see a ruddy thing up here."

The officer of the watch repeated his orders, and then reported them done.

"Very good Lieutenant Kirkmeister! That's exactly how its done. That's why I've chosen you as my 3rd Mate." Meir purred, as he took more bearing fixes with his compass that was mounted on a gymbal.

"Port 10. Steer 275."

"Ten of port wheel on, and to steer 275. Sir!" the Bosun replied evenly.

"Navigator! We have just passed the outer dock lighthouse, approx 1000metres to our starboard. I want to maintain this transit bearing before I need to alter course onto that bearing towards Cuxhaven. Lay in a course from that point to Rooghorn

The Black Rose

Island then down to the main harbour lighthouse at Wilhelmshaven. Report to me when you have reached that point at Rooghorn." Meir said placidly to him, then looked around to find Schenk looking out to sea through his binoculars.

"First mate. Secure from sea stations, and set cruise watches. Get the galley flashed up and the men fed. I want a ships muster on the after cargo deck at 1100hrs. All officers to wear sidearm. See to it!"

"Aye Captain!" Schenk responded quickly as Meir stepped into his bridge cabin, shutting the door quietly behind him.

"Here's some breakfast for you Captain." Winkler greeted as he appeared up out of a hatchway carrying a silver tray of food, taking Meir by surprise.

"Where have you just sprung from Winkler?" he gasped.

"You've got a special escape ladder and hatchway that takes you down into your day cabin. I'm the only person to use it apart from yourself!" Winkler said slowly.

"Well make sure it stays that way Winkler." Meir said quickly as he started to strip off his still wet uniform.

"I've put your 'Steaming Gear' out onto your bunk. But get some food down you first." Winkler said dryly and started to potter around whilst Meir ate his food.

"The men are keen to prove themselves, and there's a good spirit between them, not like it was on the *Danzigger*." Winkler volunteered.

"Thank you for your, shall we say, inside information, Winkler. If you can serve me as well as you apparently did the Admiral, then I'll see that you retire a rich man if not a famous one. Remember, you address me in military terms and not as you have done in the past." Meir said softly as he started to appreciate his father's gesture of lending him, his old and trusted manservant.

Winkler looked at Meir, took off his glasses and putting them into his top pocket, gave Meir a big smile.

The Black Rose

"Captain. I've known you as a boy, and watched you rise up through the officer corps to reach your present rank. If you're as good as your father was at his age, with his ships company, then I'll sleep easy in my bunk." Winkler said almost condescendingly.

"Thank you for your history lesson Winkler! I'm sure that we'll get along fine, just as long as you do any duty that is required. And for you specially, as that will be above and beyond all other men on board." Meir said candidly, and then concluded by saying.

"We will not ever speak of this conversation, or any future ones that we may have. Just get used to being an ordinary Petty Officer Steward from now on, as I will not be offering you any special treatment just because you are my father's manservant on loan to me. Do you get my drift steward?"

"Aye captain! So it shall be!" Winkler nodded and took Meirs' wet clothing away with him back down the hatch again.

Meir heard a constant knocking on his door and shouted his command for the unknown person to enter.

"Captain. We've arrived at the next point on our chart, where you intend a change of course."

"Very good navigator. Come and show me what course you recommend that I should take." He ordered, as he ushered the navigator out onto the bridge.

"Yes, that's a good course on this leg, which should take us about another 2 hours to transit. But I want to transit a certain part of the coastline off Sandeshaven before I swing north for my approach to Wilhelmshaven." Meir agreed, as the navigator looked puzzled.

"If you intend making a U turn, how far south on that course are we going?"

"Lay a course from the end of this one, but take tidal changes and local shoaling into consideration as we're supposed to be a deep draughed merchantman. Let me know

The Black Rose

when we're on the new course you've just pencilled in!" Meir ordered quietly.

"Aye aye sir!" the navigator replied respectfully.

"Lt. Kirkmeister!" Meir called, but there was no reply.

"Who's officer of the watch?" he asked angrily to the helmsman.

"Me. I am Captain." a voice answered from the starboard bridge wing.

"Whoever you are you'd better show yourself right now!" Meir shouted.

"4th Mate and Gunnery Officer Lt. Biederman! Captain." the luckless officer stuttered as he stood in front of Meir.

"What is it you find interesting out on the bridge wing? Have you got something else to do with your time other than look after this bridge as your place of duty?" Meir snarled and looked at the young officer who was looking very pale.

"It's my first real trip to sea, captain. I had to use the 'pig's ear' for a moment." Beidermann gasped as he held his hand over his mouth and spewed into it, sending bits of food spraying out from between his fingers.

"You're first trip to sea and you're holding a Lieutenants rank?" Meir asked incredulously, but decided to not wait for an answer.

"That's no excuse for being absent from your post Lieutenant. I will not tolerate anybody, no matter who they are and especially one of my officers, being absent without good reason. Being seasick is not one of them." Meir hissed, and sneered at the sight of the man in front of him.

"2nd Mate!" Meir shouted over to the chart table.

"Yes Captain!" Klinshoff breathed, as he appeared swiftly at Meir's side.

"Take over this watch. Bosun's Mate! Escort Lt. Biederman below to the sickbay for treatment then have him report to me immediately afterwards."

The Black Rose

The rating acted immediately and hustled the luckless officer off the bridge.

"My apologies for a double watch 2nd Mate, but you can thank your friend for that. See to my previous orders as well!" Meir said in a calmer tone of voice then left the bridge.

"Captain. It's 1050 sir!" Schenk called through Meir's bridge cabin doorway.

"I have the men mustered as ordered, sir!"

"Very good 1st Mate. Come with me to my day cabin. Send for the Bosun, and tell him to bring his big brown book with him."

Schenk turned and requested Klinshoff to summons the Bosun, before he followed Meir down the bridge ladder into the main officers quarters and onto the after cargo deck.

"Ships company, atten-shun!" the Bosun shouted to the gathered men.

Meir stood on the cargo hatchway with the big brown book in his hands, and flanked by Schenk and all the other officers.
Meir read out the ARTICLES OF WAR and ships standing orders to the men, who started to become restless due to the lengthy sermon that was exacted upon them.

Meir also read out the RIOT ACT, and reminded everybody that as their country was at war, no tolerance would be allowed to any persons present who disobeys the said acts or goes against the express orders of the captain and officers of the ship.

"I have now concluded my duty of informing you all on the ARTICLES OF WAR etc. So nobody can say they have not been incorporated within those articles, nor have not been told about them. Carry on with your duties. Dismiss the men Bosun! First Mate! Officers to muster in the passenger lounge in two minutes." He concluded, as he left with the other officers following along behind him.

"Crew Diss-Miss" the Bosun shouted in parade ground fashion.

Meir waited until the officers arrived in the passenger lounge before dismissing the stewards from the compartment.

"Whilst I know every old or new plate, rivet and weld this ship is made from, and they are proving to be of typical German workmanship, that I cannot say the same about the officers currently manning her." Meir said angrily as he looked around at the puzzled faces before him.

"I have had to relieve one of your number from his duties, which makes it very sad for me, because from what I've read from all your Service Certificates, everybody here is supposed to be a professional. How wrong you have proved me in that assumption.

"4th Mate Lt. Beiderman was found to be absent from his post, namely that of Officer of the Watch (OOW) on the bridge. He was given that very responsible duty so that whilst the rest of us can relax, no harm can befall us when we do.

"If that is the example you set, then it seems that I cannot rely or trust any of you to help me run this ship for the purpose it was sent to sea for." Meir said as he looked for any sign of reaction from the officers.

"I have the principle that every man is allowed just one mistake whilst I'm in command. Therefore, as Beiderman has just made his, and as he is one of you, it now means that his mistake is also yours. For Beiderman has made your collective mistake, and it's he that you should give thanks to. You are Naval officers, trained to set example and leadership to the crew who rely upon you to keep them as safe as possible. From now on I will not tolerate any more such mistakes, misjudgements or whatever else you care to label it, from my officers. No sir! The next culprit will receive the punishment and you all know what it entails. This is my first and final warning so take special note of what I said." Meir concluded

The Black Rose

as he left the officers in stunned silence and for them to have lunch.

"Captain! It's time to take a check bearing before altering onto our new course." Klinshoff stated as he met Meir coming out of his day cabin.

"Very good Navigator!" Meir said quietly as he brushed his hair back off his forehead and looked at his watch.

"Good timing at this speed. Let's go!" Meir replied as he sprinted up the steep steel ladders onto the bridge.

"Officer of the Watch! Get the men to harbour stations in 30 minutes." Meir ordered, as he went over to the chart table.

"Navigator. Check these bearings one more time and take two more bearing fixes as we turn. Call them out to me in true bearings."

Both men repeated their orders back, which pleased Meir, as he took on a more cheerful countenance.

"We have an evening in Wilhelmshaven to look forward to men! No leave, but plenty of good food and schnapps!" Meir announced to the bridge crew, who gave a cheer in response, as the ship neared its destination.

"Officer of the Watch! I've changed my mind. Get the crew to harbour stations now, if you please." Meir ordered.

"Harbour stations! Harbour stations! Special duty men close up." came the announcement over the ships tannoy system.

Meir eased his ship into the narrow naval base entrance and got ready for a berthing that he was not too familiar with.

"Stop engines. Port 20!"

"20 of port wheel on! Motor telegraphs ready." A gruff voice replied, which Meir guessed that it was the Bosun back at the wheel again.

"Very good Bosun! Midships, slow ahead both!" Meir orders came thick and fast as he stood in the bridge wing, and

The Black Rose

had his ship steered neatly alongside his allocated berth behind a raft of submarines.

The ship gave a slight bump as it pressed against the bamboo and rope fenders, as a signal that they had arrived.

"Secure both ends. Finished with motors. Fall out from harbour stations First Mate." Meir ordered quickly as he went down the bridge ladder towards the gangway that was being lowered onto the ship from a dockside crane.

"I shall be back in about four hours. Get all hands organised into four working parties, and ready to receive our cargo."

"Aye aye sir!" Schenk responded with a nod instead of a salute.

"Good evening Captain!" a Commodore greeted Meir as he stepped off the gangway.

"Good evening Commodore Becks! We meet again. Made good timing on my last tack." Meir started to explain but was put at ease by Becks who ushered him into an awaiting staff car.

"My men will store your ship and get your cargo put exactly right so that you can have a good trim. Come Captain Meir, we have a few guests for you to meet."

Meir followed Becks into a well kept building, which he always took for granted as a regular military navy man as opposed to the scruffy buildings he'd used as a merchantman. He looked around at the various pictures of famous officers, ships and other mementoes, as he entered a large hall full of scruffily dressed officers.

"Gentlemen! This is Captain Hans Otto Von Meir. He will be your support and supply master." Becks announced as the officers stood up and clapped him.

Becks introduced each officer in turn, although Meir knew quite a few of them, and spoke to them as he re-met them.

"Now that's over, we can now get down to business." Becks stated, as he lorded over the group of men and proceeded to go through certain plans, tactics, code words, phrases,

The Black Rose

communication arrangements, and a myriad of other topics, that took over three hours to get through.

"Commodore! I must be getting back as I'm due to sail within two hours. Maybe you can have the rest of this planning during my next phase of operations." Meir stated and started to leave.

"Captain. You're too eager to get to work again. No sense going off without your set of documents. Besides, there's no rush for you to leave just yet." Becks chided mildly.

"And anyway, there's a special person due here within the hour. It will be your duty to meet him, as he is these officers head of operations. Mine is only subterfuge and responsible for loading you up with the right cargo and papers."

"Admiral Horstenitz! You've come at last!" the officers cheered as they saw their boss come sauntering through the door.

"Evening Becks!" Horstenitz greeted and looked at Meir.

"You must be Admiral Meir's son Otto! Pleased to meet you."

Meir saluted but shook Horstenitz's offered hand.

"Your father and I went to naval college together. We've got together for this show, but I understand you've got a special ship that will be my U-boats depot ship whilst at sea! Good for you! I need someone capable of keeping these reprobates of mine in order."

The U-boat officers jeered and whistled at the reference of reprobates.

Meir smiled at the apparent camaraderie between the admiral and his officers, but declined to answer him.

"For now, you will have six of my grey wolves to cater for Otto. But if things go to plan then you can add another 12 for your area. As you can see!" Horstenitz began as he unrolled a large sea chart out and pinned it onto the wall behind them.

"Each area, or chunk of Atlantic, has an emblem with its appropriate code name as shown. This one is the Orchid, this one is the Daffodil, and so on. The patrol area allocated to you and to supply our friends is this one here that has its symbol of a rose, but will bear the codename of '*THE BLACK ROSE*'. Also for you to know and for future reference, wherever area you have been allocated to, you will keep your codename at all times.

"For your first assignment you will need a base to operate from, so as you can see from the charts, we have a special forward base built on the West coast of Ireland that you will use and get your supplies from.

"There are three other such vessels already using this base, and each of you will be operating totally independantly, and will not even be allowed to know of each others existence or movements.

"You will observe radio silence, but will keep a 24hour radio watch for signal traffic. Our friends will have a special frequency to contact you on, to tell you what stores or support they need. The reason for that is because you will rendezvous (R/V) with each boat in turn as you make your outward leg.

"If for some reason you miss one or cannot get in contact with him, you will continue to the end of your run and get him on the way back. You may send your own supply replenishment signal when you're in sight of mainland Ireland again.

"You have your orders from your own HQ command, so these are mainly a supplement to them. When you get to your forward base, you'll find more special operational orders from both sources. I wish you luck Otto!" the admiral concluded.

Meir was taken to a side office and given his false papers, ship manifesto, a collection of ships photographs, their names and brief history to each one.

"You will be disguising your ship as any one of these you see belonging to our friends in the Castle Line, and you will be given the stores to effect these changes to whatever ship would be appropriate, plus of course some items of stores that you'll appreciate when you see them.

The Black Rose

The Castle line ships are already using your supply base, but you'll need this to be able to mingle with them." Becks said as he handed Meir a large brown envelope, which he opened up and looked inside at the contents.

"Between myself and my officers we are fluent in about eight Languages, but I'm blowed about speaking Irish, Commodore! Why couldn't you give us an American identity instead of this Irish one?"

Becks chuckled at this revelation and told Meir that from the twenty officers he met tonight, several of them can speak in a broad Irish and even Yank accent.

"They will be on deck when you transit the Dover Straits and English Channel. Besides, the real ship is in Sandeshaven being scrapped, and that gives us the opportunity to assume her identity before someone realises the truth. She trades between Hamburg, Amsterdam, Bergen, Cork, and sometimes across the Atlantic, but crucially she's Dublin registered, therefore deemed as a neutral ship.

That will be important to the success of our operations if you can maintain the outward facade of being from a neutral country, such as Ireland.

Your ship was extended and given a false hull and funnel to look like her, and you'll be carrying about 6,000 tons of supplies. Remember that all stores and supplies are quoted as foodstuffs. So apart from your obvious deck cargo, your ship will be seemingly stuffed with food for the starving Irish people due to the potato famine they've had again."

Meir listened to Becks going on about things he had already been briefed about, and wished he was back on board again enjoying a brief moment of luxury in his day cabin without someone demanding his attention.

"Now that you're private briefing is completed, Otto! Get your passengers on board and yourself underway by 0100." Becks finally ordered, as he shook Meir's hand and left the room.

The Black Rose

* * *

Meir walked along the naval dockyard looking at the sleek and deadly U boats huddled together, ahead of his ship, until he finally arrived on board where he met Schenk waiting for him on the gangway.

"Evening Captain!" Schenk said breezily.

"We're all loaded up and trimmed well. We were ordered to put a false Plimsoll line and depth markings onto our bow whilst you were away. We've got 6,000 tons of supplies and 28 special passengers with their baggage as our passengers."

Meir gave Schenk a puzzled look and queried his passenger total.

"I have their names all here."

Meir looked down the list and saw his extra eight passengers were in fact female.

"Women on my ship! But we're going to war, Schenk!" Meir spluttered as he recovered from his surprise.

"I'll see about this!"

"Captain Meir! There is no real need for you to be offended. After all, what's a passenger cargo ship without women amongst them." A gentle but cultured voice came from behind Schenk.

Schenk turned and gazed with Meir at the tall, slender, fur coated woman smoking a cigarette from a long cigarette holder.

"And just who might you be, lady?" Meir demanded sharply.

"Never you mind, dear boy. Just sail your little boat down the English Channel to the big sea and I shall get off when we reach Cork." the woman responded casually, which made Meir even angrier.

"First Mate! Get this woman ashore and take up the gangway. She is not sailing on my ship!"

The Black Rose

"Oh there, there, little man! Did poor little Lenka upset you then!" The woman pouted, but started to squawk like a chicken as Schenk grabbed her roughly, and frog-marched her over the gangway and dumped her unceremoniously into a puddle by the gangway.

"You can't do this to me! I have to sail aboard you. If I don't then you'll be in big trouble." the woman shrieked as she stood up in the puddle and shook her fist at him.

"Pah! Women!" Meir sneered then waiting until Schenk got back on board before he signalled the dockside crane operator to hoist the gangway off.

"We're loaded with enough cargo to cause a great deal of trouble without having her to add to it, First mate. If there's one thing I can't stand, it's women who don't know their place in this man's outfit, especially on my ship." Meir snorted, as he made his way up onto the bridge wing to start undocking his ship again.

Hans Otto Von Meir left Wilhelmshaven under the cloak of a dark, rainy night to begin his part in the Nazi's *Third Reich* war effort to dominate the world.

Chapter III
Friends

The ship with many names sailed slowly towards the Dover Straits, where they met a British warship coming swiftly towards them, with their aldis signal light blinking furiously at them.

"We have the pleasure of the British Navy to escort us in convoy through the straits." Kirkmeister said loudly towards Meir's bridge cabin.

Meir came onto the bridge putting his cap on and went out onto the bridge wing to look at the grey man of war bearing down on them.

"2nd Mate, get those two Irish speaking officers onto the bridge on the double, and ask the First Mate to see me also on the double." Meir ordered, as he looked through his powerful binoculars at the crowd of British officers standing around on their open bridge.

"Bad idea for open bridges in this weather, Tommy. That's why my passengers are all inside, and I've got a sheltered one." Meir said to nobody in particular, but Schenk answered anyway.

"Yes Captain, they prefer an all round view. It is one of their Battle class destroyers, steam turbine, with 2 twin 4.5 inch gun turrets, and does a good 30 knots." Schenk explained then asked why he was sent for.

"We may be boarded to have our manifest and cargo inspected. In which case, make sure any non-British speaking crew stay out of sight. We're looking damn good enough to get past their muster, so they might just marshal us into a tight westbound convoy, passing the eastbound convoy somewhere in the middle of the strait." Meir surmised.

"But do it anyway, as it makes good practice as we go through the channel. Bound to be stopped somewhere, knowing the British."

"Aye Captain. I have a young cousin in their mob as an engineering Sub Lieutenant, on one of these type, but can't remember which one."

"Now that's a thought. Well done Schenk, maybe we can capitalise on info like that from the rest of the crew. But there's still one problem that I cannot solve for the moment. How did that woman know where we were going, when I was only told the hour we sailed? We could have gone up the North Sea and around Scotland for all we knew at the time."

"I've been thinking on those lines too, Captain. But duty first." Schenk said as he went below into the bowels of the ship.

A loud voice came from the warship, as Meir looked over to see an officer speaking through a loud hailer.

"Speak to your Captain!" came the almost audible request. Meir was tapped on the shoulder by one of his passengers, Lt Kaufman, who also had a loudhailer ready to reply.

"Captain Dermot here. What can I do for you admiral?" Kaufman responded in a broad Irish accent.

The British officer asked the name of the ship, from where it came and where it was bound.

"*SS Kilkenny Castle*. Dublin registered. Out of Hamburg, bound for Cork."

"That's two fine looking engines and carriages you've got on deck. I know one, but what was the other?"

"Aye to be sure, tis a Gottenmuller type steam box engine we picked up from Hamburg. The new owner is the Galway Bay Railway when we get it there. Would you like a quick look at her?" Kaufman asked daringly, drawing a gasp from Meir who was standing behind him.

"Thank you for your offer Captain. Maybe next year sometime when this spot of bother is over, in the meantime duty calls. What speed can you make?"

The Black Rose

"Am doing my best now at 10 knots, sorry about that."

"No problem Captain. We're marshalling a westbound convoy of three lines of ships through the Strait to protect you from enemy mines or submarines. If you join the front of the central column, you won't get run over by the faster outer columns or slam into the back of the ship in front of you." the British officer explained.

"Just keep in line, at a constant speed of 10 knots for the distance of 40 sea miles before we disperse you. Okay?"

"10 knots in line for 40 sea miles. Got that. Thank you admiral!" Kaufman saluted jovially.

"Just doing my job to make you safe Captain." the British officer replied before the ship altered course outwards and doubled back to herd anymore ships for the convoy.

Meir grinned and thanked Kaufman, but said it was a hairy trick to invite the enemy to board you.

"It showed that we had nothing to hide. Besides, that officer knew his steam engines enough to know there was a new Gottenmuller steam engine just being built, but nobody has seen one yet. And the fact that there was until recently such a railway company. My uncle owned it up to this year, before he sold it off and came back to Kiel to live, but the British won't know that yet, anyway."

Meir grinned at the subterfuge and realised that this would be his answer to bluffing his way out of danger in future occasions.

The transit down the channel was slow and harrowing, as several Royal Naval warships came upon them snooping and sniffing around them. Their disguise as an Irish tramp steamer proved to be just right and Meir got used to answering the challenges himself, in his newly acquired Irish accent. But Meir was suspicious of the keen interest the navy was showing him, as if they knew something was not quite right. This set Meirs determination to find out why.

The Black Rose

* * *

He had the bags and belongings of the woman he threw off in Wilhelmshaven searched, to discover that she was not what she seemed. She was in fact a top Gestapo Agent with connections in Cork and other places. He decided to solve the mystery when he reached his forward base, in the meantime to be extra vigilant when he did arrive there.

Three days after entering the Dover Straits, and as the ship neared the Southern Irish coast, before Meir opened his next set of orders:

'You will not enter Cork harbour, but you will off-load your female passengers by launch off Bantry harbour, then proceed around the western coast of Ireland and up to Black Rose Bay. There the fishing boat' Ballymuffin', will meet you and take you to a secret location

'You are advised that you may experience unwanted attention from the Secret Police or Gestapo. Be on your guard, as they could make your operations or command untenable, as they seem to have the political rank above us regular servicemen.'

Meir called for Schenk, Emst, and Klinshoff and Kirkmeister to see him in his day cabin.

"Victor, Richard, Heinrich, Jurgen, close the door. You four represent my senior and oldest friends on board, that I need to rely upon at any given circumstance or event. Please read these orders that I have been given, especially the last paragraph. It will explain the investigations I have been doing these last few days." Meir said softly, for fear of being heard in any adjoining cabin.

The three officers read quickly through them and whistled at the mention of the Gestapo.

"But we're regular sailors! Our guests are regular U-Boat officers and men. What does the Gestapo want with us?" Emst asked as he scratched his head.

"It appears that this operation is strictly hush hush. Not even our Fuhrer knows about it, and the Gestapo must have got wind of it to investigate us. If we succeed in our support vessel operations, maybe they'll take all the credit and leave us alone. Otherwise if we fail then each one of us will be shot, for misappropriation of the Fuhrers funds." Meir answered.

"My father and the other two admirals are out on a short length of rope, so its up to us to damn well make sure we succeed, not only for them but for our sakes as well."

"Bloody hell Otto! If we fail then all our families will be ridiculed and be treated as criminals of the state. Do the U-boat crews know about this?" Schenk asked, wiping the globules of sweat appearing on his forehead.

"No! Those men are merely hitching a ride. We'll be the scapegoats. So we'd better watch who we might confide in, be extra careful and watch our backs from now on. Do we agree on this? " Meir whispered.

"Agreed!" the other three whispered back, they shook hands in a private deal of mutual help.

Meir had his ship steer into Bantry Bay and to the harbour entrance of Bantry where he met a fast moving launch waiting for them.

The women climbed clumsily over the side of the ship and down a rope ladder into the launch; the launch skipper shouted up to Meir who was on the bridge watching the event.

"When you arrive at Black Rose Bay, approach on a course of 095, to arrive 10 kilometres off Arghillen Island head, where you will then be met by a fishing boat called the *'Ballymuffin'* to guide you into harbour. R/V with it at 0400, and at their high tide." the skipper advised as he concurred with the orders Meir was given earlier.

Meir thanked the man who then spun the craft around and sped away into the night.

The Black Rose

"Thank god we've got shot of those incessant moaners. Nothing pleased them, captain." Klinshoff muttered as he stood by Meir watching the boat leave.

"2nd Mate, you're right yet again. Amen to that too. Maybe we men can get on with some real work now.

"Lay on a course for Black Rose Bay, and let me know when we're 10 kilometres off the offshore Island headland of Arghillen." Meir replied, then turned to the officer of the watch.

"Half ahead together. Tell the engine room to stop making smoke, and set revs for 18 knots. I'm fed up of crawling along like a cripple, lets get some decent speed out of her. Then ask the Chief engineer to come and see me in my cabin." Meir ordered.

He waited for his orders to be repeated back and carried out before grunting his satisfaction as he left the bridge.

"Chief! Can you tell me how fast I can really attempt with this false bow? This ship can fairly shift with its original bow, and I've known it to do over 30 knots."

"We shall have to give her a speed trial, captain. But her special bow is a reinforced one for northern waters and nearly two inches thick. The bow is detachable and easily re-rigged again if you need to remove it. We have a spare on deck, ready to assemble if that one gets jettisoned. But according to my own calculations, she can do a good 28 knots before anything drops off her."

Meir looked at the ship plans as Emst traced the outline of the bow, and nodded his satisfaction.

"That's very good Richard. An engine speed trial is definitely needed, as are the weapons. In fact we need to get ourselves into fighting shape, once we've gone on our first patrol. Anyway Richard, that will do for now." Meir stated as he rolled the plans up and put it with the pile of others.

"If that's all you want Captain, I can get back to my duties." Emst responded.

The Black Rose

"Yes Chief! But be good enough to increase speed slowly up to 25 knots, I don't want to lose any part of the ship. Inform the bridge and the navigator. No smoke if you can help it, and thank you. See you in harbour." Meir said gently as he shut the door behind his departing friend.

Meir felt a great tiredness overcome him, and decided to take a much-needed nap in his day cabin.

The Bridge cabin was too noisy and too handy to be disturbed by someone with stupid questions or problems. The only people allowed to waken him were his steward Winkler. The Chief Engineer, and the Officer of the Watch, (OOW) could do so but only in an emergency, or as ordered. Everybody else had to wait.

The slow and sluggish movement of the ship was replaced by a more pleasant rocking movement, as her engines started a quicker and less vibrating rhythm. This was amenable to Meir, helping him to sleep easier.

"Captain, we've arrived off Arghillan Island, but there's no fishing boat." Klinshoff said softly, as he entered Meirs cabin.

"What time is it? What's our speed?"

"0200 Captain. Speed 25 knots."

"Hah! That's very good! We've gone from a lumbering tramp steamer plodding along at 10 knots, to a racing clipper doing 25. We're two hours ahead of schedule, which means that the *Ballymuffin* is still tied up alongside." Meir said gleefully, as he climbed down off his bunk and started to get dressed.

"Tell the OOW to stop engines, and darken ship. Switch off all navigation lights. Lay a course of 095 when we get within 10 kilometres off the island, I'll be there in a moment."

"Aye captain!" Klinshoff replied, shutting the cabin door on his way out.

Meir arrived on the bridge, which was still in bright light.

"OOW! I ordered the ship to be darkened. Get these lights off and switch to blue lighting, now if you please." Meir growled.

"Then get yourself off the bridge and check that all deadlights are used. I don't even want the navigational lights shown. Nobody is to smoke on deck, and make sure all the passenger lounge windows have their blackout screens rigged. Come back to me when completed."

The OOW repeated his orders and disappeared down the bridge wing ladder.

"2nd Mate, send for the First Mate and the Chief engineer if you would." Meir's requests to his officers were in fact orders. Some of his officers were still uncertain about which of his requests were just that instead of an order. That is what he liked, as it kept them on their toes.

Schenk and Emst arrived almost together on the bridge and found Meir peering over a blue-lit chart table.

"Captain?" Schenk asked politely.

"Morning gentlemen! Sorry to get you up so soon." Meir apologised quickly,

"I intend surprising everybody by turning up unexpectedly. I've had a good look at these charts. They are, shall we say, rescued charts from the British Admiralty, which are the best charts in the world. So I'll use them to find my way into this harbour. We'll anchor off Kildrum until our pilot gets to us. Good night-time navigation practice in unknown waters and islands, what do you say?"

Klinshoff, Emst and Schenk looked in horror at their captain.

"But Captain. It might scare them half to death, and might start a shooting match." Schenk said.

"We'd need a lead swinger in the bows to check our depth. We're almost 5 metres deeper than normal and need plenty of sea-room." Klinshoff added

"Aye Captain. And I can only give you one hour manoeuvring capability for your slow speeds, else it'll be main engines and stacks of smoke."

"It seems that you've come up with sensible objections to my plan, I wonder if our U-boat friends in the lounge would attempt it. Go and ask Schmitz and Kaufman to come and see me Navigator." Meir said as he stroked his chin, still in thought.

"You sent for us Captain!"

"Ah yes! Good morning gentlemen. No doubt you both have conducted periscope reconnaissance patrols before, so I need your expert guidance on a certain matter.

"I have a suggestion of a plan that involves me entering unknown waters with little sea-room to manoeuvre in and under total darkness from the moon." Meir explained as he showed them the chart.

Both officers looked at the charts, and asked certain questions before giving their answers.

"It is our opinion that whilst a U-boat can slip in and out again, due to our low profile in the water, and we have a higher and longer power available in our batteries to be able to move around quietly. But in your case, you do not have such advantage. You'd be spotted several kilometres off shore even before you make your run-in. You'd be a sitting duck if some trigger-happy coast watchers happen to be on guard. Not something to risk even for a measly few hours captain." Kaufman advised.

Meir looked at the group of officers and decided to take their advice just as a lookout whispered that there was a craft coming straight towards them. Which distracted Meir momentarily.

"Thank you for your advice gentlemen. However, it's strictly academic now." Meir conceded as he went over to the starboard bridge wing and looked out through his powerful binoculars.

"OOW. Give a blast on the horn and have all lights switched on!" Meir said sadistically.

The sudden appearance of a large ship right in front of the little fishing vessel made its skipper veer sharply and Meir saw the skipper shake his fist at them, before it came round full circle again to come alongside.

"Who the bloody fuckin' hell is the captain of this fuckin' bloody ship?" an irate man screamed as he arrived onto the bridge.

"I am! Captain Meir." Meir said calmly as he hid his amusement.

The large burly man swung round and lashed out at Meir but missed as Meir ducked the lunging blow.

"You stupid fuckin' bastard! What the fuckin' hell did you want to pull a fuckin' stroke like that? You are a fuckin' idiot! Do you realise there's several fuckin' high calibre guns pointing down on you and if you'd entered the harbour you'd be blown out of the fuckin' water let alone from the mine field we've got laid." the fisherman shouted, before Schenk and Klinshoff grabbed hold of him to restrain him.

"That is the last time you take a swing at me, mister." Meir snarled.

"I arrived early and hid myself until you arrived. No sense advertising the fact that I was waiting to enter a strange area that's not supposed to have a harbour facility, now is there." Meir stated coldly and logically, which made the fisherman calm down.

"Well think yourself fuckin' lucky this time. The last fuckin' ship tried it, was sunk off the headland only a few fuckin' cables from you. You'd have gone into it and wrecked your fuckin' self had you not stopped where you are. Nobody comes in here without my fuckin' escort, as I'm the only one that fuckin' knows where the hazards are. I'm talking hazards like the fuckin' mines and the fuckin' outcrops of rocks let alone all the fuckin' heavy guns that are hidden." the fisherman said, his sentences holding more expletives than proper and civil language

"I take it that you'll pilot us in from here then skipper?" Meir asked politely as if nothing happened.

"That's why I'm fuckin' well here. What fuckin' engine power have you got and what's your fuckin' draught?" the fisherman asked as he moved the helmsman out of the way and took over the wheel.

"No offence helmsman, but I need to feel the fuckin' ship through her wheel. Have a fuckin' seat and relax for a while."

"Captain, get me your fuckin' navigator and his fuckin' notebook!" the fisherman ordered belligerently.

Klinshoff looked at Meir with surprise.

"Better do what the fuckin' pilot wants, 2nd Mate. You might learn a few fuckin' things, even if it's only how to swear in a fuckin' Irish accent." Meir said as he impersonated the fisherman, and handed the navigator his pen to write with.

"And don't forget where you got the fuckin' pen from." He added.

The fisherman showed the navigator certain points and angles to look out for, as Meir stood on a bridge wing, peering at a knobbly black lump that was land almost within reaching distance from him. He too was furiously writing notes as each object attracted his eye.

The ship came round a spur of land and made an S bend turn around two more, until they reached a stretch of water with a stone jetty at the end of it. Meir could see large cylindrical shaped things, under heavy camouflage netting, and deduced it was fuel bunkers.

He also saw some holes in the bottom of the large hill above the jetty, and surmised that they would be the stores depots. But what surprised him most was the closeness of the mines

The Black Rose

that the ship skimmed past and the several guns poking themselves from behind yet more camouflage. He'd spotted four large naval guns on the way into the inner harbour, and the integrated signal system that worked as the ship passed certain points.

The ship bumped itself against the new jetty and was securely tied up against it before the fisherman announced that he was finished, and that they could shut down the engines.

"Captain! You should advise your engineer that no fuckin' smoke should be made nor the fuckin' funnel cleaned until after the moon goes in and it's totally fuckin' dark that you can't see a fuckin' thing in front of you. Although the island and the hills around them are pretty fuckin' high, smoke can still be fuckin' seen out at sea for more than 15 fuckin' miles."

"Thank you for driving me pilot, and I'll certainly tell my fuckin' engineer. It makes fuckin' good sense not to advertise your fuckin' secret bolt hole with fuckin' smoke." Meir concluded sarcastically. The fisherman scowled and muttered to himself, knowing that Meir was sending him up.

"I shall be berthed down the fuckin' harbour for when you want to leave. Remember Captain. It's your fuckin' precious ship, not mine. So don't fuckin' leave here without me." the fisherman retorted, as he picked up his binoculars and left the bridge still swearing his head off, and went over the gangway, which had been placed on the ship.

"Secure from harbour stations. Finished with engines. First Mate, have our passengers disembarked then get the hands turned in until 0630 hours. No leave. Navigator, leaving out the swear words, get those fixes and angles plotted, before you get turned in. Helmsman, get me the steward." Meir ordered swiftly before he entered his bridge cabin.

"Captain!" Winkler asked sleepily as he entered the cabin.

Winkler. Get me my uniform and a cup of strong coffee. I have to be ashore in 15 minutes."

The Black Rose

Meir stepped ashore and walked a short distance along the dockside looking at the ships hull and its bows, before a staff car arrived and stopped by them.

"Captain Meir?" a voice from inside the vehicle asked politely.

Meir went over to the car and looked inside the back to see two admirals looking at him.

"Admiral Volginen, Admiral Horstenitz!"Meir said with surprise

"What brings you here? In fact how did you get here before me?"

"Morning Otto! Glad you made it. Welcome to my little end of the operations. Jump in, we've got some orders to go through." Volginen invited.

Meir was escorted into a decorated and well-furnished room with a large picture of Hitler at one end, that seem to dominate the whole room.

Under it, sat a group of officers that Meir recognised as his former passengers.

"As you know everybody Otto, I'll get straight down to business." Horstenitz started, as he dumped a large pile of documents onto the highly polished table.

"I, that is We!" Horstenitz corrected himself and coughed to clear his throat

"Have a squadron of six Uboats operating out of here, but that will change as from today they will be kept at sea, now that the *Schelzwig* has arrived. These passengers you brought Otto, are in fact my 'Spare Crew' Officers and men. Which means that every time you go out on your patrol, you will be taking them out to relieve officers and crew on those boats and bring them back for rest and recovery (R&R).

According to war conventions, we can get away with a merchant ship coming and going, but U-boats are not allowed, especially after the furore one of them caused when it sank a

The Black Rose

large passenger liner off the coast about 90 kilometres south of here, a few weeks ago.

Therefore, you wlll take supplies out to them and bring back the crews for R&R. The cargo you brought will be offloaded and stored in our special containment areas. But you will be reloaded with supplies and spare U-boat parts each time you come back. You will also be having dummy deck cargo now and again, so your cargo weight will vary accordingly.

As far as your replenishment signals are concerned, so we can get things ready for when you dock again, and because there is a war started, everything will be quoted as foodstuffs, but coded to mean specific items. For instance, 4 crates of Tinned Fish means, 4 crates containing 12 torpedoes each, whereas 2 boxes of Fresh Fish means 2 boxes for eating. Or 1 crate of Tinned Milk means 200 tons of diesel fuel, whereas 1 Urn of Fresh Milk means 40 gallons of milk for drinking, etc etc. Here is a copy of the codes for each of you." Horstenitz droned on, as he handed out copies of orders, codes, positions, and R/V procedures and asked Volginen to take over the briefings.

Volginen took over the meeting and finally completed the briefings which had taken him over 2 hours to complete, including answering the pertinent questions raised by the officers.

"The dockyard workers from the nearby village of Kildrum will be coming in now on the 0730 ferry, and will do your storing etc, Otto. You will be sailing in two days time, but in the meantime, get yourself on board and get some shut-eye. I shall be sending for you at 1400 today, for further discussions concerning your shake down, and so on. As for the rest of you, you will be billeted ashore for that time, so follow the steward and he'll take you to your quarters and some food.

"We will have a friendly get together here tonight, and I have arranged a special gaggle of 'ladies of the night' who

The Black Rose

shall be in attendance for those who wish to partake in their delights." Volginen said and smiled at the whoops of joy at his special surprise. Then turned turned to Meir and handed him a large cylindrical package.

"This is for you Otto. Open it and show the rest of us."

Meir opened the package and unrolled a large coloured flag, and held it up for everybody to see what it was.

"That Otto, is your Castle Line House flag, done in the Irish green white and gold. Look closely at the little flag on the end of the mast sticking out of the top of the castle. It has your symbol on it. Any mail or stores or anything you send us will have that little emblem stamped on it."

Meir looked at the gold castle with the little white flag above it, and saw a black flower imprinted on it.

"It's the Castle line flag with your designated codeword on it, Otto. And for the rest of you, take note of it, as it will be your recognition signal so as not to sink his ship by mistake, despite his unique cavitation sounds." Horstenitz said, as the U-boat men gathered around to get a good look at the flag[1].

"Well that's all for now. Must dash, unless there is something someone has something else to add?"

"Yes Admiral! I have a peculiar incident to report and need to have it resolved." Meir said as he told about the fur-coated woman.

Volginen clapped Meir on his shoulder and with a big smile stated

"That was the right thing to do with people like them. We are professional military men, they are just a pack of scum with their own secret agenda. But be on your guard as each one of them can bring you deep trouble with a capital T. So put it from your mind young Otto, and just get on with your mission."

"Thank you both. Give my regards to Admiral Meir." Meir nodded as he clutched his present.

---

[1] The sounds made by a ship propelling itself through the water.

The Black Rose

Meir and the U-boat officers stood up smartly and saluted the admirals as they left, followed closely by Meir who found the car outside to take him back to his ship again.

The Black Rose

Chapter IV
First Time

The ship finally sailed directly west out of harbour on her first patrol, in the morning light, with Meir watching attentively as she swam primly over the big grey Atlantic waves.

"OOW! Pipe action stations at 1000. Tell the engine room to make smoke for another two hours, then increase speed to 25 knot. Tell the lookouts to keep a sharp watch for any sign of smoke from any direction. I'm going below!" Meir ordered.

"Captain! Here's your fresh steaming gear, and your breakfast. I have your mail and the Radio Officer Lt Brantz, has some signals for you." Winkler announced as he laid the plate of food onto the rubber surface of the table.

"Skid mats on the table already Winkler? We've just got to sea." Meir said in surprise.

"Tell the Radio Officer to bring me his signals after I've had my food."

"Aye captain." Winkler acknowledged and disappeared down his little hatchway.

"Captain. I have one plain language signal and one decoded one for you." Brantz said as he entered Meir's day cabin.

Meir read the decoded one slowly, then glanced through the other one.

"Thank you, er Lt." Meir started.

"Lt Brantz!" the man reminded Meir.

"Ah yes! Willy Brantz, I remember! Yes that's it, you were in the Munich Olympiad." Meir said pleasantly.

"Yes, I remember now. You won the K class sailing gold medal. Nice to have you aboard, although it's all diesel these days."

Brantz's eyes lit up and smiled at the recognition Meir gave him.

"A sailing job never the less, Captain!"

"Modern German transport at it's best, Brantz." Meir enthused as he signed his name on the signals.

"Thank you Brantz. That will be all. Tell the 2nd Mate I wish to see him on the bridge in about 15 minutes."

Brantz repeated his order, saluted his captain and went to leave the cabin.

"There's just one thing though, and I need to remind you so that you can remind your friends. No saluting on board from now on, as we all know who we are and what our ranks are. But that doesn't mean there'll be no discipline, as it will be implicit at all times. Do you understand this?"

"Yes captain! I shall do what you ask!" Brantz said as he stood ramrod straight in front of Meir.

"Very well! Shut the door on the way out!" Meir replied as he dismissed Brantz, and turned to his sea charts.

"Navigator, these are the special charts we shall be using, so plot these co-ordinates I have written down. Our area is this square piece of ocean with the symbol of a black rose, here." Meir pointed to the chart with his protractor.

"That's a mighty big chunk of ocean, captain. We'll need to be on our toes for our daily sun sight fixings and star plotting." Klinshoff whistled.

"The main thing you and I have to remember is that no matter where we are on the chart, our codename will always be, and for us to be known as **The BLACK ROSE.** Even though we might have a pretend name just like the *Kilkenny Castle* or whatever will be written on our stern."

"Yes captain. We seem to be collecting names like a common Berlin whore on a bad night, trying to shake up some business."

"Very aptly put 2nd Mate." Meir replied with a smile, then showed the plain language shipping report for the whole expanse of the ocean.

The Black Rose

The two men worked steadily through their charts, paying no heed to the comings and goings of the bridge crew.

"Ship at action stations Captain!" Schenk advised as he coughed politely to draw Meir's attention from his charts.

"1000 already First mate?" Meir asked with surprise, as he looked over to the bridge clock.

"Very good. We shall start with gun drills until 1200. I intend to secure from action stations only when I'm happy, and especially the torpedo drills. You will see to it that a rating with good writing, to operate a special 'Attack log' to record all the commands given during action stations. This log is needed for analysis purposes, and for future references. " he ordered.

"Aye aye sir." Schenk replied as both men commenced their arduous weapon drills.

Meir ordered and scolded his officers who re-drilled the men so that they could perform like a coiled spring ready to let loose, and in the process almost into a state of exhaustion.

"We've cracked the timing you gave us captain. Can the men secure now?" Schenk hinted politely.

"Yes thank you First mate. I am happy with today's performance, but there are some items that still bother me. I want to see the 5th Mate in my cabin later, I wish to discuss the merits of his calculations. Say during the first Dog watch."

"Aye captain!" Schenk responded dutifully.

"Who's got the watch?" Meir questioned loudly.

"I have Captain!" Kirkmeister replied swiftly as he removed his binoculars from his eyes.

"Oh it's you, 3rd Mate! Well keep a good eye on the horizon, any sight of smoke drop your speed to about 12 knots. Let me know if you happen to do so."

"Aye aye captain!"

"Very good then." Meir said as he left the bridge and went down to his day cabin, two decks below the bridge.

The Black Rose

* * *

Meir enjoyed a customary stroll on the upper deck after supper every night, even if it was a storm lashed ship heaving under him. But this night was a calm one given that the ship was in the middle of the unpredictable North Atlantic.

He came upon a sailor smoking a pipe and whittling a piece of wood with his knife, and challenged the man to identify himself.

"Evenin' Captain! I'm the for'ard derrick winch operator, Petty officer Voss." the man explained as he stood up slowly from his makeshift bench.

"As you were Voss!" Meir said gently and motioned Voss to sit back down again.

"How long have you been to sea, Voss?"

"Me sir! This is my 8th commission. Due outside this Christmas after 25 years, although I can't see me getting home for that. What do you say Captain?"

Meir looked at the weatherworn face of Voss and marvelled at how at ease he was with himself and in front of his captain.

"I have been assured that we'll be back home in the Fatherland by then. If not, then the *Third Reich* will be paying us all overtime. Where is it you come from Voss?"

"My family home is in the village of Blexendorf near Bremen."

"I know that place. I have family living there down near the old water mill." Meir confided as he gazed out to sea.

"Then you must belong to old man Walter Voss who owns the mill." He added

"That's right captain, he's my father. But not any more, it got taken from us last year by the Brown Shirt brigade, when I was out in the Orient serving on your elder brothers ship the gunboat *Hapschiffer.* All my family and friends living around there were relocated to some farming community near a place called Buchenwald. I haven't had time to visit them since the *Hapschiffer*."

"Yes I heard about all that myself when I was the First Lieutenant on board the battle cruiser *Scheering*. Never mind, I expect they're doing well and things can only get better when we've thrashed the British once and for all."

"Well, those fine ships we were on are now scrapped, and here we are sailing on a merchantman, full of cloak and dagger stuff."

Both men chatted for a while before Voss spotted a column of smoke almost invisible to the naked eye, and reported it to Meir.

"Voss. You might be an old sailor, and as far as I'm concerned it doesn't matter what religion or creed you come from, you have certainly made your captain proud of you, well done. I was looking in the same direction but saw nothing. How did you manage it?"

Voss declined to answer except to shrug his shoulders and claimed a bit of good luck.

"Luck my arse, sailor. I shall speak to you later, in the meantime, keep track of that ship!" Meir directed abruptly, as he stood up and walked swiftly towards the bridge ladder.

"OOW! Who's the OOW? Have you sighted anything yet?" Meir demanded sharply.

"Nothing reported from the bridge lookouts captain." came the reply.

"Reduce our speed to 12knots, maintain present course. Who are the lookouts? Get them mustered in here right now."
The startled OOW did his bidding and had four seamen lined up in the bridge.

"You are all very young sailors. Still suckling on your mother's tits by the look of you. I have just come from the for'ard cargo deck and saw a column of smoke approx green 30! Why didn't any of you see it?" Meir demanded crossly.

The Black Rose

The sailors looked at each other and shrugged, claiming that they saw nothing, which angered Meir even more.

"OOW. Hands to action stations. I want these men removed from duty and placed on report on completion. Do you understand?"

The equally bewildered OOW meekly carried out his orders as the 4 men rushed off to their stations.

Meir looked at the bridge clock and at his watch.

"Ship at action stations captain!" Schenk said calmly even though he was breathing hard from his exertions.

"It took the ship 15 minutes to close up, First mate. That is not good enough. I want it down to at least 10. We have an unsighted ship to starboard which nobody but Petty Officer Voss and I saw. We have to assume it's a British warship, as we're still within their patrol areas. Given that they can steam at a good 30-35 knots, it would mean that they'd be on us within another 5 minutes. One can only surmise at that and let's hope for our sakes it's only another lonely merchantman." Schenk merely nodded but decided to keep quiet.

"The ship will remain at action stations until 0600 tomorrow morning. Then I want you to clear lower deck at 0700 to witness punishment, stand fast our passengers." Meir paused to let the implications sink in to everybody listening on the bridge.

"Bosun. Get yourself relieved off the helm and prepare charge sheets for the four lookouts that were on duty prior to action stations. I wish to interview them in 30 minutes."

"Aye aye captain!" the bosun responded.

"First mate. Get Petty officer Voss relieved from his post and get him mustered on the bridge, now if you please."
Petty officer Voss shielded his eyes as he emerged from the darkness into the bright lights of the bridge.

"You sent for me captain!" Voss asked unhurriedly.

"Petty officer Voss. Tell everybody here on the bridge what we saw before action stations were called. Speak out loud and clear." Meir demanded, as he looked around defiantly at the others on the bridge.

Voss did as he was told and stood impassively for his next order.

"You have heard from the man just what I had said. Is there anybody here that doubts his or my word?" Meir challenged, and received the silence he expected.

"First Mate. I do hereby promote Petty Officer Voss to an Acting Sub Lt, and as the 6th Mate. He will assume the responsibility as Foredeck Load Officer. Whilst at sea he will train all seamen to the proper ways of keeping lookout especially whilst on a war patrol. 6th Mate, Sub Lt. Voss do your duty."

"Aye Aye captain" Voss said woodenly and shuffled off the bridge to assume his new post.

"You are all witness that I have promoted Voss in recognition of his good work, but tomorrow you will also witness the punishment of four men who did not. Carry on First mate." Meir concluded.

"But captain. We're supposed to be, and act like a neutral merchantman." Shenk said as the hapless ratings were led away from the bridge.

Schenk followed Meir to his cabin and continued to appeal for clemency on behalf of the men, but got short shrift from Meir. "Those men will be needed when we R/V with our friends tomorrow." Schenk pleaded.

"You of all people should know that unless I keep proper discipline, the crew would forget themselves and start taking liberties when you least expect them. They know the score, and everybody expects whatever punishment is meted out, that is part of the life in the Kriegsmarine. And that is mainly because everybody knows that we are all military, not merchantmen. Do not ever lose sight of that fact. Get to your duty First mate." Meir shouted and slammed the door on his friend.

The Black Rose

* * *

"It's 0700. All hands mustered aft for punishment Captain!" a bleary eyed officer reported as Meir was looking over his sea charts on the bridge.

"Very good. Send me the Bosun." Meir replied curtly.

Meir arrived with the Bosun on the after cargo deck.

"Ships company, atten-shun" Schenk ordered as he turned and saluted Meir.

"Very well First mate. Bring forward the offenders Bosun." The four men stood in a line in front of Meir with their hands tied behind them and their heads bowed.

"In accordance with German Naval laws and under the Acts of War, you have been found guilty of gross negligence to duty.

"But which one of you will receive the punishment for all of you, that is the question?" Meir stated coldly, as he turned round and looked at his officers.

"4th Mate, Lt. Beiderman, two steps forward." He ordered. Beiderman stepped forward, and looked blankly at Meir.

"Now then Lt. Tell the ship's company what your specific duties are on board this vessel."

"I'm the gunnery Officer sir." Beiderman whispered, but Meir demanded that he should speak up for the benefit of the men standing at the back of the assembly.

"I'm the gunnery Officer, sir!"

"Very good Lt, it's good you know your job." Meir replied patronisingly.

"It is a good profession to be in, as I too am a gunnery officer." Meir admitted.

"Bosun. Take that weapon you have in that bag and give it to the Gunnery Officer." Meir said as he turned back to the Bosun.

Beiderman looked bewildered and hesitated to take the weapon from the chief Bosun.

The Black Rose

Meir explained in a loud voice to everybody, that 4th Mate, Lt Beiderman was also guilty of neglect of duty. That he put the ship and its crew into great danger in that he had left his post as OOW without permission or relief. Therefore, he had 1 officer and 4 ratings to punish to set an example to the rest of them.

"What is the principal duty of a Gunnery Officer, Lt? Tell the men what he does." Meir snapped.

"He, he, orders guns to be fired." Beiderman stammered.

"Repeat that loud and clear if you please. Even I can't hear what you said." Meir shouted.

"I control the guns for firing. Sir!"

"You shoot guns Lt. Very good!" Meir taunted.

"Then why do you hesitate to take hold of that weapon, unless of course you're not familiar with standard naval issue firearms?"

Beiderman grabbed hold of the weapon and pointed towards Meir, but found that Meir had his own machine pistol pointing into Beiderman stomach.

"Okay then Lt. Now we know what it's like to handle little pop guns. I would like you to show me just how good you are." Meir said as he sneered in Beiderman face.

"Bosun! My back is turned to the offenders, so I want them to number themselves in line."

The four men shouted in sequence as ordered, but Meir wanted them to repeat it as he could not hear them properly, which they did.

"Now then Lt, unless you are good at your job and can tell me how many rounds there are in that weapon you have, you had better open the magazine and count the bullets."

Beiderman took his time and stated that he found only one bullet.

"Very good Lt! Now spin the revolving magazine barrel several times. Bosun! Alter the position of the offenders.

The Black Rose

Meir watched Beiderman fumble with the revolver and heard the men count out again.

"Lt. Kirkmeister! You will step forward and remove the coat and hat from Lt. Beiderman." Meir ordered, but kept his eye on Beiderman and watched the order being carried out.

"I am still with my back to the crew and I am facing my officers. Lt.Beiderman! You have only 1 round in your revolver. If you fail to do your duty then I might as well shoot you as a useless and pathetic gunnery officer. Do you understand?" he snarled, as he finally extracted Beiderman's spluttered answer of compliance.

"Very good Beiderman. We will now play a little bit of a Russian Naval Officers game, called Russian roulette. All you have to do is, spin the bullet chamber and shoot a rating with a number I give you.

"If the weapon does not fire, then simply move onto the next rating, spin the chamber again and repeat the drill until the weapon does fire. In other words, neither you nor the ratings will know who will get shot." he explained.

"Now you will go and shoot rating number." Meir paused as he heard muffled gasps from the men.

"You will shoot the rating number 3 in his left ear, now if you please." Meir barked, as he saw the looks of alarm and disapproval from his officers.

"But Captain! I can't shoot a man in cold blood." Beiderman protested.

Meir exploded in a fit of rage, drew his revolver and aimed it at Beiderman forehead.

"By the very definition of your trade as a gunnery officer, you live by shooting large calibre guns to kill lots of the enemy. Yet you cringe to shoot just one man with a little one. There are four targets but only 1 bullet. By heavens man, unless you do your duty, then I will shoot you here and now myself, then the rating." Meir bellowed.

The Black Rose

Beiderman looked at the terrified ratings, and at the shocked horror of the onlookers for what he was ordered to do, before he pulled the trigger and blasted the hapless mans brains out, which made some of the men vomit at the sight of the blood and gore.

"Well done Lt. Beiderman! You hit with your first shot. Now you can call yourself 'GUNS' like me." Meir said soothingly, then turned to the men.

"The rating that was shot was chosen at random as you have witnessed. The officer who shot him, was himself involved under the same punishment laws. That was why his rank was removed from him, to conduct the shooting. It means that he could now possibly stand trial as a war criminal." he shouted, and paused whilst he stuffed his pistol back into its holster.

"I meant what I said to you all on the dockside in Hamburg only two weeks ago, so let this be your solitary lesson, and I strongly advise you all to learn by it.

"I don't care about the colour or creed a man is, providing he performs his duties in time honoured naval tradition. But I will not have nor will I tolerate idlers, shirkers, sexual perverts, troublemakers or religious nuts on my ship, no matter what rank they may be.

"Therefore, each and every one of you had better buck your ideas up as of now, next time I'll do the shooting." Meir hissed menacingly, then paused as he turned to the Bosun.

"Bosun! Dismiss the men, then see to it that the dead body is ready for a military burial at sea at 0700-tomorrow morning. First Mate, I shall be visiting our guests and all off-duty officers at 1030 in the passengers lounge." Meir ordered as he made his way towards his bridge cabin without waiting for any replies.

Meir was eating his breakfast, with Winkler flitting about, when he heard a knock on his cabin door.

The Black Rose

"Captain. By our dead reckoning, we are at the edge of our patrol area, and recommend that we return to our base course for the run in to our first R/V position." Klinshoff advised as he stood in the cabin waiting for his orders.

"Thank you Navigator. Get yourself a relief OOW, have your breakfast then we'll take a look at the chart again in about 30 minutes."

"Aye captain." Klinshoff replied and left.

Meir and Klinshoff worked on their charts again as the ship moved its way ever westward, until Meir was satisfied with his course and position.

"It's 1030 Captain. Our guests are waiting for you now as ordered." the OOW informed politely.

"Very good. Reduce speed to 10 knots, and steer 275. Tell the lookouts to keep a sharp eye out for any floating objects in the water. They are to look out for white rubbish bags or other debris of that nature." Meir replied as he went below to the lounge and was met by Schenk.

"Good morning gentlemen. Hope you've had a pleasant few days cruising. I have to thank you all for contributing your Submariner expertise and knowledge during this time. The torpedo firing instructions were of particular value, as were the special techniques we had to learn, to be able to supply your needs.

"The time has now come for us to make a glorious history for ourselves as we are about to enter our designated R/V slot to meet each of your friends in succession." Meir said amiably, which raised a hearty cheer from the men.

"I will always be on call with your supplies as and when you need me, but make sure you don't sink us by mistake if you find us in company with other surface vessels, and especially if I get roped into a convoy."

That suggestion drew more ribald remarks from the men, as one of the officers stood up.

The Black Rose

"I'm due to take over command of the U21." Kaufman started and commenced to ask pertinent questions of Meir, who gave his answers, which seemed to satisfy everybody.

"Any more questions gentlemen? Only next time we meet, is when you first see me in your periscope." Meir replied, then asked a few questions and gave suggestions of his own, which drew an equal response from the Submariners.

"Remember this. This ship is like an actor, all dressed up and pretending to be what she's not. She is a proper merchant ship but manned by military men pretending to be merchantmen. In reality, this ship is the fastest merchant ship in the world, excluding certain large ocean liners, that is. And due to our special effects, if you like, we are able to match or outgun any destroyer and even outmanoeuvre any light cruiser that our illustrious sea enemy, the Royal Navy, can send our way. We will protect you when you're vulnerable and we will expect a reciprocal kindness from you. What do you say Captain Kaufman?"

Kaufman stood up, saluted Meir and started to sing the Submariners anthem, spontaneously joined by the rest of the men.

Meir looked round at this special breed of men, saluted and left them to their last moments of fresh air, before they would be ensconced in their steel coffins some hundreds of feet below the waves.

"Captain! Debris sighted fine off the port bow!" the OOW reported excitedly, as Meir emerged from his bridge cabin.

Meir went slowly out onto the bridge wing and looking through his binoculars, saw the telltale streaks of a periscope moving through the water just in front of the flotsam.

"OOW. Come here and look again at something that you have probably not seen before." he invited as he showed the officer where to look.

"Why yes! It's a submarine periscope. I can see it."

The Black Rose

"Very good! Now that flotsam you see is the ships rubbish called gash. They have ditched it to mark its position and dived again to keep hidden. It's giving us a good look to see if we are friend or foe." Meir informed.

"Signalman. Use your small signal lamp and flash our recognition signal towards that line of flotsam over there. Lookout, hold our special 'house flag' over the side." Meir ordered, which the signalman did.

"OOW! Get hands to Replenishment stations. Ask Captain Kaufman to come to the bridge immediately."

Kaufman stood by Meir and looked through a set of binoculars at the periscope, then started to wave his white-topped hat at it.

Meir was not alone to be surprised and marvelling at the sight of a surfacing submarine, almost like a whale coming up out of the waves.

Meir manoeuvred his ship so that the boat could come into its sheltered side and almost alongside it.

"Hello the **Black Rose**! I'm Captain Hilsinger U21. Glad to see you. Need a full plate today." Came the loudhailer-assisted voice.

Meir waved his hat over his head, and replied in the same manner.

"You will receive your hardware supplies from the for'ard derricks. But your food will come from aft. Fuel and water will be from midships. I have some friends and mail on board for you. Prepare to receive them once we've replenished you. You will be advised, that should we meet strangers, I will leave you and come back on my return leg."

"Thank you Captain! How long will you take?"

"About two hours, depending on progress. Let me know when you're ready."

"Ready now. Commence replenishment." the U-boat captain replied as Meir saw several men emerge onto the submarine casing from two seemingly narrow hatchways.

"OOW! This is a piece of history. It is the first time for a German ship attempting this and our first time on a real transfer. I have the conn. Get your camera and use it to good use, and get someone to record in writing all that is taking place. It will come in useful later." Meir ordered as he watched the proceedings.

Both vessels were almost lashed together with huge fenders between them to prevent any hull damage, as the derricks dipped and swooped over the much smaller but more deadly U-boat.

Meir watched the torpedoes and ammunition being swallowed up by the forward hatch, as the food went down the after one. At the same time, two umbilical hoses were pumping fuel and fresh water into the boat's tanks.

The replenishment went without a hitch, including the transfer of the men, their belongings and the long awaited letters from home.

Meir watched as Kaufman arriving up into the conning tower, waved to him, and shouted.

"See you in one month Captain. Good luck, and don't shoot any of my men when I'm away."

Meir smiled and waved back, as he saw the submarine start to sink slowly under the waves to disappear into the murky depths of the ocean.

"OOW. Secure from Replenishment duty. Set Patrol routine again. Steer 285 speed 25 knots. I'm going below to meet our new guests."

"Aye aye captain."

Meir arrived into the passenger lounge and found it buzzing with excitement and camaraderie amongst his officers and the newcomers.

"Welcome aboard gentlemen for the start of your R&R. You will be excused any duties, despite what the rest of us might get up to. I hope you will be comfortable, as this will be

The Black Rose

your home until we get back to Kildrum. We have just completed our very first transfer at sea, and we can thank our enemies the Royal Navy as they invented it. But we're a long way behind learning their skills, so hopefully we can improve on the timings and techniques as each drop is made." he announced, then went among the new passengers and stayed a while with them before he finally left.

"We're about there for our next R/V Captain!" Klinshoff advised, as he showed Meir the position on the chart.

"Very good Navigator. OOW! Same drill as before if you please." Meir commanded, which had the ship bustling with activity.

Meir stood on his bridge wing watching the transfer, as the passengers lined themselves along the passenger deck to witness this new naval practice.

They cheered as the replacement officers scrambled over and down the scramble nets onto the U-boat, to relieve their opposite numbers.

Again, Meir went through his welcoming speech, and did so every time a fresh transfer took place.

"2nd Mate. We've completed our first mission now it's time we went home." Meir said to Klinshoff as they both leaned over their charts.

"OOW. Set a course of 085 speed 25 knots and tell the engine room to make a little more smoke now, any sign of strangers then slow down to about 12 knots. Any other urgent problems call me!" he ordered as he left the bridge with the Navigator.

It was dark when the ship reached Kildrum, and met the *Ballymuffin* steaming around the headland.

Meir sighed as he heard the swearing Irish fisherman coming up his bridge ladder.

"Here we go again First Mate."

"Maybe he's in a good mood this time." Schenk replied hopefully.

The Black Rose

"Evenin' Captain. Just as well you fuckin' turned up when you did, as I was on my fuckin' way home for my fresh fish supper, cooked over a fuckin' peat fire."

"Hello pilot! Fish for a change?" Meir baited, but got no reply as the fisherman took over the wheel and steered the ship neatly down its S shape course and into the little harbour.

When he was finished, the fisherman turned to the navigator with a smile and said.

"How's about that then. No fuckin' compass, nor nothin fancy, just plain steering and fuckin' speed control!"

"How about mid ocean navigation then skipper. Do you think you could navigate your way across the Atlantic and arrive at your destination on time?" Klinshoff asked, as he winked at Meir.

"Don't fuckin' have to. I does my fuckin' fishin around these waters, not a fuckin' thousand miles away. Anyway me little boat only carries a fuckin' ton of coal. I'd need a vessel the size of the fuckin' Queen Mary to get across. She's due to pass here in the next few hours, so it was just your fuckin' luck you weren't spotted coming here."

"What? Other liners pass here skipper?" Meir asked quickly as his ears picked up the name of the Queen Mary.

"Fuckin' loads of them pass here about six hours steaming away to the south of us. You're too fuckin' slow to catch up with them anyways.

"Ask the fuckin' admiral, he'll tell you what you want to know. Me, I'm fuckin' off home now." The fisherman concluded as he walked down the gangway and got ashore.

"That's interesting news. If those liners are fast enough, then they would steam independently instead of in a slow moving convoy." Meir said almost absent-mindedly to Schenk, as he saw a small group of officers waiting on the jetty for him.

"First mate! Secure from harbour stations. Get our passengers ashore. No leave, but plenty of schnapps, see to it.

The Black Rose

I'll be ashore visiting the admiral for a while." Meir ordered as he picked up his large brief case and left the bridge.

"Evening Otto! How did it go?" Volnigen asked eagerly, as he ushered Meir into his car.

"Went like we planned Admiral! I have some photos, maps and sketches to show you. Took as many records and details as I could, and even managed to adopt some of the Royal Navy's skills to good effect." Meir said almost nonchalantly, but feeling very pleased with himself.

"You've made history young Otto. And you've made three old admirals very proud and pleased that you were able to pull it off. The proof of our overall success will come when you've completed 4 more runs, before we can announce, secretly that is, our operations and triumphs."

"That's no problem, but I'm a bit concerned about my return leg. I would be the only ship entering a war zone in ballast, instead of loaded to the waterline with cargo. And from what our pilot has said there's a lot of fast ships passing our place only about 60 miles south of us. The Queen Mary being one of them." Meir replied with concern.

"Is there by damn. Didn't know that. We'll set a coast watch up beyond our little area. Pointless sinking them on the way out, and they'd be too fast for our grey wolves but not for you. You might be able to bag a couple on their way back when you return from your patrol."

"Yes. Our friends can make a mess of the convoys, and I'd come along and sweep up after them to ensure none gets away. Good idea admiral." Meir acknowledged, making the admiral think it was his idea in the first place.

The admiral had Meir join him at his quarters, where the admiral gave him a welcome home banquet, in company of other staff officers.

When it was over, Meir started to show the photographs and details of his patrol as the champagne flowed and the cigar

The Black Rose

smoke billowed from the smokers.

Everybody made suggestions and comments to the admiral and Meir, and uncertain relevant details were cleared up in the usual brainstorming manner.

"I think that about raps it up for tonight gentlemen. Tomorrow's another day, our Captain has to get his ship back to sea again. You sail again tomorrow night, to another patrol area as we've placed another squadron of six to mirror our friends already out there. That way your ship won't need altering every time you come back in again. At least that is the plan."

"Can I have your permission to engage the enemy whilst on patrol, or do I have to remain passive?"

"You will only engage the enemy if it's a straggler with nobody else around. No smoke to be seen over the horizon I mean. You're existence has to remain secret until you've done your four trips to each patrol area. That, as I've said, will give us time to assess the impact your ship makes in keeping our squadrons on station. If they can remain on station, then it means that the more ships they sink, the less the enemy will have to send their supplies and re-enforcements with. We could starve the British into giving up. Anyway, that's the game plan."

"Thank you for taking me into your confidence admiral. Now I know why my ship is so special. Although I cannot think why we can't have more of them built to this calibre of ship."

"Ah, now that would be telling you things that are only on a need to know basis, Otto. Anyway, how are you getting on with our Irish pilot?" Volnigen asked to change the subject.

"He is the most offensive low life I've had the misfortune to meet. I shall be glad to get shot of him, if in fact I don't shoot him anyway."

"He's the best there is on this whole coastline. I've been out on his little puffer and he can tell what the weather's going to be like long before my so-called weather boffins can, just by looking at the colour of the water."

The Black Rose

"That good is he!" Meir marvelled then changing the subject told him about Voss, Beiderman, and the shot sailor.

Volnigen merely smiled and told him that unless he controlled his temper he'd end up sailing the ship single-handed with an empty gun by his side.

"Okay then Otto. Time for you to get back. I'll have you loaded in the morning. I'll come and see you before you sail at 1900. In the meantime, get your engineer to have a portable pump rigged so that you can take on seawater to compensate for your weight loss. That is to say, you will fill up the empty fuel tanks with the seawater to make it look that you seem to be loaded up on your way back."

Meir smiled as he saluted the admiral and began his walk back to the ship.

It was nearly midnight when he arrived back on board, feeling elated and pleased with himself.

"Good morning captain! Here's your breakfast and a fresh pot of Brazilian coffee and the local papers for you to read. It seems that our friends are creating havoc out there." Winkler said amiably as he pottered around the cabin.

Meir yawned and stretched himself as he climbed out of his bunk, before he looked at the banner headlines proclaiming that the British merchant ships were being massacred and a picture of a U-boat captain with his crew being decorated by the Fuhrer himself.

He didn't offer a reply, merely ate his breakfast, and read the inside stories of the paper instead.

The ship was a hive of activity again when the local dockyard workers arrived. Soon the ship was loaded and spruced up ready for its next patrol by the time the workers left for home.

"OOW! Have the ship's company to supper one hour early, and get the passengers embarked by then. I want to sail on the next high tide."

"Aye Aye Captain!" the OOW responded after repeating his orders back.

Meir went onto the bridge and found the navigator with his charts again.

"We've got a storm coming our way, navigator. Judging by the tide we'll be heading into it for its duration. I want you to plot the new R/V co-ordinates and work out a good course and speed to get to the new patrol area. Our speed will be around 20 knots but reduced to about 12 during the heavy seas."

"I've already plotted the R/V's and made you two courses captain." Klinshoff replied.

"Very good 2nd Mate. Our foulmouthed pilot's little craft is only an inshore fishing boat, not built for heavy seas. Have you gleaned enough information from him to be able to enter this harbour on our own?"

"No captain. He's very liberal with his swearing but like a clam when it comes to bearings and courses."

"Damn him. We'll have to keep a closer watch on what he looks at when he takes us out tonight. Get a couple of extra lookouts on deck and tell them to note the different landmarks or whatever. Our friend must fix onto something for him to choose his course."

"Aye aye captain." Klinshoff replied as Meir left the bridge.

Meir was on the dockside with the admirals getting his customary send off, whilst the ship was being prepared to cast off and sail away.

"There might be storms in your area, in which case you might not be able to supply them with their torpedoes. If that is the situation, keep going to the end of your run, then try it again on your return leg. Here are your codes for this patrol, and good luck. See you in 15 days."

"Thank you admiral. I could do with a bit of a challenge this time. Maybe I can get to engage the enemy on my way back.

The Black Rose

Might as well use the torpedoes up as return them again."

"You have the patrol Otto, but first and foremost, look after your ship." Volnigen stated.

"Aye aye sir." Meir replied as he saluted the admirals, boarded his ship and started to rattle off his orders when he reached the bridge.

"The pilot's not on board yet captain." Klinshoff stated calmly.

"Admiral! Where is our bloody pilot? This is not a very good arrangement if we're solely reliant on a foulmouthed fisherman."

Before the admiral had a chance to reply, Meir heard someone swearing below him.

"Ah stop yer fuckin' moanin, and let me get onto the fuckin' bridge." the fisherman shouted as he came up the starboard bridge ladder.

"Pilot! Get this ship out of here right now." Meir growled and looked ominously at the fisherman, who seemed to take no notice of what was said, and carried on with his job.

Much to the relief of the bridge crew, the fisherman climbed back into his own little ship, tooted his ships horn then turned his ship around to go back in to harbour again.

Meir turned to his OOW with his set of orders.

"Full ahead together! Tell the engineroom to set speed for 25 knots. Bosun! Starboard 10 and steer a steady course of 275. OOW set PATROL routine watches. I'm going below."

"Aye aye captain." The OOW responded.

"Ask the 4th and 5th Mate to see me in my day cabin in 30 minutes."

"Aye aye Captain" came the required response again, as Meir went down the steep ladder into the ship and to his main cabin.

Meir was able to have a leisurely shower, change into his clean steaming gear and have some hot food before the two officers knocked his cabin door.

"Guns, Torpedoes! Come in!" he invited as the men stepped inside.

"I have some good news and some not so good to tell you. The good news is that we have now been given permission to use our weaponry.

But the not so good news is, that we need to get our attack strategy and timings corrected to have the desired effect I want to achieve." Meir announced, which started a full-blown discussion on the subject lasting well into the night.

Meir decided that the only way to hone up their skills was to get as much practice in as and when it presented itself, which concluded the meeting and all three went to carry out their other duties on board.

For Meir, it was a few hours welcome sleep, before someone else decided to waken him with some tale of woe or whatever. Such was the life of the captain of a ship.

Chapter V
Calypso Queen

"**C**aptain on the bridge." the OOW announced, which meant that everybody was to be extra alert.

"Good morning 3rd mate. What is our progress?" Meir asked politely as he went and sat in his special chair bolted to the deck in the middle of the bridge.

"On course and maintaining speed. Weather picking up and coming from our port quarter!" Kirkmiester reported calmly.

"Yes. I was expecting a bit of blow. Any strangers about?"

"Smoke reported five minutes ago, but way over the horizon fine on our starboard bow. I have posted a lookout on a specially constructed crows nest on the for'ard derrick mast to get a better look, but he could still only see a wisp of smoke."

"Crows nest? Who thought of that old idea?"

"I did Captain." Beiderman answered as he came into the bridge.

"I needed a higher vantage point to help the range finder I had made during our last visit in Kildrum. I shall be able to triangulate my bearings to give me much better range calculations with it."

"That sounds good Guns! Maybe you will acquaint me into its mechanism soon. Well done for once!" Meir drawled.

"I have now been relieved by the 4th mate, captain. Do you require me any further?"

"Thank you 3rd mate. Go and have your breakfast. Ask the 1st mate to come and see me when he's had his." Meir said pleasantly.

"Aye aye captain!" Kirkmiester replied as he handed his binoculars over to Beiderman before leaving the bridge.

Meir sat in his high-legged chair, looking out of the bridge windows through his binoculars, feeling the ship corkscrew its

The Black Rose

way up and over the grey marbled waves that met the ship. This was his undisputed domain, and his kingdom as the captain.

He was only in his early 20's but he was God over everything and everyone on board his ship. As it was he that decided who lived or died on it, and that included any other vessel he met that did not obey his orders.

"OOW! Get the foc'sle and both cargo deck working parties to have the cargo and all other hatches firmly secured. In fact, have the entire ship secured for bad weather. I think you'd better get that lookout down from his perch too." he ordered.

"Aye aye captain!" Beiderman replied as the order was announced over the ships tannoy system.

"Captain! I have just intercepted several distress signals on the 500Kc International ship distress frequency. Our nearest one is about 60kilometres away fine on our port bow, and another one more or less on the same bearing according to my DF ranging.

"From their call signs, one's a 15,000ton tanker called the *Calypso Queen*, the other one is a freighter but can't find her on the list. Here are their positions." Brantz announced as he approached the captain.

Meir took the signal and going over to his chart, worked out the position relative to his own.

"We will go to that position, then the other one. But do not to answer their calls, we're not supposed to be on this part of the ocean. Just keep listening in case someone else answers." Meir said coldly as he handed Brantz back his signal.

"Do you hear that 4th? It seems that we have been given a present from our friends' night encounters. We will take advantage of our new tactics and your new fangled range finder. What do you say to that?" Meir chortled as he rubbed his hands in glee.

The Black Rose

Beiderman agreed, sharing the little moment of excitement with his captain.

"But let's not be too hasty Guns. We don't want any witnesses or onlookers just yet."

Beiderman looked at Meir and replied swiftly.

"But captain if there is a witness and close by, can we sink it too? Two in one go so to speak!"

"Stop and think Guns! We've got to consider our friends needs first. Besides, it's a good two hours steaming away even at our best speed. Just wait and see what our fortune brings us. In the meantime, get the hands to early supper and to Action stations in 90 minutes." Meir insisted with a smile, which made Beiderman respond in the same manner

"Aye Aye captain!"

This news of possible action went through the ship like lightening and had everybody buoyed up and feeling more cheerful just thinking of the prospect of a gunnery action.

Even Winkler was in a good mood when he served Meir with his lunch.

"About time we used those ornaments on our decks captain. Maybe a good gun action is what we all need to justify sailing around the ocean like a grocery boy on his bicycle."

"You too Winkler! It must be a long time ago since you to saw action. It's not all that great. When you sink just one ship then you've sunk them all."

"Maybe so, but it's the morale of the men that's the more important element. Especially with the recent shooting of one of their number." Winkler hinted, as he carried on tidying up the cabin

Meir looked at Winkler with surprise, but did not comment, as he finished his meal.

"Action stations! Hands to Acton stations!" came the raucous voice over the tannoy.

The Black Rose

Meir arrived onto the bridge and saw Klinshoff looking ahead through his binoculars, and went over to the chart to check his position.

"We're almost on the eastern edge of our friends' patrol area. We have a base course to maintain, so you are to plot each change of course and speeds as of now navigator.

What have you in sight!" he asked, taking up his binoculars and scanning the horizon.

"Ship fine off our port bow, range of 15 kilometres captain!" Beiderman responded quickly.

"Guns! You made good timing to Action stations! Now get your new range finder going and let me know how it works. And I agree on your range. Navigator, start the attack log." Meir said as he offered the navigator his stopwatch.

Klinshoff stated that he had his own and declining the offer walked rapidly towards the chart table.

"We have another ship about 15 kilometres astern of this one and to our starboard, Guns! Therefore we shall use the torpedo weapon system only on both of them. If there are any survivors who make the lifeboats, they will think they have been torpedoed again. That way we can maintain our cover for a little while yet. If we use our guns then we'd have to slaughter every person on board both ships." Meir ordered, which made Beiderman scowl.

"But we need the shooting practice captain. Can't we use it on the rear one?"

"You appear to have caught the lust for blood ever since you shot that rating, Guns! Not this time I'm afraid." Meir teased and turned to issue changes in course and speed.

"Range 5 kilometres Captain! For'ard and port tubes ready!" Beiderman advised, as he stood back to let Flens take over for his action.

"Very good Guns! Keep your eye on the other ship and report if she alters course. 5th Mate, the ship is listing heavily

The Black Rose

to port. So I shall be coming in on her high side. I intend firing 1 and 2 at 3 kilometres. Set their angles to 1 degree either side of the bow. We'll shoot them down her throat, then alter to her starboard to fire 3 & 5 as we reach their critical angles. Our range will be 900 metres. We have a 2 metre wave depth, so set torpedo depth to 3. All 4 torpedoes should hit within 10 seconds of each other. Stand by with your stopwatch.

"I make range of 3 kilometres Guns! Confirm that!" Meir ordered, as he made his mental calculations and ready for his first attack.

"Confirmed!" Beiderman replied excitedly.

"Fire 1 and 2!" Flens shouted down his telephone receiver. The ship gave an extra shudder than it would expect from an oncoming wave, as two torpedoes sped towards its victim.

"Starboard 15! Half astern Starboard! Full ahead Port!" Meir snapped, which drew the repeated orders back to him. Meir looked at his watch again.

"Midships. Full ahead together." he ordered which was followed by Flens own command.

"Fire 3." He paused and counted five seconds

"Fire 5!"

Again the ship shuddered as two more deadly torpedoes went swiftly towards mass destruction.

The tanker's bow disappeared instantly in a ball of flame as both torpedoes destroyed it, just as the other two torpedoes slammed into its side. The ship erupted into a huge fireball as it exploded from stem to stern, then disintegrated and sank within seconds of being hit.

The men on the *Black Rose* stood in awe at such a sight and danced with glee as they realised that it was their first successful action. Beiderman reminded them that they were still at action stations for them to return to their posts.

Meir saw a bright round object hanging off the DF aerial and climbed up and retrieved it. He brought onto the bridge and showed everybody what it was. The large round lifebelt had the name '*CALYPSO QUEEN*. BOSTON N.Y.' written on it.

"It seems as our so called neutral Yanks are trying to get in on the act." Beiderman cooed, as he stroked the fuel stained lifebelt.

"Our first trophy gentlemen! Have it put somewhere appropriate in the passenger lounge. Let's see how many more we can win!" Meir said with satisfaction, as he handed it over to Flens and said.

"Between you and guns. That's one nil to you. You keep the score and the ships names. I'll keep the tonnage and glory!"

Beiderman scowled but took it gamely, then reminded Meir that the second ship was now at 10,000 metres but starting to attempt a zigzag.

"Very good Guns! Torpedo Officer, I hope your men have reloaded 1 and 2. I intend using the starboard tubes this time. Same drill only we'll wait until she zigs towards us."

"She's asking us to stop and help her, Captain!" the signalman shouted from the starboard bridge wing.

"Tell her there's a U-boat on my tail and to get the hell away from here!" Meir shouted back, and saw the signalman flashing his aldis.

"That should take any suspicions off us, if they saw that the other ship got torpedoed. Imagine if we used our guns, Guns! We'd have to slaughter this next lot, instead of letting them get to their life rafts."

Meir had the same drill performed and slowed his ship down to see the outcome. The ship had almost disappeared beneath the waves as Meir watched a lifeboat picking up some of its survivors.

"At least you're safe, only another 500 kilometres to go before you reach Ireland." Meir muttered to himself as

The Black Rose

Beiderman brought back yet another souvenir. It was the house flag of the hapless ship.

"Put it with the other one Guns! Find out who she was and tell me her tonnage." he suggested, then turned to the navigator.

"We should be near our patrol area and our first R/V. Get us back onto our base course and speed, navigator. Guns! Secure from Action stations, and prepare for replenishment stations in about 1 hour. I'm going below to my cabin. Send me the Radio Officer!" Meir ordered.

"You sent for me captain?" Brantz asked politely as he entered Meir's day cabin.

"Yes Brantz! Did you find out the details of that second ship?"

"Yes captain. She was a 7,000-ton cold store ship that was sold from one company to another.

"I had to look into my Lloyds supplemental books for her. Is that all you need captain, only I've got a schedule with our friends to keep in about 15 minutes!"

"Yes Brantz, that's all. You may go now and tell our friends we're on our way." Meir concluded as Brantz left his cabin.

Meir conducted his next six R/Vs with no problem, despite the heavy seas, and turned his ship back to Kildrum with his ships company in very high spirits.

On return to Kildrum, it was Horstenitz that greeted Meir, but with concern written on his face.

"It appears that we are being too successful, as we've got yet another two squadrons on station to the west of both our northern one and southern one. I have two problems. First is that you can supply one 'string' only at once. Which means that the other 'string' will be left stranded, or having to come back into port for their supplies. The other one is that the base supply dump is getting lower and lower by the week, every

The Black Rose

time one of our ships fails to make the run through the Orkney or Dover Straits."

Meir thought of the two ships he destroyed and the waste of good supplies that perhaps Volnigen could use, and told him of a new plan he'd thought of whilst on the run back.

"We only have a limited area to hide in Otto. What would we do with the carcasses of what you bring in? Besides, not all tankers carry diesel fuel, mostly bunker or furnace oil."

"According to one of my U-boat passengers, there is a new U-boat being built that can refuel their boats whilst at sea. He called it a 'Milchcow!' Apparently he'd been doing trials on the prototype and reckons it's like a very large and fat whale that can stay under water for very long periods.

"It has a snorkel mast to get the air for its diesel engines to charge its batteries whilst it's submerged. But it is a very slow moving vessel of about 10 knots, whereas our friends can do a good 18.

"Therefore if it was brought into immediate use, I would only be required to refuel those who missed their R/V and to re-arm or feed them as required." Meir said at length as the staff car arrived back into the HQ building complex.

"It appears Otto, you must have read my mind on the refuelling, but we'd have to think about the food problem." Horstenitz commented and changed the subject abruptly.

"What's this I hear about you engaging the enemy twice in one go Otto? Tell me more!"

Meir didn't have to, as the two officers entered the Officers mess they were met with salutes and cheers, as everybody extolling Meir's tactics.

After the excitement died down, Meir and the admirals went through to the Admiral's big office where there were lots of sea charts and maps pinned up on the wall. One of them depicted the list of names of ships or their tonnage that had been sunk by the ever-increasing squadrons of grey wolves.

The Black Rose

"This coming year is going to be a very lucrative and happy time for us submariners, and a pretty dismal one for the British. But there is something in your plan, and whilst it has a great deal of merit, it needs a special operation of its own to succeed. I shall think on it during your next patrol, which will be a quadruple one. You'll be taking a full cargo out to all our friends in time for Christmas, but on the way back you'll be laying secret minefields in positions that I have plotted for you. Nobody is to know about this, and all of which should take you about six weeks to complete. This is our big one 'tour de force' if you like, and the one that we'll be presenting to our Fuhrer, so our success is riding on your back."

Meir contained his grin but not the satisfaction he felt, when he told the admirals that all three of them involved with this special operation would be able to retire very rich and famous men. Volnigen merely chuckled and told Meir that they were already Baronial Grand Admirals.

The Black Rose

Chapter VI
Jezebels

Meir sailed his ship out to sea fully loaded with fresh supplies, including, according to the signal, 20 dozen hens and 30 dozen duck eggs. He had over 30 special passengers and this would be his last time before Christmas and good will towards all men. How ironic to celebrate such things in the middle of a world war.

The officers and men were busy with their now familiar daily routines, even sharing the odd moment to have a skylark from time to time. Meir advised his officers to let the men have their fun, as the task they were about to do would certainly make men of them all.

This went on for the three days transit, with Meir looking for his friends, yet with almost nowhere to hide, in almost 3,000,000 square kilometres of nothing but ocean. His daily sun and star fixes kept him on track to his first string, but it meant that he'd have to cross the main convoy shipping lanes to get to the other side for the return leg.

"As you know in times like these gentlemen, I get you together to sound you out on certain tactical ideas of mine, I give you the idea and its up to you to pick holes in it. You passengers are welcome to join in to give your tactical brains a bit of sharpening." Meir smiled then started as the officers relaxed in the passengers lounge.

The session went on until Meir's plan was shaped, refined and agreed upon. The U-boat skippers thought it was a crazy idea, but then most crazy ideas worked as long as the results were obtained.

It was the end of the first string of R/Vs some five days later when it was time to effect this tactic.

"Who's the OOW?" Meir asked as he entered the bridge.

The Black Rose

"I am captain" Voss replied smartly

"Hello 6th Mate. Get the lower deck cleared. Half on the fore and half on the after cargo decks.

"Fetch the first mate if you would, and then get yourself relieved, you're required on deck as of now."

"Aye aye captain. Our speed and course is unchanged." Voss replied then left.

"First mate. I want you to start converting the ship, using model 2. We have about four hours daylight left to complete it, and another four hours to get ourselves onto a suitable north easterly course." Meir ordered as he held up a picture of ship model 2.

"Aye aye captain. We'll have to dismantle our after derricks to do so, and even jettison some of our empty Tinned fish crates."

"No First mate. Just lower the booms down to deck level and use the empty crates to shore up the false side and deck panels. I will inspect it afterwards."

"Aye captain. The men will enjoy the next bit of the plan. Pity about not having real ones though." Schenk smiled as he left the bridge.

Meir watched the ship miraculously change itself from a tired old tramp steamer into a modern cargo passenger ship, as he worked with the navigator on their return course that would take them along their second string of grey wolves.

"Ship ready for inspection sir." Schenk reported.

"Very good first mate." Meir said as he commenced his inspection.

Meir was very critical about certain items that the men had to re-adjust or do again, before he was satisfied with everything.

"Well done First mate, now its party time. Break out the special boxes of clothing and have the crew come and see how

77

well they can dress up. I fancy it will be a very interesting time for us all, so get organised and I will be along to judge the best looking ones in two hours from now. But remember, only non-sounding German voices are to he heard." Meir grinned as he patted Schenk on the shoulder.

"We don't want mixed marriages now do we Victor!"

Schenk chuckled as he left to get the party organised in the passenger lounge.

Meir was summoned to judge, and was amazed by the transformation even the passengers lounge had taken on.

"Never have I seen such an ugly bunch of painted jezebels on one ship as I can see here tonight!" Meir laughed as the men greeted him with ribald remarks and saucy suggestions.

It was a beauty competition to see which of the crew got to dress up and act as female passengers during their transit back to Kildrum. This was a much sought after prize because it meant that each one would be excused duty for that time.

Meir inspected the 'ladies' and even got a slap on the wrist for 'being too forward with the merchandise' or had puckered lips thrust in his face, as he made his deliberations.

"I have selected the following numbers as winners." Meir announced, as he rattled off each number, getting howls of laughter and antics from the winners.

"You will be required to parade about, and act as a normal passenger would, either on deck or be seen in the windows of the lounge, until we get accepted into and given our place in the next convoy going east! The rest of you will resume your duties." he concluded, as the party feeling was shattered by Voss who came dashing into the lounge.

"Captain, I was on my way back onto the bridge to resume my duties as OOW, when a lookout reported smoke ahead of us and to starboard. It's a long way off, probably a coaler. What are your instructions?"

Meir left the lounge and walked swiftly along the narrow

The Black Rose

corridor and up the central stairway onto the bridge where he grabbed a pair of binoculars and scanned ahead of him.

It was getting dark but Meir spotted a few tale-tell signs of ships ahead of him and noted which way they appeared to be going.

"6th Mate. Get me the navigator and the radio officer." Meir ordered sharply.

Within moments both men were standing alongside Meir waiting orders.

"Navigator. We have three or more ships approx 20 kilometres ahead of us, moving left to right across our course. What courses are they headed? Brantz. I want you to monitor the signals from that area, and see if you can pick up anything that will give us a clue as to who's there, warships included. OOW! Hands to patrol routine.

"Excluding the passenger lounge, go to night lighting. Its Lights! Camera! Action time gentlemen." Meir chuckled as the officers obeyed their orders.

"Captain, we've spotted several more ships ahead stretching from Red 10 to Green 15. It might be the formation of another eastbound convoy." Schenk advised, poking his head into Meir's bridge cabin.

"Brantz has picked up a few names and types of ships too, including one warship!"

"OOW get the hands to Action stations. Its time to strike up the band. Make sure we're not lit up like a Christmas tree otherwise we'll annoy our neighbours."

"Aye aye captain."

"Ship at action stations" Beiderman reported, as he stood by Meir's chair awaiting orders.

"Very good Guns! I'll make a good OOW of you yet! If this is a convoy, then expect a warship to come snooping around us asking damn awkward questions just like the Dover Straits. Once we've got into our allocated position we can relax. It might take all night, in which case you will know all about that from an earlier occasion. Right Guns?"

Beiderman grunted his acknowledgement, as he was too busy looking through his binoculars.

"Captain! We have a row of starboard lights ahead of us about 15 kilometres and one port one. It looks like an escort coming our way. Bearing green 10." the signalman shouted from the starboard bridge wing.

Meir looked out towards that angle and saw a ghostly grey shape come out of the gloom with its signal lights flashing, and its searchlight flickering over the ship and to the bridge, almost blinding him.

Meir was handed his loudhailer and went out onto the wing waving his hat in the air with the other.

"He asks us what ship and where bound. But asks us to heave to!"

"Stop together!" Meir ordered then whispered to the Navigator who was standing next to him.

"Have some of our passengers come out onto the starboard passenger deck. Make sure they've got drinks or whatever in their hands."

"Hello *Killarney Castle*! Speak to the captain!" a voice from the warship shouted, but was intermittent due to the noise of the wind and splashing of the waves.

"Speaking! Captain O'Fool here." Meir said in his best Irish accent, and mentally thanked his foulmouthed pilot for it. There was an awkward pause from the warship before a reply came back.

"Hello Captain O'Tool. Where's Captain Dermot?"
Meir had remembered Kaufman's conversation with this officer as he nudged Klinshoff and gave him a wink.

"Captain Dermot? He's on the *Kilkenny*, admiral. But he's still trying to get his little train set working. I'm now on my way back, loaded with foodstuffs you can't seem to buy in Dublin."

The Black Rose

"Sorry Captain. I thought you were the *Kilkenny*. Maybe Dermot could do with a spare engine captain. What type of engine did he say he got?"

Meir smiled at this trick question and replied loud and clear. "Someone called Gottenmuller."

There was another long pause before the reply came back.

"Yes that's the one. Tell him he's a lucky man to own one of them. Anyway can't stand chatting here all day. We have an eastbound convoy up ahead that's in four lanes of 10 ships each. What speed can you do?"

"With wind and tide I can do 15 knots now I've had the boilers fixed."

"That's good. You can join lane two on the other side and slot yourself in behind the *Dalmatian*, and be third from last. Any sign of trouble, veer north towards Iceland out of the way, as there are other ships coming in behind you that you might not see."

"The *Dalmatian* from Liverpool did you say! The last time I saw her was in Pennsylvania about a month ago. A lovely cargo ship she is too."

"Yes, well good luck. Remember to keep in lane and at the mean convoy speed of 12 knots. Keep a base course of 095 from the one in front. We have 5 escorts to take you across and will meet a further three if all goes well. As I've said, any engine trouble then you're on your own, nobody will be stopping for absolutely anything until we get to the Clyde."

Meir shouted his thanks and waved to the officer as the warship veered sharply and raced away towards the convoy like a sheepdog rounding up its flock.

Meir turned to his grinning officers and members of the bridge crew who were cock-a-hoop at the deception, and even joked about it.

"Its Captain O'Fool be jasus and begorrah!" Klinshoff mimicked and ribbed Meir about it, who grinned as much as the rest of them and took it sportingly.

"Right then Navigator! Lay out that course we were given. Guns! I shall be going to the end of the convoy and work my way up between the 1st and 2nd columns. As we pass each ship, note down its name, port of registry, and type of ship, then give a copy to Brantz as well as myself. I shall be too busy to take notice, as I'll be conning the ship in the meantime. I will not be disturbed until such time we are in convoy position."

Meir steered his ship slowly through the waiting columns of ships and took up his position, as Beiderman chanted out the particulars of the ships.

"Guns! We're now under starters orders, so keep a good lookout for some signal flare or other as that's when we start moving."

"Aye aye captain"

"Navigator. It's now 2300. How far to the edge of the northern strings' patrol area?"

Klinshoff took a moment and gave his reply.

"Very good navigator! Guns! Secure from patrol routine until 0600. Try and redeem our ladies back into proper rig again and go to Action stations at 0630. Call me at 0500."

"Aye Aye captain."

Meir went to his day cabin and took a shower, as Winkler brought him a snack. He was feeling good with his plan and everything was working like clockwork for him. He even smiled again at the ruse he had pulled off with that stupid British officer, and at the vital piece of info about the *Dalmatian*. His personal journal would be full of such notations.

"0500 Captain! Here's some breakfast. Get it down you. It's bitterly cold and wet up on deck and the wind is rising." Winkler advised softly as he switched on the overhead bunk light.

Meir looked over to see Winkler smiling and laying out his foul-weather gear to wear, and looked at his barometer.

"Thank you steward. Make sure you've had yours because this is going to be one very long day. It looks as if we're in for a gale. Any snow yet?"

"No captain, but according to the wireless office, the new weather forecast is for snow blizzard conditions and very heavy seas. That's why I've laid out your thermals and cold weather gear." Winkler informed, as he left carrying the empty plate and cup away.

"OOW! Get hands to breakfast. Action stations will be delayed. Ask all ships officers to report to my day cabin immediately including the special officers."

Meir took the special convoy grid chart off the navigation chart table and went swiftly back down to his cabin again.

All the officers arrived within moments, some still with food in their mouths.

"My apologies gentlemen. Finish what you're eating and take a look at this chart." Meir soothed as he unfolded the ships' positions in the convoy

"It appears that we won't be able to make our R/V's with our northern string, unless we double back after what I propose to do." Meir started, as he went briefly through his plan.

The officers made counter suggestions on certain aspects of the plan, then after a brief show of agreement, they went to conduct their captains plan of action.

"Very good gentlemen. Lets give the men a good Christmas present. Navigator, relieve the 3rd mate and have him sent to me" Meir concluded.

Kirkmeister reported and quickly grasped the plan and his own involvement in it, before saluting Meir and rushing to do his duty.

"OOW! Darken ship, then have hands to Action stations!" Meir ordered as he arrived back onto the bridge again.

He waited until the bridge was fully manned and settled before issuing a string of orders that had men running around everywhere.

The Black Rose

"Bosun, tell the engine room to stop making smoke on the forward funnel, and reduce the after one by 50%. Then full ahead together, speed 25 knots. Guns! Get your mortars ready. Torpedo officer! Stand by all tubes. Tell the 6th mate to stand by to lay an egg pattern when I give the signal. Navigator, get ready to plot all changes of speed and courses.

"I want to leapfrog around the vessel in front and veer round beyond the outer columns and double back behind the convoy before turning and escaping due north." Meir's orders came like bullets out of a machine gun.

"Bosun have your men on their toes. Stand by to execute Operation Jezebel." Meir paused and felt the extreme tension and anticipation from all men on the bridge

This would be his pattern of rapid fire orders issued each time for this type of action.

Meir would be like the conductor of an orchestra as he kept himself in unison with the ebb and flow of his attack that would be measured in heartbeats.

"What's our speed? Signalman, where are the escorts?"

"18 knots and rising!"

"One up ahead, one astern, one in and around the convoy, the other two are tracking a parallel course on the outer lanes." Came the answers.

Meir looked through his binouculars and made a slow sweep of all around his ship before he started to give a rapid fire of orders.

"Torpedo Officer! Fire stern tube 8 in 5 seconds, then count 5 seconds and fire 7 at an angle of 20 degrees outward from the stern. Helmsman! Full ahead together and tell the engine room to make speed 30 knots!

"Torpedo Officer! You will then fire for'ard tube 1 at an angle of 15 degrees outward from the bow, then port tubes 3 & 5 as a broadside when the angles are at optimum angles. Reload when fired, you've got exactly five minutes to get each

The Black Rose

tube fully reloaded."

The ship gave a shudder as the first of the torpedoes were fired followed by the second salvo.

"Starboard 20! Slow astern starboard, full ahead Port! Tell the 6th mate to start rolling the eggs!

"Guns! Fire all four mortars with H.E. in between columns 3 and 4 to create a diversion whilst we get over to the outer lane."

No sooner had the ship raced across the bows of the ship that was ahead of their column, when there was several loud explosions as each torpedo found its target.

"Fire tube 1. Count five seconds then fire 2 then 3. Keep those eggs rolling. Fire tubes 4 then 6 when reached critical angles."

Meir torpedoed four more ships as he weaved through the lines of the convoy and turned full circle around the outside of it. He noticed the freshly scattered mines were starting to take their own toll as the following ships blundered into them.

"Midships! Steer 010. Make full smoke on both funnels. Keep those mines rolling.

"Guns! Get your main weapon systems raised and ready in case we're followed. Load with armour piercing. Stand by after tubes." Meir shouted, as he watched with pleasure his handiwork and the absolute destruction he had created.

"That should give them something to think about!" he muttered as he watched yet another ship blew up in spectacular fashion, to sink before his gaze.

The ship raced away northward for several hours, and away from the noises of explosions and the carnage they left behind them, but nobody followed them.

"It appears that we're safe Guns! Nobody suspected anything else but U-boats. Your mortars gave the impression of U-boats on the surface, which helped create mayhem and panic and the ships to break ranks and race in any direction but where they thought the U-boats were."

The Black Rose

The reports came in from the lookouts, who had counted each ship hit and sunk by torpedo, and those that hit mines. Meir and Klinshoff crossed each ship off from the grid and stood mesmerized at what they had done.

"Do you realise gentlemen! We have torn the heart out of a convoy of 40 ships, by sinking 18 of them, all on our own and all within two hours of starting the operation. We managed to sink 14 by torpedoes, and can account 4 more by mines.

"That means, some 400,000 tons of fuel and supplies can now been crossed off the British shopping list. The cherry on the cake is that we sank an escort destroyer into the bargain, before escaping.

"We now have 20 ships and 1 destroyer as our tally. But just you wait until HQ hears about our action today. I wonder of our other brothers sailing dedicated ships such as this one could match that score!" Meir bragged, and smiled broadly as he held up the convoy chart for everybody to see.

"Slow ahead both. Port 15. Navigator, find us a course to get back onto R/V base track. Secure from action stations. Patrol routine." Meir ordered as he let everybody see the records for themselves.

"Bold and ruthless as the hawk, gentlemen!" he whispered as each man was amazed by what they saw.

Meir went into the passenger lounge to explain to the guest officers that they would be a bit late, but showed them exactly what had taken place.

To a man, they were astounded and started to cheer and clap him.

"You'd make a good U-boat captain." the senior of them admitted as he unpinned his submarine badge and pinned it to Meir's chest.

"I was presented with this many years ago by Admiral Horstenitz. You have sunk more ships in one action than a whole squadron of U-boats."

The Black Rose

"I thank you for your generosity Captain, but it was only an opportune moment for me to try out one of my theoretical tactical moves."

The modest speech Meir made, drew mild rebukes and ribbing from the rest of the passengers, as they started to sing the submariners anthem again. This time Meir managed to join in with the words instead of miming them as before.

Meir left the euphoric atmosphere of the passengers' lounge feeling that he mush have somehow missed his vocation, U-boats, instead of a captain on a pretend merchant vessel.

He arrived into his day cabin feeling exhausted and with a sense of anticlimax, as he had wanted to try his retreat tactics on the escort who really should have followed him. He felt incomplete and unsatisfied, but shrugged his shoulders and put it to one side for some future encounter, perhaps.

The ship made its full string of R/Vs and was on its way to its secondary patrol duty, laying the hens eggs.

It had to pass through the Northern Channel between Scotland and Northern Ireland, before it made its way down the full length of the Irish Sea and back to base again.

Fortunately it was very rough weather and poor visibility enabling Meir to lay his 'Duck egg' mines in the entrance of the famous Belfast Lough, before racing full speed home to his secret bolthole.

Whereas the duck eggs were magnetic mines, which laid on the sea floor, the hens' eggs were contact mines, which floated on or just under the surface of the water.

Meir saw a little puff of smoke coming from the island and cheered as he recognised the *Ballymuffin* dancing its way over the big waves.

The fisherman stepped onto the bridge and was given a cheer by the bridge crew, as Meir greeted him with his best impersonation.

"Well if it ain't the fuckin' *Ballymuffin,* skipper and all, begorrah!"

The fisherman just scowled and swore in his usual manner, which delighted the bridge crew who cheered him on.

"Pilot! May we have the pleasure of you taking us into port now, we want a taste of dry land for a while!" Meir said as he saluted the man and ushered him to the ship's wheel.

"You fuckin' lot must'a been on the fuckin' wakky bakky or sometin'!" he growled, but gave a big smile in response, as he guided the ship into its little harbour with ease.

Volginen greeted Meir with a salute as somebody reeled out a large red carpet for them to walk on as they stepped out of the car at the HQ compound.

All who attended the celebrations feted Meir, as his convoy action tactics were explained and retold all evening. The champagne and caviar was in abundance everywhere as Meir was brought into a side office where several newsmen and cameras were waiting to ambush him. They surrounded him as the flash cameras popped and men asked various questions for several minutes when there was a hush, as a big door opened to reveal Admiral's Meir and Horstenitz standing there.

"Captain Hans Otto Von Meir! It gives me great pleasure to decorate you with Germany's highest bravery award. The Knights Cross with swords with gold Laurel leaves!" Admiral Meir announced as he placed the medal around his son's neck.

Meir stood ramrod still and looked incredulously at the three admirals, who also wore the same highest accolade their country could award its citizens.

"Congratulations Otto!" they said in unison as they clapped politely. Meir stood dumbstruck at this surprise investiture, but merely saluted them, as the cameras flashed again and again.

The night wore on until the party drew to a close, leaving only the three admirals, Captain Meir and the ever-faithful steward, Winkler.

The Black Rose

"Now that everybody has gone, we can get down to some urgent business. Winkler, finish clearing away, and take the rest of the night off and spread the word that everybody's got the day off tomorrow. Send for my Flag officer and tell him to bring my brief case, on your way out." Admiral Meir stated quietly, as the four men walked out of the party room and into an unlit side office.

The flag officer appeared with the brief case and handed it to Admiral Meir

Meir showed the admirals all his documentation, marked 'OPERATION JEZEBEL' with the symbol of the *BLACK ROSE* stamped below the writing. It included maps, charts, diagrams, and tactical orders given and other items that were recorded.

All of which drew more noises of encouragement and a job well done, before Admiral Meir gave his son a wax-sealed envelope.

"This is from the Fuhrer himself" he explained as Meir opened it carefully and commenced reading it.

"But Admiral! That's one big area for me to cover, just for one squadron of U-boats. Where is the logistical support and friendly port like we've got here?" Meir objected strongly.

The admiral's spoke in turn but did not criticize the document, merely offered their support in any way they could. They explained that it was the Fuhrer who latched onto their successful operations from Kildrum and because of it he would be expanding the entire concept in a much bigger way than what they had tried or imagined they could do.

Meir raised several operational matters and problems that the admirals tried to overcome. But it became clear to him that he was talking to a brick wall.

"Otto! It's a matter of 'You will do this by order of the Fuhrer, or else you die like a dog!' Besides, you've proved even to us that you're the best man to make this operation succeed.

Your last engagement proved that." Horstenitz said evenly but with a deadpan face.

"Just sleep on it for a day or so. There's no rush to start. Besides its Christmas!" Horstenitz said expansively as he put an arm around the smaller man and hugged him.

"Yes son! The Fuhrer has already given us, and now you, a handsome present in recognition of our part in the pursuance of the new order of the *3rd Reich*! We three admirals can now enjoy his full support.

"The ship's company's present from the Fuhrer, is a months wages plus three weeks leave as of tomorrow once we've de-stored and settled your ship down for the festive period.

"There is a special plane to take them all home. All except we admirals, yourself and about seven others within our operational command, that is." Admiral Meir concluded as the men left the offices for the night.

Meir went to his ship to say goodbye to his men before they left on their well-earned leave, with his Father's words echoing in his ears.

"We are mere regular sailors obeying the Naval Officer Academy code of honour. Therefore any Jewish or Polish shipmate within our command will not be going on leave, but kept behind for their own safety, Otto!"

Chapter VII
Corkscrews

Meir spent his Christmas ashore in the HQ complex whilst he had several modifications made to the ship. He went through several tactical ideas that he had written up, all of which was closely scrutinised by the admirals.

This time, also meant for planning for the next stage of Meir's operations, was, much to the impatience and the annoyance, finally put on hold.

"Never mind Otto! This means that you can go out on your patrols with a free hand to support our surface raiders up north, as long as you meet your delivery targets." Horstenitz stated stoically, and the others echoed that remark.

The crew arrived back full of joviality and in good spirit just waiting to have another crack at the so-called 'invincible rulers of the waves'.

The ship was given a quick hull scrape and was eventually loaded up with supplies, ready for her new patrol as Meir received his usual set of orders and special code words.

"You have been given a list of passenger ships to look out for. But do not attempt any main armament or gun action until you're on your way back, and even then make sure its only troops embarked. We are still part of a Sovereign Navy Otto, only doing our job, and not butchers!"

"Very well admiral. Must leave now." Meir stated, as he saluted Horstenitz and went back onto his ship as the gangway was being hoisted off.

"Prepare to get under way, First Mate. Never mind the fisherman, we can do without him from now on. Darken ship. Tell the engine room no smoke."

"Aye aye captain."

Meir conned his ship through the harbour and out into the ocean, and into the teeth of a full gale and under the cover of

The Black Rose

the pre-dawn darkness.

"Secure from Harbour stations. First mate, get the deck watch to double check the deck cargo and that all hatchways are secured. Then Patrol routine. Navigator, we shall go anti-clockwise, so set a course for our northern string of R/Vs. Make speed 18 knots." Meir ordered as he left the bridge.

The ship punched her way up and through the big waves and clawed her way back up again as she re-emerged from plunging deep into the troughs on the other side. The shuddering, juddering, corkscrewing motion of the ship was to be endured by any ship in those waters.

The storm lasted for nearly three days before it passed them by. It left the ocean calm as if the storm had swept all the lumps and creases out of the water.

"OOW! Increase speed to 25 knots. Call the navigator and have him to assist me in a position fix."

"Aye aye sir!" was the standard reply.

Meir and the navigator took their midday position and entered it onto their sea chart.

"We have to alter course to starboard to compensate for our last three days blown off course, 2nd. Given a speed of 30 knots and on that new bearing, so we can come back to the base course again.

"Thankfully it will take us a few hours less to reach our first R/V than we anticipated."

Meir gave the orders for the new speed and course and was about to go below again, when a lookout reported a ship sighting. He went out to the bridge wing and looked at where the ship was located, to discover that it looked like a fast moving troop ship coming their way.

"OOW! Hands to action stations! Get all weapon systems closed up!"

Meir sat in his chair with Beiderman and Flens flanking

The Black Rose

him, and Klinshoff standing by the chart.

"Guns! As soon as we fire our first salvo of torpedoes, I want you to blast the bridge and wireless mast with 'A' turret, then as we pass, let rip with the rest of your weapon systems. Make sure of your first shot, I don't want them to be able to use their radio. This is a troop ship, so I want no survivors!" Meir ordered coldly as the others looked at him in astonishment.

"These are my orders gentlemen. Kill troops on ships, but sink the others. Now don't just stand there looking at me, get to your duties." He snapped.

"5th Mate. We shall meet starboard to starboard but I want to circle the ship and fire into her other side. I want at least 6 torpedoes in her. Range Guns?"

"8 kilometres. Captain"

"Stop together! Stand by for'ard torpedo tubes! Set range 1,000 metres, and 2 degrees from the bow. We're going down her throat before we alter to port, Guns. We shall be losing speed rapidly so that I can be able to dance around her other side. Make your calculations for firing accordingly." Meir hissed as he kept looking at the increasingly larger ship bearing down them.

"Fire!" Flens shouted down his command telephone. Followed seconds later by Beidermans commands

"2 rounds H.E. 'A' gun Fire!"

"Starboard 20, full astern port, full ahead starboard!" Meir ordered.

"Bofors and Mortars commence firing! 'A' and 'X' turrets rapid fire! Commence when in sight. Heavy machine gun systems, in automatic, Fire!" Beiderman shouted in quick succession as both ships passed within 2 cables of each other.

Three torpedoes, and a hail of 4.5 gun shells, mortars, bofors and the 50mm machine guns struck the large troop ship simultaneously. It seemed to stop almost in its tracks as if hitting a brick wall; with people screaming and shouting so loud it almost drowned the gunfire.

The Black Rose

"Full ahead together!"

Meir turned his ship quickly around and sped up on the other side of the hapless ship, firing another broadside of torpedoes and bullets at it, before it sank rapidly leaving a pool of blood where it sank.

The machine gunners were shooting and strafing at those who managed to get away from the ship until there was no trace of life or signs that a ship was once in that spot.

"Cease firing. Cease firing!" Meir ordered, as their guns fell silent.

A seaman came up into the bridge and gave Meir a lifebelt and told him that there were no survivors.

Meir looked at the name and declared that it was a despicable action, but one that was necessary.

"This tactic, like the convoy one, will be named in honour of the ship that was killed. Our convoy tactic was named the *Dalmatian*, this one gentlemen will now be called the '*Windermere*" he said as he held up the belt for the others to read. *SS. LAKE WINDEMERE*. Southampton.

Brantz came onto the bridge with his ships' register and pronounced that it was a 27,000-ton Blue Liner Passenger ship, licensed to carry up to 7,000 troops.

The bridge crew fell silent and looked crestfallen at what they had done, but Meir turned round to Brantz and announced loudly.

"That action only took 30 minutes Guns. We've saved our own troops that little bit more, so well done everybody. Secure from action stations. Go to replenishment stations in one hour. Navigator, get us back on course for our 1st string R/V." Meir said brightly, then left the bridge feeling pleased with himself for an action well conducted.

The ship had completed her first pass and started on her way for the 2nd pass for the southern string when a warship was spotted on the horizon coming up behind them.

The Black Rose

Meir heard the report to the OOW as he was in his bridge cabin at the time, and came dashing out to look for himself.

"Hands to action stations. Tell the engine room to increase smoke gradually, from both funnels. Make your speed 12 knots!"

"Ship at action stations captain" Beiderman reported.

"Guns. Get the 6th mate to start rolling a pattern of eggs. But tell him do it only when the smoke is nice and thick and is touching the water. That way, our stranger won't be able to see what we're up to."

Beiderman left to carry out the orders as Meir turned to Flens.

"It looks as he is the lead ship to a convoy and is overhauling us to see who we are. We will let him make his overtaking manoeuvre before you fire your broadside torpedoes. That's if one of our mines doesn't get him."

Flens nodded and got his weapon system ready for firing.

Beiderman came back and received his gunnery orders, which kept him busy whilst Meir studied the horizon behind the oncoming warship.

"Guns. Get a lookout on the top of the bridge and have him look behind the warship. I can't see for smoke, but I've a hunch we need to get to our R/V's before this bloody lot approaches. If not then their shooting opportunity will be lost because of it."

Beiderman sent one of the bridge lookouts on the errand, who came back within minutes to report that there were several columns of smoke over the horizon but he couldn't see the ships themselves.

Meir brushed his long black hair back from his forehead, then stroked the end of his short but hooked nose.

While he was contemplating his next move, a splash rose up in front of their starboard bow.

"That is a warning shot gentlemen, which means unless we stop we will get the next one. Slow ahead together and get ready to starboard your helm Bosun. We're going to turn beam on and give them a full broadside. She won't be able to bring her aft armament into use, so stand by all guns. Keep out of sight until I give the word, then open fire with everything you've got, but make sure her radio antennae are destroyed in the first salvo."

Meir watched the warship range close down to almost 1 sea mile, before he ordered his ship into action.

"Starboard 20. Full ahead port, full astern starboard."

The ship pivoted and swung swiftly round in front of the unsuspecting warship, then unleashed a hail of bullets and torpedoes at her.

The warship was taken by surprise and was too late to react, as two torpedoes slammed into her and her bridge and forward guns disintegrated in a hail of high explosives. The warship started to move slowly round, another two torpedoes slammed into her side, stopped her dead in her tracks, as more shells slammed into the rest of the ship. She exploded into a fireball then sank within seconds, leaving no trace, except a smudge of oil where she sank.

The men gave a huge cheer and hugged each other with delight, including the bridge crew.

"Scratch a 'W' class off the Royal Navy's repair bills, and add it to our tally gentlemen. Secure from action stations. Replenishment stations in half an hour." Meir smiled as he went over to the chart and marked the position where the ship sank.

"OOW! Ask Brantz to speak to me!"

"Aye aye captain!" came the pleased reply.

"Brantz. Tell our friends that there's a convoy behind us and we'll be coming in at full speed. I will take two boats at a time, if they can make the same R/V spot. They have four hours to reach me, here are my expected positions." Meir ordered, as he handed the co ordinates to Brantz.

Brantz came back an hour later telling him that the first two were waiting for him, and the others were getting paired off.

The Black Rose

"OOW! Hands to replenishment stations! Standby to receive two boats, both sides! In fact, have all all hands mustered on deck for this one."

"Aye aye captain."

Meir signalled to the two boats' captains that he would need to keep moving, and for them to keep a steerage speed of about 8 knots.

This had never been attempted before in calm waters let alone in a lumpy ocean, but Meir was determined that it was done, in order for him to complete his run.

He watched impatiently as the two U-boats took their supplies off him and completed their personnel transfers before he finally waved them off and moved onto his next pair. It was a race against time for Meir and he knew it, so he kept his men at replenishment stations until all the string was supplied. The last pair of U boats were being being done in the early morning light of the second day after sinking the destroyer.

"Hands secure from replenishment stations. Set patrol routine. Navigator, set a course for home. Using a speed of 25 knots, let me know our expected time of arrival (ETA) Kildrum." Meir yawned as he walked wearily towards his day cabin and a much-needed shower.

"If you feel like that captain, how do you think the crew feel?" Winkler asked quietly.

"No doubt they feel the same. But just think of the rest they will get when we dock again. Besides steward, it was the sinking of the destroyer kept them going." Meir replied philosophically.

Winkler just grinned and nodded his head, as he knew that Meir was totally right.

Once more the ship came back into Kildrum and docked for a little rest before being loaded for her next run.

"Otto! It appears that the world is shouting foul over the sinking of an unarmed liner full of American tourists. Judging

The Black Rose

by my calculations, it must have been in your sector. Either you sunk it, or our friends did, which is it?" Holsenitz asked angrily.

Meir stated that he was the one responsible, and anyway he had only carried out his remit, by sinking any vessel used against the German people. It was a troop ship laden with soldiers, he declared and produced the lifebelt and some khaki tunics that some of his sailors fished out of the water.

One piece of khaki had a red flash naming a Canadian Province Regiment that was carried on board.

Horstenitz looked at Meir's impassive face and smiled.

"Well, you certainly have been busy this time Otto! You've also sunk a destroyer too. On top of that, you've managed to supply two U-boats at once and under way too just like the British Navy. If you keep on going like that, we can stop the war soon and all go home."

Meir just looked at the admiral, nodded his head and handed over his sealed documentation, which contained the records of his last voyage.

The ship was kept in harbour for a few days, for the crew to enjoy time ashore before Meir was called for a special briefing with the three admirals.

Meir went through the main operations room into the admirals' large meeting room, where he saw them looking intently over a large sea chart.

"Afternoon Otto! We have a special operation for you to undertake, but first you must look at our map to see what we'll be briefing you on." Volginen greeted, as he gestured Meir to come over to the large table.

"This is your current patrol area as you can see." Horstenitz said as he pointed across the chart with a slender stick.

"Thanks to you we've managed to develop it but it has become too cumbersome for you to handle now, because we have a double string of 40 U-boats each, across the Northern Atlantic.

The Black Rose

They will be covering the northern shipping route, and will be supplied directly from the newly acquired French ports on the Atlantic seaboard. We don't have to make the long journey around the top of Britain to get on patrol now, which means that our boats can spend longer at sea and dodge back as and when. Because of this wonderful piece of fortune, we can set up another string to the south, to cover the British southern supply routes." Horstenitz paused to show Meir the new position.

"Otto! This is where you come in again." Admiral Meir said.

"I wondered when I'd be mentioned." Meir said sarcastically, but smiled as if to take the sting out of his seeming insubordination to his admirals.

"Yes, quite Otto!" Horstenitz said flatly then continued with the briefings.

"They will be operating in a line from Cadiz to the Azores. But you will be operating either from the Grand Canarias, or a special place that we're building for you on the Spanish Sahara coast. It will be just like this place, fully fortified and equipped to take supplies. We get most of our diesel fuel from Morocco and the Spanish Sahara oilfields, so you will not be short of fuel. Once that has been established, the other plans we talked about will then be initiated in the same way but across to the other side of the Atlantic."

Meir listened to the briefings, raising suggestions or objections as he saw fit.

"It appears that Otto wants to run his own show, gentlemen." Volginen sighed at Meirs continual objections.

Admiral Meir turned to his son and told him that it was more of a political thing than mere naval tactics. That is why he was to pick up some special passengers from La Corunna and take them to Cadiz.

"So I'm to become a spy runner and a Gestapo cruise ship! Is that all I get for my troubles in the Northern Atlantic?" Meir demanded angrily.

The Black Rose

"Not at all Otto! Once you've disembarked your special passengers at Cadiz, you can proceed towards your special operations base. That is the plan anyway." Admiral Meir said re-assuringly.

Meir looked at the map and the places marked on the North African coast, then looked across to the Caribbean Sea.

"I wouldn't mind a few cruises over there. I haven't been there since I was a midshipman on leave with Uncle Heinz."

"Unfortunately Uncle Heinz will not be there, but you still have his ship, which is almost as good, Otto."

"That's providing I'm not sunk, nor set upon by the Gestapo, dear father."

"Just as long as you are doing your duty and helping the cause of the *Third Reich* as you have been doing these last seven months, they will leave you alone. In fact they'd probably help you in more ways than you think." Horstenitz rejoined as the admirals felt that Meir was coming round to the new concepts of a war that Germany appeared to be winning.

The briefings went on for several hours more, with only brief interludes for refreshments, before the four men had exhausted their salient points or critical items that needed to be sorted out.

Meir left the HQ building and decided to walk back to the ship, almost robotically, his mind still on the various important points that stuck in his mind that needed time to think about. He finally arrived on board and was greeted by his least favourite person, standing at the top of the gangway.

"Evenin' Admiral! It's been a fuckin' lovely day, spoilt because I've been fuckin' detailed off to come and see you." The fisherman greeted affably.

Meir sighed wearily, as he turned to the man.

"Well if it isn't the fuckin' bog stomping trotter, smelling of fuckin' god knows what." Meir replied tersely, and looked at the QM for some sort of support.

"What is it I can do for you pilot?" he asked condescendingly.

"I've been given special fuckin' orders to join you for some cruise that your admirals have been promising me ever since you fuckin' lot arrived. I've come aboard now in case you fuckin' lot sail without me."

"QM! Get this foulmouthed person off my ship and tell him to come back tomorrow and see the Bosun. Tell the Bosun to expect him. Also spread the word that I'm not to be disturbed tonight." Meir said with gritted teeth, as he barged past the man and made his way to his day cabin. He did not suffer fools gladly, and would probably have shot him there and then had he been armed.

"Morning Captain! Its 0700, I have your breakfast ready and a copy of today's newspapers. You take time and enjoy them, the ship can wait another couple of hours." Winkler said, as he scraped a chair towards the table.

"Morning Winkler." Meir said groggily, as he felt bone weary and mentally tired.

"My father sends his regards. I'll be seeing him later on today, so you can accompany me to see him for a while if you wish."

"Why thank you captain. I'll do just that." Winkler said appreciatively as he went to leave the cabin.

"Oh steward. Before you go, ask the First Mate to get all the officers together in the lounge to see me at 0830."

"Aye aye captain. If you promise me to have an hour to yourself first." Winkler replied with concern for his captain, as he shut the door quietly behind him

Chapter VIII
Little Balls

Telling his officers to settle down, Meir unfolded a large chart with several coloured lines, crosses and places marked on it, and pinned it upon the bulkhead behind him. He picked up a black pointer stick and started to explain the key codes of the chart, stopping to let each officer take in what he said. He explained exactly what the three admirals had told him and the problems or unforeseen gremlins that might crop up during their operations. Then went on to find out their opinions.

"It has been my custom to invite my officers to attend these briefings, mainly to express their thoughts on the matters in hand. We have had several such brainstorming sessions in the past, which meant that my actions taken were on the consensus of my officers. That way, any unpleasantness or backlash to our endeavours encountered, everybody shares the blame for and not just the captain. In other words gentlemen, you carry the can just as much as I do, even though the buck stops with me.

"I am the captain of this ship and what I say goes. However, I shall leave you all to make up your own minds as to who is coming with me or not. It's your decision gentlemen." Meir concluded as he left his officers to discuss things amongst themselves.

Meir was tutored by his father since he was a midshipman, that commanding a ship was a privilege and only enjoyed if he had the complete trust and backing from his crew, especially his officers.

If that was true, then the captain would enjoy immense popularity within the fleet, and if the Kaiser got to know, and was pleased, could rise to a very high rank with all the trappings to go with it. This was why he adopted the age-old and foolproof method of his father's teachings.

The Black Rose

Meir returned to the lounge seeking his officers decision, and was met by Schenk.

"Captain. We are of a unanimous decision, that we ask you to lead us into glory for our Fuhrer and our Fatherland.

"We will serve you and you have our unconditional support in whatever future you map out for us."

Meir looked at each mans face around him and saw pride and pleasure written across their faces.

"Very well my officers. We sail tomorrow morning at 0500. But you are warned that we have a very difficult time in front of us. Starting with the company of our pilot." Meir said earnestly but with wickedness in his voice, when he mentioned the fisherman.

"Oh no! Not the fuckin' fisherman!" Several of the officers shouted in mock horror.

Meir grinned and told them all that the admirals had promised the fisherman that he'd have a special holiday, and a cruise on the ship, to pay him for his good services. So who was Captain Meir to deny that mans holiday?

This gave way to hoots of laughter and derision until Meir indicated that the briefing was now at a close, and he left his officers to celebrate their next victorious voyage whatever it was. He left knowing that whatever the future held, he had the undying support from his officers and men.

The ship was prepared and fully loaded for its next voyage to an unknown destiny as Meir attended his final briefing at the HQ complex.

"I shall be seeing you again in Mazanan soon Otto. But for Christ sakes, keep a cool head when you take on board your special passengers. They seem to have the knack of usurping our command even though they may be of a junior rank to us, such is their power." Horstenitz stated ominously as the other officers looked on, straight-faced and without a flicker of emotion.

Meir felt a shudder go down his spine and knew he was in for a torrid time, but merely nodded his head in acknowledgement and took his pack of sealed orders.

"Ship ready for sea captain! We have a full cargo but on an even keel. Tide turns in 15 minutes." Schenk reported as Meir arrived onto the bridge.

"Very good First Mate. Have we got our Irish pilot on board?"

"I'm standing by the fuckin' wheel, admiral." came the reply.

Meir looked over to the man and groaned, but decided to let him take the wheel for his last moment of glory before he became part of the Kriegsmarine discipline.

"Thank you pilot." Meir responded as he manoeuvred his ship out of the harbour, and waved to the three admirals who stood on the dockside watching him go.

"Relieve the pilot and get him below. Steer 180. Speed 15 knots. Navigator! Lay a direct course to our next R/V. Set passage routine." Meir ordered, as the bridge crew made their immediate change over.

The ship sailed steadily southward towards the northern coast of Spain, enjoying a carefree and leisurely time, with little or no concern to bother them as they went.

On the third day out, Meir opened his sealed orders and read them carefully, to make certain that he understood exactly what was required of him.

'On no account should you get yourself entangled into a compromising position. You are a professional navy man, protect it.' Meir read, as he remembered what was said and what he felt back in Kildrum.

There was something ominous, and a foreboding that was telling him something was not quite right, but he could not figure what it was. He decided to leave well alone until whatever was nagging him, manifested itself up for him to deal with it.

"Captain. Approaching our R/V point. We have a pilot launch waiting to take us in." Kirkmeister advised, as he poked his head through the bridge cabin doorway.

"Thank you. Get our guest pilot onto the bridge, but tell the Bosun to take the wheel. Hands to harbour stations."

"Aye aye captain!"

Meir strode out of his little cabin at the back of the bridge and saw the harbour entrance to La Corunna beckoning him.

"OOW! Get me a Spanish speaking officer on the bridge to translate for me."

The fisherman stood by the Bosun, watching the proceedings, but went over to Meir and interrupted his orders

"Captain! I've met many a fuckin' Dago, fishing off my waters many a time. I can speak their fuckin' lingo and I can pilot, as you know. I've looked at these waters and feel good about what I see. Without that, I just don't fuckin' sail into them."

Meir was taken by surprise by the fisherman's revelation.

"Okay Bog stomper, you're on. I have perfectly good officers and helmsmen to do the job anyway. Any wrong move and I'll shoot you like a dog." Meir replied angrily.

"Captain! That's no fuckin' way to answer me. I'm only trying to be fuckin' helpful to you. Just give me a fuckin' go that's all. I've always fancied myself in fuckin' strange waters anyway."

"Very well pilot. So long as you stop your fuckin' swearing!" Meir replied, as the fisherman smiled back at him.

The Spanish pilot came on board as if he owned the ship, full of self-importance, and totally ignorant to who may have understood his language.

"Who is el Capitan? I will pilot dis sheep into harbours." the Spaniard stated in a bombastic way, before the fisherman shouted at him.

The Black Rose

Meir could understand most of the Spanish spoken, but was in tears of laughter when Klinshoff translated what the fisherman said.

It was obvious to Meir that the Spaniard was verbally put into his place, as he adopted a more civil and polite manner.

The fisherman steered the ship as instructed, translating engine or other course changes as he went along, until the ship finally arrived alongside a deserted stone jetty, save for a few men as the shore berthing party.

The Spanish officer saluted the fisherman, and flicked two fingers at Meir as he left the bridge, swearing as he left. The fisherman responding in kind and with his own gestures back to the astonished Spanish pilot.

Meir walked over to the fisherman, still chuckling as he put an arm around him.

"You are a fuckin' mad Irishman. You can fuckin' steer my ship into any port we visit. How would you like to become my own fuckin' special pilot, Pilot?"

"Well I'd be fuckin' delighted admiral. I was getting bored with this fuckin' cruise anyway."

"First mate. See to it that our pilot here is given a courtesy title and made a 'Special officer' commensurate with the Supply Officer. Just one slight thing for you to realise, I don't take to swearing on my ship, have you got that, pilot?"

"Thank you captain! That's a fuckin' deal, happy to oblige." the fisherman beamed as he held his hand out for Meir to shake.

"We do not shake hands on this ship. A salute is more our style, pilot. But just this once." Meir chided softly, still with a smile, and shook his hand to seal their bargain.

"Finished with main engines. Fall out from harbour stations. Leave for non-duty men until 0700 tomorrow. Navigator, ask the 1st Mate to see me, I shall be in my day cabin." Meir ordered as the bridge was being emptied of crew.

"First mate! Come in if you please" Meir acknowledged, as Schenk appeared.

"We are to standby to receive a few special guests shortly. They appear not to have been on the dockside when we arrived, so be on the gangway to meet them. I shall receive them in the lounge, and make sure it is clean and clear and ready for guests. Tell the supply officer to cater for an impromptu cocktail party when they arrive."

"Aye aye captain. Do we need any special linguists?"

"No. We have the German Consul and his staff plus a few of our Spanish friends who speak our language anyway."

"Aye aye captain!" Schenk responded and left as Winkler came through the doorway.

"Get me my best uniform out and prepare to receive guests in here. I don't want it looking like a pigstye."

"Don't worry captain! You seem to forget that I've had several years looking after a Grand Admiral. Leave everything to me, including the cocktail party in the lounge. Just you calm down and be natural." Winkler said calmly as he started to lay out Meir's best uniform, and his new set of bravery medals.

"When they see your new collection of medals, they will be like putty in your hands captain, so use it to your best advantage at all times. Do not let them dictate to you, or let them make you bend to their wishes. These people are our slaves, not the other way round. That is the advice I give to you as told to me by your father."

Meir looked at Winkler and nodded his appreciation.

"I'm glad you came on board, Winkler. Now leave me to get on."

Meir stood on the gangway with Schenk as several well-dressed people walked happily up the gangway and onto the ship.

Unknown to Meir, Winkler was standing behind him and

whispered to him, as to who the persons were coming towards him.

Meir whispered his thanks, as he saw Winkler disappear through a hatchway.

"Good evening, captain!" The first person greeted condescendingly.

"Good evening Consul and Lady Steiner. Good evening Commodore and Lady Lutz!"

Meir greeted each dignitary as they arrived on board much to the surprise of the visitors as they did not expect Meir to know them.

"It appears that the Kriegsmarine has sent us their top man." Commodore Lutz stated as he recognised Meir's medals and sashes.

Meir invited them to accompany him to the passengers' lounge where they would be received rather than on a drafty gangway.

"Are you sure we're invited on board your little ship, sailor Boy? Only last time, I was thrown off it." came a sarcastic voice and a ring of smoke that drifted over Meir.

Meir turned to see the same fur-coated female smoking probably the same foul smelling cigarette.

"But of course Ms Wintemann, unless you find it more pleasing standing around in drafty doorways!" Meir retorted, which drew a scowl from the woman.

The guests arrived into the lounge and saw all the trophies Meir and his ship had won, which drew whistles of incredulity from the guests.

"Sunk two destroyers I see." the commodore commented, sounding very impressed with what he saw.

"What you see is only a few mementoes of what my men have achieved. It is the ship that should take the credit." Meir said humbly, but was pooh-poohed by all.

The Black Rose

The short welcoming party came to an end as Steiner called time for everybody to get ashore.

"Captain. Come and see me at my office tomorrow morning about 1100. I have a diplomatic bag arriving with special orders for you. Good night, and thanks for having us!"

"I shall be there. Thank you for meeting me, Consul." Meir replied, as he escorted his guests back across the gangway, making certain that Ms Wintermann was with them, before he himself left the gangway.

Meir had this weird feeling again, and sensed that something was afoot, that would come and plague him. He spent ages agonising on what this feeling was, and put it all down to that woman.

But what could a slip of a woman do to a national hero was his thoughts, but remembered his fathers words of advice.

'*Keep it military. Let others do their own work.*'

Meir took Schenk with him to the meeting at the Consulate, they stepped out of the limousine and into the cool marble hallway, which had a large picture of Hitler suspended under an even larger wooden eagle representing the German Eagle.

They did not have time to gaze or take in their surroundings, as a neatly dressed lady came and ushered them into Steiner's office.

"Good morning gentlemen. You are on sovereign soil of the German *Third Reich,* therefore we can speak openly without any fear of being overheard." Steiner greeted, as he indicated to them to take a seat.

Steiner pulled a large black canvas bag from under his desk, lifted it and placed it heavily onto his highly polished table.

"Here is your diplomatic bag. Excluding Ms Wintermann of course!" Steiner joked and looking for a favourable response, but got none.

"Well never mind!" Steiner continued, annoyed at not

The Black Rose

having his jokes laughed at.

"You already have your basic operational orders, but these are the special ones from your HQ in Kildrum. You will take it with you and open it outside these national waters. I don't want us to embarrass our Spanish friends unduly, so it's a matter of courtesy."

Meir looked at Schenk and saw the amazement on his face when he saw the large bulky bag.

"It appears that we have some weighty and lumpy problems to overcome, to receive such a bag, Consul. I am wondering if we could open it here first, to examine its contents. That way we could return anything that would not fit our orders. That is of course, if you already know what's in the bag from your own briefings and orders." Meir enquired civilly.

"I have an idea as to its contents, but I really do insist you take it on board and open it there. I am only carrying out my instructions from my own superiors as you must yours gentlemen."

Meir looked again at Schenk, shrugged his shoulders, and repeated his fathers words.

"Let's go 1st Mate. Let us keep this military. The consul is the diplomat not us."

"Before you go, you will be taking some special passengers with you when you sail. Six special ones will be put ashore in Cadiz and Morocco, but the rest will stay with you. Your despatch orders for them are here." Steiner stated, as he reached into a small drawer under the table and threw several passports and a sealed envelope on the top of it.

One passport fell onto the floor which Schenk picked up, looked at and showed Meir.

"It appears that we've got the privilege of special female company, Captain."

Meir took the passport and gave it back to Steiner.

"I do not want this female, nor any other female on my ship

when I sail, Consul. Can't we just take our stuff from this sack, and you send her in it by sea mail instead?"

Steiner took it as a joke and laughed at the idea, but told them crossly that she was one of the highest-ranking spies in Germany, and could demand more or less what she wanted or where she went.

"I command my ship, nobody else. Nobody tells me who comes aboard unless I agree to it. I do not want this woman on my ship and that's final. She can catch the next fishing boat as far as I'm concerned." Meir hissed as he stood up, grabbed the bag and started to leave.

"Captain Meir!" Steiner stuttered, "I demand you to reconsider!"

"Stuff your considerations, Consul. I will not have women on my ship whilst I'm in action!" Meir shouted, and left with Schenk carrying the heavy bag between them.

When the two officers arrived on board, Meir ordered the ship to prepare to get underway, but to have a thorough search in case of a certain stowaway.

The male passengers arrived and were searched before they were allowed on board, then the gangway was removed and the ship sailed hurriedly out of port.

"This port is easy as pie Captain! I can feel the current and the ship swimming easily through it!"

"Thank you pilot. Keep up the good work." Meir responded, as he did not hear one swear word uttered from the usually foul-mouthed man.

The ship sped down the Portuguese coast and docked in Cadiz where there were a few people to meet them just like in La Corunna.

"Thought you'd get away from me sailor boy?"

Meir stared at this woman who seemed to haunt him everywhere he went.

The Black Rose

"Ms Wintermann. Let me get this straight. I have no quarrel with you, but I do not have women on my ship when I'm at sea. Find yourself another way of getting to wherever your destination is, but not ever on my ship."

"That dear boy is not up to you. You are only a little boy sailing a rusty old ship around the sea. I out-rank you several times over and can come and go as I please. That is on special orders from the Deputy Fuhrer himself, see my special pass." she sneered as she showed him her pass with the special seal indented upon it.

"I shall put it this way. The person who gave you this pass is not here to say that they gave it to you. It means nothing to me, so kindly be on your way before I throw you overboard to the sharks." Meir snarled.

"Okay then sailor boy, have it your way. One day you'll be coming crawling to me begging for forgiveness. It's what all you men do anyway when I have your little balls in the palm of my hand. If you're good you get to keep them." she jibed, as she walked slowly off the ship in a cloud of cigarette smoke.

Meir sailed his ship out of the so-called neutral Spanish port of Cadiz, but was in fact very much pro Nazi, and headed it towards a specially made bolthole where his next series of operations would take place.

Chapter IX
Spanish Drum

The transit from Cadiz to the Moroccan coast was a short one, but was full of ships loaded with all sorts of cargo, and Meir it found almost irresistible to let them go. He got several men on deck with binoculars to jot down what type and possibly what the ships names were.

"First mate, we will have a good night-time engagement among these ships. No wonder our Admirals wants us to plug the hole this end. There must be millions of tons of freight going north to the British. I can't wait until we are on patrol again."

"We all share the same thought captain." Schenk replied as he read out the name of a large tanker.

"It's a British Shell tanker, probably over from Venezuela, or from even round the cape from Ethiopia."

The two-day crossing had whetted the voracious appetite of Meir, which was apparent by his impatience to get back into action again, when he left his passenger drop-off point at Mazagon abruptly to make for his new bolthole.

"OOW! We are at the exact position our instructions gave us, but I can't see any port or any signs of one along this coastline. Port 10 steer 175 I want to get further inshore. Get extra lookouts posted, including one up in the crows nest."

"Captain! Beggin yer pardon. I've got a fuckin' notion that we'd have to be almost on the beach to spot our opening. Just like Kildrum. Maybe if we send out a couple of launches and look for a concealed entrance somewhere near to where your position is."

Meir looked over and saw the fisherman at the helm steering the ship but with someone telling him when he came to the course.

The Black Rose

"OOW! Get the pilot relieved. Irish come over here and show me exactly where on this chart you'd expect to find such a place. Better still, lay on a course for me."

"I can't do that Captain!"

"You do as I ordered Pilot!" Meir shouted.

"Captain. Our friend here may be a brilliant helmsman, but he's telling the truth. The fact is that he can't read nor write, just a good fisherman and knows his angles." Klinshoff interceded

"Aye captain! I had an Uncle who taught me how to steer a ship, and he was just like that. It happens sir." The Bosun stated, as he too spoke up in defence of the pilot.

Meir looked at the Navigator, the Bosun, then at the fisherman and shook his head slowly.

"No wonder you were not able to tell the navigator the angles you used to get into Kildrum. It also explains your awareness to strange harbours. Different angles would only confuse you." Meir said softly as he walked over to the man.

"Very well pilot, we wait on your command. Find this place and take me into it."

The fisherman started to hum quietly to himself as he started to manoeuvre the ship directly towards the vast coastline of sand.

"Captain. Somebody watch my course and note down what I do or tell you. I can take you in and out of Kildrum blindfolded, but I'd need a little while in these waters to do that."

"Pilot. You get us in and I'll see to the rest." Meir said grudgingly.

The fisherman pointed to several little lumps on the coastline, to his compass, telling what speed to do, and what water to look out for, as the ship went between two small islands and skirted around another before coming into a large lagoon.

Meir looked around the lagoon and noted that it was almost like Kildrum, except instead of greenery, there was nothing but hills of sand and a few palm trees dotted over the place.

"Pilot. There is a place ahead of us that looks like our jetty. Just to the right of that promontory. It looks long enough to take us." he said at length as he finished his careful scan around this new base of his.

The ship bumped itself gently against the sandstone jetty as a small crane lifted a gangway over onto the ship.
Meir saw there were a few officers waiting to greet him, and waved to them.

"Thank you pilot, job well done. OOW! Secure from harbour stations, finished with engines." he ordered, then signalled the first mate to come with him.

Meir and Schenk walked over the gangway and ashore to be met by the waiting officers.

"Greetings Captain Meir." Commodore Becks said pleasantly as he introduced the three other officers with him.
Meir, in turn, introduced Schenk to them as they walked across the hot dusty jetty towards a building carved directly into the sandstone cliff towering above them.

"Glad you spotted our little marker to guide yourself in through the difficult and winding entrance. That was an impressive entrance you gave, and our very first proper ship to make it. I shall give you a map of the place when it is eventually completed." Becks declared pointing out various features whilst they walked the short distance to the building.

"Its pretty warm here commodore, is it always like this?" Schenk asked, as he started to sweat profusely. His answer came as they stepped into the building, which was almost like stepping from a hot shower straight into a wall of ice.

"As you can feel First mate, it has its own built in air conditioning, and also that's why we're wearing light tan uniforms to help keep us cool when we're out and about." Becks smiled, as he ushered everybody into a large room.

Looking around the room, Meir saw not glass in the windows, but louvered panels, which were opened outwards to let the light in. He went over to one and looked out to see a panoramic view of the harbour, but could not see beyond the facing islets and the ocean beyond them.

"A very clever piece of civil engineering don't you think Captain?"

Becks asked as he came over to look out with Meir.

"It's what I'd expect from German engineering Commodore."

"German? No! Just a couple of us, and an army of local tribesmen willing to earn a few Marks a day that's all. As I've said, we've a long way to go to complete it, which is where you will be coming into the picture."

"Me commodore?"

"Why yes captain. Apart from your supply runs to our friends, you'll be required to bring us various items we need to sustain and complete the place. Anyway, that's enough of that subject until later. Come and have a cool glass of wine, its Moroccan red and a present from the local sheik who apparently owns this place."

Meir and Schenk were offered simple hospitality by Becks and his staff officers for a little while before Becks announced that it was time to get down to business.

"We will start operational planning tomorrow Captain. In the meantime, you can have time off to study your new orders and familiarise yourself with the place."

Meir thanked Becks and left with Schenk, taking a good look at his new surroundings as they walked back to the ship.

It had been a long hot day for the ship and its crew, and all were thankful for the cool of the evening, as everybody settled down after their supper and watched a film that was shown under canvas on the upper deck.

Becks arrived on board the ship the following morning, with two of his officers. Meir and Schenk escorted them to the lounge, where Becks and his officers were amazed at the trophies put up around the bulkheads.

"You certainly have been busy Captain! But it will be small fry when you see what has been planned for you." Becks announced as he started to brief the ships officers, which took most of the morning.

"So we are expected to provide you with a supply of workers and stores during our time off?" Meir challenged.

"Your orders were well defined before you left, as you read in your not inconsiderable sized diplomatic bag full of them, Captain. All you are doing is to help supplement the supplies for our friends out on patrol. You will note, that we have tapped into the oil pipeline to siphon off any diesel you care to need, so it's just frozen foodstuffs and ammunition."

"We help our friends sink ships yet we turn pirate and loot them, or bring them into here." Meir observed.

"After the first couple of ships lying around in this lagoon, what then?"

"We need to sink three to seal off our northern end, by creating a sand bank with them. Then sink two more in the false channel and plant with sea mines. The rest, you will take to another secret location and dump them by scuttling them."

"Yes commodore! Go on!" Meir said slowly as he felt his anger rising.

"The people found on board will be used as workers, whereas the crewmen will be press-ganged into service for our harbour defence and other such occupations."

Meir told Becks that he was never a pirate, but an honest military man, and would much prefer to sink the ships than rape them into the bargain.

The Black Rose

A deep voice boomed from behind Meir telling him 'enough was enough'!

"Admiral Horstenitz! How did you get here?" he asked with surprise.

"I came by way of U-boat then by seaplane. You will carry out your duties as Commodore Becks dictates. He is our Civil Engineer who creates our dockyards for us. If he needs supplies then you just go out and go shopping amongst all those lovely freighters that pass these waters unescorted and unmolested. Remember, this is your training ground for your Western Atlantic operations." Horstenitz said harshly as he took off his cap in the heat of the day.

"But what about my replenishment routes Admiral?"

"They've got other arrangements with our friends in Cadiz and the Canary islands. You dear Otto, have higher goals to attain from now on, so just do your duty, and all will be fine. Besides, as an Irish freighter, rescuing ships in distress could be a very lucrative and rewarding sideline. Think about it Otto, being a dove for a change instead of a hawk!"

Meir just bit his lip and staring at the liners lifebelt thought of all those passengers.

"But how would you dispose of the people Admiral?"

"By natural wastage. Besides we have other little surprise harbours to build further down the coast and across the other side in South America. Estimated work force of about 500 for starters."

"Yes, by the time we have sorted out the Jews and Poles there might not be enough people to go round." A newcomer stated coming from behind Horstenitz.

"This, gentlemen is SS Army Captain Hans Luchens. He will be joining your ship as 'Morale Officer' and will take care of your political guidance." Horstenitz stated, introducing the fairly small, scrawny and pimply-faced man.

Meir sighed as he saw this specimen of German manhood,

The Black Rose

for he knew that this man was also a Gestapo agent who his father had warned him not to cross.

"It appears that we have a new but very, very, special officer on board gentlemen." he announced.

"Thank you captain. I too have a duty to perform whilst on board your fine looking ship." Luchens said with a weedy voice, as he made himself comfortable next to Schenk.

"You sail tonight Otto! I shall be on board for part of the way as you'll be transferring me onto one of my new type of U-boats operating in these waters." Horstenitz concluded leaving with Becks and his staff.

Meir saluted them as they went off the ship, and waited until they had gone before walking swiftly back into the lounge, to find exactly what he had feared.

"Captain. I have the list of your crew here, and I want to see these men that I have underlined. You will see to that for me yes?"

"Chief steward! Kindly escort Captain Luchens to our special deluxe cabin suite for unexpected guests, and stay with him until I get there." Meir ordered as he took the list off Luchens.

The steward looked vaguely at his captain for a moment, then nodded as he realised what was asked of him.

"Cabin deluxe it is sir! Follow me if you would Mr Luchens. Only civilians and special people like yourself get to use this exclusive one."

Meir went to his day cabin swiftly and used his sound phone to contact the sickbay, glad the Doctor was still there.

"Doc! Come and see me here immediately if you please, and bring a special knockout injection with you."

"Very good captain. The dosage will vary according to the size of the person, so I'll bring the entire bottle in case."

The surgeon Lt arrived, wearing his white overcoat and carrying his standard doctors black bag.

The Black Rose

"Follow me if you would doc!" Meir said with relief, as he led the surgeon down and through the foc'sle to a special compartment normally used as a prison cell.

Meir looked at the bulkhead door, which had a brass plate on it stating it was the 'chain locker' where in olden days, a person clapped in irons was normally kept.

"Captain Meir! It's pretty dark in this cabin. I was hoping for better, shall we say, like in the passengers lounge area." Luchens said petulantly.

"Sorry Luchens, this is the best I can do for passengers who turn up uninvited and without a prior booking.

"We're fully booked up for this cruise." He replied swiftly as he nodded for the steward to leave them, before Meir introduced the surgeon.

"Hello Captain Luchens. I am the surgeon on board this vessel. We have had a touch of scurvy on board, and we don't want a risk of another epidemic. Can I see your papers and passport please." the surgeon said placidly, which was quickly produced by Luchens.

"Scurvy did you say? What's that?" Luchens asked in total bewilderment.

"Captain Luchens. This is only a preliminary medical check on you, in case you have something that the rest of my men might catch. I don't want men dying on me at the wrong moments." Meir said softly as he re-assured him that it was only a routine visit by the doctor.

"It seems Captain Luchens." the surgeon said, as he looked through Luchens passport.

"That you've travelled extensively in the past year. And to places that are rife with Beri Beri, Sleeping sickness, and other nasty diseases that can cause one mighty eruption in your body when you least expect it." the surgeon said slowly and gave Meir a sly sideways wink.

"Hmmm!" the surgeon said slowly and rubbed Luchens pimply cheek.

The Black Rose

"It appears that I was right. This heat will kill you within two days. So I suggest that you only stay somewhere where it's very dark and shady. In the meantime, as your temperature is very high, I shall give you something to cool your blood down a bit just to settle you. Okay?"

"Yes thank you doctor, I need to be fit for my duties." Luchens said quickly taking off his jacket and rolling up his sleeve as he saw the surgeon reach into his bag and bring out a small syringe.

"It's only liquid aspirin, Luchens. It will help you." the surgeon said soothingly as he injected Luchens with the serum, then wiped the spot with a clean bit of cotton wool.

"Here, just hold this to your arm for a while." the surgeon said with a smile and put the needle back into his bag and left.

"There you are Luchens. I always look after my passengers. I will have your fresh bedding and other home comforts brought down here for you. Maybe when you have time after evening dinner, we can go through that list of yours. Okay?" Luchens just smiled and sat on the wooden pallet that was his bed, then flopped sideways as he passed out.

Meir left the cabin feeling very pleased with himself, and went back to enjoy what was left of his day, before sailing out on his new patrol area.

"Ship ready for sea, Captain!" Schenk reported, who then went down onto the forward cargo deck to his place of duty.

"Pilot. You have the conn. Take us out of here. Navigator! Check each bearing as we leave.

"Bosun, see to it that our pilot has instant response." Meir ordered rapidly, as the admiral sat in Meir's special chair looking around and taking everything in.

The ship emerged from its little haven and sailed out into warmer and calmer waters than what it had experienced up in the Arctic.

The Black Rose

"Our pilot is worthy of his name Otto! He was my parting gift to you when you sailed from Kildrum. He is also a Sinn Feinn party member, with a worldwide brotherhood who can be recruited at any time to blow the British out of their beds as they sleep. That way we don't have to send many good Luftwaffe men to their deaths crossing the British mainland. Only five of their men can pin down at least 1,000 badly needed troops in search for them. You are advised to keep a look out for them, as they are so devious and treacherous they'd even blow up their own granny just to look big. They could blow up a church parade today, then go and confess their sins to the local priest what they'd done, and get the priests blessings, just so that they could go and do it over again without any feeling of guilt. That is the Catholic Religions' way of life over there." Holstenitz stated.

"Who needs enemies when you've got back-stabbing IRA in your street. But then I suppose it's the same with our German born Jewish families, who find themselves murdered by their own neighbours!" Meir said quickly trying to concentrate on matters in hand as opposed to delving into the semantics of the German/Irish Political harmonising pacts.

The two lookouts started to report several ship sightings spurring Meir to call for action stations, while the admiral watched at all that took place on the bridge.

"Ship closed up for Action stations captain" Beiderman reported.

"Very good, Guns! I want to cross over the shipping lane and disappear westward, but double back under the cloak of darkness with the ship blacked out. We have one hour to effect a slight transformation of silhouette before we can return and nail those ships that we already see."

Meir saw the sideways glance he was given by Holstenitz, but paid no attention to it. Instead he resolved to show the admiral just how his ship performed without a 'Morale' officer on board.

The ship turned around beyond the horizon of the passing ships and sped back again ready for action.

"We have 3 columns of 6 ships sailing on a parallel course, it appears that it's a loose convoy, so lookout for some escort of any kind, Guns! 5th Mate, stand by with all tubes. Have the 6th Mate standby with eggs laid astern."

"Aye aye captain." Both officers replied.

"There's an escorting warship bearing green 50." One of the lookouts shouted, prompting Meir to look at the bearing immediately.

"Port 15. Speed 25 knots. Tell the engine room to stop making smoke. Navigator! Plot all changes of course and speeds. I shall execute the *Dalmatian* procedure once I've got into the convoy."

The ship darted between the front and second columns of ships then turned to race down in between the 2nd and 3rd columns keeping themselves out of sight from the escort warship.

"5th Mate. We have our torpedo system altered to use pretty much like a rifle magazine. You can fire tubes 3 to 6 when the angle is critical, then follow it up with 7 & 8 so that we have 2 torpedoes each target. You can reload and ready to fire again in only 3 minutes. Set your range at 2 kilometres and set torpedo depth of 3 metres. Make each torpedo count."

Flens repeated his orders and got himself busy with his calculations.

Meir raced his ship down between the two lines of ships, firing his torpedoes as he went, only to come around the back of the convoy to sneak upon the escort.

"Guns! The escort is looking for U-boats, and won't have his guns ready for us. We will do what we did before. Cross the 'T' and disable him from the front."

The Black Rose

Beiderman licked his lips and muttered his response.
"Starboard 15. Speed 30 knots. Fire when ready Guns."

Whilst the merchant ships were exploding and being blown up by the mines all around them, Meir unleashed another deadly hail of bullets and torpedoes at a ship that never knew what hit them. The destroyer sank with such a spectacular explosion, as did one of the merchant ships, that Meir knew they were full of ammunition.

Meir took his ship around again, firing his weapons at the ships still floating, until there were no more to fire at. The whole action took less than 2 hours.

Horstenitz did not say one word all through the attack, merely looked at each sinking ship and the devastation Meir had caused.

"Captain Meir. You have sunk almost the entire convoy on your own. I am now considering why I should have a squadron of my newest U-boats stationed here to do exactly what one ship is able to do. That has given me an idea which will suit our beloved Fuhrer."

Meir looked out to sea through his binoculars, and grinned to himself. He was feeling absolutely pleased with himself making him even more confident when he turned to face the admiral.

"But we have only just begun my patrol, admiral. Besides, all I did was to use the *Dalmatian* tactics that you yourself had devised, several years ago." Meir lied, but said it convincingly.

Horstenitz looked puzzled for a moment, before he shrugged his shoulders to admit that he couldn't remember the *Dalmatian* Tactic.

Meir's officers grinned at each other realising that their captain had bamboozled the admiral, before they requested to secure from action stations.

"Secure from action stations. Set course for the admirals R/V. Speed 30 knots. Set patrol routine." Meir responded, then went over and asked the admiral to leave the bridge to the watchmen.

The Black Rose

"Otto. You have displayed the actions of a brave man, and its no wonder we all got the Knights Cross. Just wait until I tell your father, he will be very proud of you. Our only problem is, is that we needed some of their cargoes and some of their crew. Please try and save the next lot for us, dear Otto. In the case of the people on board those ships, best leave that to Luchens when you decide to let him loose again. That man might have troops of his own to call upon to enforce his own regime. So you'd better watch your step or he'll have you shot on sight as a traitor." Horstenitz said ominously.

"Come and have some champagne with me in the lounge to celebrate your victorious action Hans. My men will no doubt cheer your efforts from what they witnessed with their own eyes. You might use your ship as a destroyer in its pure sense, but it performs like a U-boat." Holstenitz added magnanimously, as he put an arm around Meir and led him off the bridge.

Meir made his R/V with Holstenitz's U-boat and transferred him along with the requirements of his boat, then left the area to carry out his new orders of trying to capture 'suitable' ships.

"First mate! I wish to have a special meeting with our officers in my day cabin this evening. Make sure Luchens is, shall we say, unavailable for comment."

Schenk looked at Meir's troubled face and acknowledged his orders.

The closed circle of officers met as arranged, with Winkler standing outside, keeping guard.

"We have been given a 'shopping list' to get from the ships passing our patrol area. For that, I'll need to put a prize crew on board those ships and escort them back to our new bolthole, and to be known as the 'Spanish Drum'. Our Army friend Luchen has given me a list of our crew that he wants to send back for political processing. However, what I intend doing is to have

The Black Rose

those listed put on board the prize ships, if only to protect them. They are good men, each and every one of them, and I don't intend the likes of Luchens get hold of them." Meir explained.

The other officers agreed whole-heartedly on that idea, before Meir went on to discuss in greater details on how he intended capturing the ships and getting Luchens off the ship at the same time. Again the officers agreed, but offered alternative suggestions as to how certain procedures and events may take their course of events.

The officers talked for a long time, and were about to complete their meeting when Luchens burst through the door.

"Having a private meeting are we?" Luchens asked bombastically, and sneered at the officers as he came through the cabin doorway.

"Captain Luchens. How dare you interrupt this meeting. Unless you step back outside this cabin this very second, I will shoot you between the eyes." Meir hissed as he levelled his machine pistol at Luchens.

Luchens went pale and started to stammer as he tried to impose his 'Gestapo' authority on the officers.

"By the authority invested in me by the Fuhrer himself, I am the captain of this vessel. Any person not obeying my orders will be shot. Ask the crew about that. You have three seconds to clear this cabin." Meir said angrily as he gripped his gun and aiming it at Luchens started to count.

Luchens turned and ran out of the cabin, threatening to get even with Meir.

The officers concluded their meeting and left quietly, knowing what they were going to do was common sense, to help protect their fellow regular sailors.

Meir went onto the bridge and asked the OOW to summon Luchens to the bridge.

Luchens arrived timidly, looking around to see anybody

lurking around to ambush him.

"Ah Captain Luchens! Come to my bridge cabin. I have some special orders for you, and some briefings like the ones I was giving my officers when you rudely interrupted us." Meir said with annoyance and showed Luchens a seat with total disdain.

"My special new orders are that I am to detain certain ships passing through our patrol area. These ships will be re-manned exclusively by my men, until they reach harbour when they will return back here again." Meir said testily, which drew the anticipated response from Luchens.

"It's quite simple Luchens. You will be accompanying my prize crew aboard these ships. So that when we dock, you'll have the prisoners duly sorted into whatever category your personal agenda requires. That is to say, the so-called criminals or enemies of the state we find will be your personal responsibility, others who can be used militarily will be handed over to Commodore Becks. The personal belongings of those people, or valuables found on board will belong to me. The cargoes will go towards our operational needs." he said at length.

"That, Captain Meir, sounds like we've got a deal. The more spies or enemies of the state I can process the better it will look on my portfolio in my own HQ with the Deputy Fuhrer." Luchens said as he rubbed his hands together, greedily.

"So we can agree on this course of action Luchens?" Meir asked swiftly whilst Luchens was gloating over his newfound fortune.

"If you do, then please sign this agreement document like the rest of my officers have." Meir demanded as he handed the document over, for Luchens to sign. This he did, and thanked Meir as he left happily out of Meir's cabin for his own.

The Black Rose

A lookout reported a ship ahead of them, which galvanised Meir into action once more.

"OOW! Hands to action stations! Guns, get your range finder set up. I will be closing on that ship fine on our starboard bow, in about 1 hour from now. The object will be to knock out her radio mast with mortar shells, then to grapple her when she heaves too. Stand by with your 50mm guns and small weapons."

Beiderman acknowledged his orders and left, as Flens approached for his.

"You will not be required for these actions 5th mate, but I'll need you to assist in getting our springs and breasts secured on our target. Get me the 3rd mate if you please." Meir ordered.

Kirkmeister arrived promptly and stood impassively, waiting for his orders.

"3rd Mate. You've seen Luchens list, and know what we intend! When we've secured alongside our target, I want you to take those men from that list as your prize crew. You'll rejoin me once we get back into harbour. In the meantime, have them ready as boarding party, fully armed etc. I want all their officers brought over here."

"Aye aye captain. We'll follow you in." Kirkmeister responded.

"I shall be coming with you to make sure Luchens does not get too hasty in pursuing his duty.

"Besides, I want to see the ships manifest for myself. I also want to get all, and I mean all, personal effects etc from each person, for security reasons, just in case our friend Luchens gets ideas about them."

Kirkmeister looked at Meir questioningly, but saluted him and left to prepare for the boarding of the very first ship that they would not try to sink first.

"Signalman, hoist the 2 black balls. Helmsman! Starboard 10. Stop together. Tell the wireless office we have fire in our

The Black Rose

engine room and to send out a short range, voice message, requesting assistance." Meir ordered, as he prepared to get his ship close enough to be able to surprise this oncoming ship.

"Signalman! Can you make out what flag she is flying?"

"No captain. But she is a freighter, with what looks like timber on her for'ard deck." came the reply.

Meir kept scanning the area, thankful that there were no other ships around to witness his first piratical act. He felt ashamed with himself as he was a military seaman who fought honestly against whatever odds the situation presented itself with.

"Captain! We have a short-range voice contact. Its from the ship '*El Manyana*'. She's a Mexican registered ship of 10,000 tons. The captain is a Manuel Ortega, who says that he will alter course to assist, but not for long as there are U-boats in the area." Brantz reported, holding out the signal for Meir to read.

"Very good Brantz." Meir said cheerfully as he turned to the fisherman.

"You hear that Pilot? You have my permission to swear as much as you like when our guest arrives."

The pilot just grinned and started to practice his Spanish swear words again, describing them in English for the benefit of the others. Meir chuckled at the impromptu lesson on swearing in Spanish, as he looked towards the ship coming his way.

"Signalman! Use your best Spanish and tell them in semaphore that we need them to come alongside, with water hoses directed at our rear funnel."

The signalman spelled out his message and read the reply.

"Will come alongside starboard side and board you, and to stand by with fenders."

"Tell him will do. Also that I need to speak to the captain personally, when they do come on board."

The Black Rose

The signalman reported the reply, which meant that Meir could do the business without any ugly scenes or bloodshed. This was his plan, but was reliant not so much on the coolness of his officers, but that of Luchens.

"Navigator. Get Luchens up here immediately."

Luchens arrived on the bridge with his army uniform on and his gun ready in its holster.

"Captain Luchens. You will get below and get dressed in your civvies immediately. You will not carry any weapons of any description. You will report to me immediately when done so." Meir ordered.

As Luchens went to leave as Meir asked him.

"Can you speak Mexican or Spanish?"

Luchens nodded and stated that he could speak most of the S. American languages. Meir dismissed him, telling him that he had five minutes to get back.

"3rd Mate. Have your boarding party hidden on the port side. I'll give you the signal of one blast from the foghorn, for you to get on board.

"Guns! Use the same signal for you to knock out the radio shack and its aerials with the nearest 50mm gun. Have your machine gunners spray a few shots at the men on the deck, then get their hands tied behind their backs for when I get on board, but do not harm them as I want them alive. Navigator! You will use the megaphone to tell those on their deck to stay still or they'll be shot. Pilot! You'll wear my coat and sit on my seat, for when their captain arrives.

"I'll stand by the wheel pretending to be your helmsman. Remember I can speak Spanish too! Get ready!" Meir said calmly but he was feeling all aglow inside, as this was a tactic that he'd only read about used by real pirates against sailing ship in the days of yore.

The Spanish freighter stopped and tying itself alongside the *Kilkenny Castle* began to render aid to the billowing smoke

The Black Rose

coming from the false funnel.

Their captain came up onto the bridge and greeted the pilot who carried out the subterfuge as Meir swiftly executed his plan of action.

The Spaniard was taken completely by surprise with the sudden appearance of Meir, who introduced himself and told the surprised man what he intended to do.

"Oh Si! Si! Signor. Et is a surprise no? You are only pretending to be buccaneers No?" Ortega asked worriedly as he saw that his ship's radio masts had been destroyed by gunfire.

Meir said that he did not intend harming anybody, and as long as he and his crew did what was required of them all would be fine.

The Spaniard just laughed and told Meir that it was okay, as this was not the first time pirates had robbed him of his cargo. He was only concerned that his ship would remain afloat for him to get back home again. And that Meir was such an amateur in such matters, even he could teach Meir a thing or two.

Meir laughed at this prospect and started to make a gentleman's deal so that both ships would enter the harbour together, but a cough from Luchens reminded him of the deal they had made.

"Captain Ortego. We have a zealous man here who is full of high ideas about the Germanic Aryan Race." Meirs said as he introduced Luchens.

The Spaniard gave Meir an extremely worried look as he swore at Luchens, who replied with equal vehemence.

Luchens swaggered on board the freighter and had several men lined up ready for questioning, which Meir let him do unhindered.

A peaceful transition was made from the helped to the dominant, and soon both ships were making its way back into harbour.

The Black Rose

"I don't like thees man Luchens. He's too dangeros for me and my men. Maybe we can get rid of him, No?"

Meir sighed as he turned to Ortega and said that there was nothing he could do as a military man, as Luchens was political animal and as such had the upper hand on him when in harbour.

The *Kilkenny Castle* docked at its usual place whereas the *El Manyana* got docked at the other end. Meirs was met by the waiting Becks, who clambered swiftly on board and congratulated him for bringing his first prize ship into port.

Becks explained what was to happen, but Meir asked about the fate of the valuable crew that Luchens had designs on.

"Never mind those! We shall have plenty more men to replace them. Besides it's a political thing and nothing to do with you."

Later on that evening Meir heard shots coming from the captured ship, and saw bodies being thrown overboard. Luchens was having his first taste of being God and enjoying his glory.

The ship sailed the following morning with her crew intact again as Meir set out to trap another unlucky ship.

This time, he sailed with Luchens who had a handful of his own men accompanying him. Luchens was more cocksure of himself, which meant that where Luchens went, so did his lackeys.

"Captain Meir. I want you to capture a passenger ship. I need to satisfy my new orders of processing." Luchens ordered as he came up onto the bridge.

"Oh do you now. My first priority is my shopping list. Once I satisfy at least half of the list, then we can start with yours. Besides, Luchens, you've already taken 20 out of the 45 crew from the *Manyana*. Men that Becks and I need to keep ourselves operational. You would only do the same again." Meir barked.

Luchens sidled up to Meir and whispered.

"Yes. But you've got all their valuables and the ships private wealth, Meir. I could have used that lot to finance my operations in this arsehole of a place."

Meir turned and looked at Luchens, and sneered.

"You forget one thing. I'm the one who faces the consequences for any actions taken on behalf of this ship. I am a military man with honour. You Luchens are scum with a capital S."

Luchens did not move an eyelid when he whispered menacingly.

"You captain, are nothing but a pirate now to add to your role as a ship with many names. International law dictates that any such ships can be hunted down and the crew hung, by any nation who gets to capture them. Whereas me, I am an honourable political person from Germany, only doing the bidding of our Fuhrer and for the Third Reich."

Meir stopped in his tracks at this sudden revelation, and wondered just how he had got himself into such a predicament.

"Ah yes, glad you mentioned that Luchens. I am a military man, licensed to kill doing my duty. What can you say in your defence to a 'War Crimes' court when they find you shot 20 or more unarmed civilians in cold blood." Meir snarled.

Luchens said nothing, instead he left the bridge with his henchmen, leaving Meir with a very nasty taste in his mouth.

Over the next few days, Meir managed to lure several more ships into his trap taking them back to their now overcrowded harbour.

The captured ships' captains were kept on board the *Kilkenny Castle* as their crews became loyal workers in the harbour and a valuable source of prize crewmen. Such was the rich vein of Germanic supporters from the so-called neutral world.

Meir was revisited by Holstenitz and given new orders that would take him across the Atlantic to support the squadron of

The Black Rose

U-boats operating off the coast of Mexico and all the way through the Caribbean.

But in the meantime, Meir was to remove all the ships from their bolthole and take them somewhere and dispose of them without anybody knowing where.

"Somewhere you can use to your advantage later on Otto. I suggest down the African coast to the renowned graveyard called the 'Skeleton Coast'. Nobody goes anywhere near that place because there's no fresh water for a thousand miles along the coast and five hundred miles of desert inland."

"I've heard of that place admiral. I'll pick a spot and give you its co-ordinates when I get back. In the meantime, Luchens is becoming unbearably too big for his boots. He's killed over 100, so called enemies of the state, yet most of them were good sailors I could have done with. Especially to operate this special tactic I have." Meir explained, showing Horstenitz the details.

Horstenitz looked intently through Meir's plans and saying that they were of high interest to him, but wished Meir well in conducting them.

"No wonder you need as many qualified sailors as you can get. To operate your own private flotilla would be a great achievement Otto. But for now you need to operate independently. Those support vessels will eventually help you when you get into difficulty with the combined forces of the American and British Cruiser squadrons based out there."

Horstenitz gave Meir a parcel of sealed orders and wished him well on his endeavours in the Carib, but told him to watch out for the British operating out of Capetown when he took ships for disposal.

Meir waved him goodbye then sailed out of harbour with his armada of empty ships, bound for a watery grave some thousand miles away.

The Black Rose

* * *

Meir had the ships manned with their original crew- members, but only enough to sail them to their next destination.

On the fifth day out, with no sightings of any other ships, Meir decided they'd gone far enough and were at a place nobody would come near.

"This looks like a good place, Navigator. Lets get inshore to see if this has the same potential as the Spanish Drum. Pilot, get yourself into the motor launch and have a good look for me. You have two hours to report back."

The fisherman came back as he was told and reported that there was a sand spit of land that was cut off by a huge current sweeping into the bay.

"The sand on the shore was moving in drifts towards the water, which also gets cut off. That's why there are little islands off shore just like the Spanish Drum." he explained.

Meir went in the launch to see for himself and decided on a plan, and got the ships officers together to discuss it.

He had two of the ships run aground on sand spits, one north facing and one south facing, but two land miles apart. They would then stop the sands from moving and at the same time become covered by it. Then the others were scuttled so that they would in time form a sand reef.

He told his officers that the tides and the sands would create a nice little harbour in a few months, and that any further ships brought down would add to it.

Thus the ship sailed back to the Spanish Drum with the crews of the sunken ships, the spare men were taken ashore and billeted in their special quarters, built from the cargo and materials taken from those ships.

Luchens came on board and ensconced himself again in his little cabin, but only had two henchmen with him.

The Black Rose

"Where are the rest of your men Luchens?"

"Taken by some fool general who wants to drive all the way to Palestine. Besides, I shall be coming across the Atlantic with you as I too have special orders." Luchens said happily.

Meir knew of his own special orders, and thought of the several islands he was able to visit, hopefully to get shot of this arrogant little man.

Becks came to visit Meir again with his amended sailing orders and had the ship loaded up with as much fuel and ammunition as it was able to carry.

Meir voiced his objections to having Luchens on board again.

"He will be your source of diplomatic contingency plans Meir. So you'll need him to get around. Besides, he will be sorting out the passengers whilst your ship escorts them across the Atlantic for docking here."

Meir grimaced and swore like the pilot as he exploded into a fit of temper.

"That's all I'm fuckin' good for. A fuckin' cattle ship to get people fuckin' killed by Luchens for nothing. What do you fuckin' well think I'm going to do for men if I get snared by a fuckin' great battle ship." Meir exploded in parody of the Irish pilot.

Becks waited until Meirs had finished his tirade, then said in a quiet voice.

"There are three admirals and a commodore relying on your conduct and ability to perform as you have been doing. Our Fuhrer has given us the go ahead for your mission, Luchens on board or not. Here are your special sealed orders. See that you carry them out."

Meir took the sealed parcel then saluted Becks as the commodore left for the ship to sail.

Chapter X
Pot People

The ship sailed in a southerly loop across the Atlantic to R/V with the new squadron of U-boats now operating in the Caribbean. They were there to sink as many US ships as possible, with the political view that the Americans would stop sending any more over to their besieged British friends. Their voyage of 7,000 kilometres lasted six peaceful days before they sighted the coast of Venezuela where the U-boat squadron had their secret base set up.

Meir had Brantz transmit his special signal to the new base "The Black Rose is blooming."

"OOW! Ask Luchens to come to the bridge. Then have the men to harbour stations." Meir ordered as he worked over the latest chart that was in use.

"Captain?" Luchens asked politely.

"Luchens, we've arrived at our next R/V point and will be met by some high powered, politically motivated people soon. As this is your domain and what you get paid for, I request that you stick around to meet these people with me." Meir responded civilly.

"Thank you Captain. I am expecting at least three aficionados, and two of my best men along with them. I have a small trip inland to make with them as soon as we dock."

"We dock in about three hours, but after sunset, and ship at blackout stations. Recommend you use the light now and get yourself ready."

"You know something Meir. We are about to make a very lucrative living over this side of the pond. When I come back from my little trip, we'll discuss it then."

Meir looked at Luchen's face and saw a sadistic look on his face, as Luchens rubbed his hands.

"What ever you do Luchens, keep our whereabouts secret.

The Black Rose

We're in the British Navy's back yard, with a base of their own just a stones throw away and an even bigger one down the coast at Georgetown."

Luchens gave Meir a smile but declined to comment further.

"Bosun. Here's the special map and sketches of the harbour, to tell the pilot what to look out for. Be ready to note his bearings and changes of speed as we go in."

"Aye aye captain!" the bosun responded as he started to show the pictures to the pilot.

"It's okay Bosun. Just be ready with the telegraphs!" the pilot said softly, spinning the ships large steering wheel in his nimble hands, and humming to himself.

Nobody took notice of his humming anymore, and were glad his swearing was now down to the odd 'F's. Even Meir smiled on times when the pilot was doing his duty, for he knew the man was priceless to him, swear words included.

The ship crept into the unknown harbour and quickly docked with the minimum of noise and lighting, just as the secret orders demanded.

Meir went down to the passenger deck as the gangway was secured onto the ship, and met Luchens with his two henchmen.

"Our guests will arrive soon Captain, as we appear to have docked earlier than expected. Your pilot has done you proud Captain, and it's a good tactical move to be there before anybody else arrives, just in case of nasty surprises, or some unwanted guests turning up."

Meir pointed to shadowy movements to the right of the gangway, as he saw an elegant limousine arrive.

"Apart from the U-boat Squadron commander, Commander Freiburgh, who are we meeting?" Meir asked quietly.

"We have 2 Venezuelan, 1 Dutch and 1 French Official to say hello to before I leave with my other friends."

The Black Rose

Meir stood relaxed as the visitors arrived on board and introduced themselves, as Meir ushered them into the passenger lounge to host them.

"You are a very brave man Captain Meir. We are glad that you have come to help." the French delegate said in awe as he looked around at the trophies put up on the bulkheads of the passenger lounge.

Meir just smiled politely and listened to the idle chat and gossip as he made his way over to the Submarine commander.

"Commander Freiburgh. I have lots of lovely tinned fish, eggs, and milk for your squadron. Do you want me to unload them here or on station?"

"I think its best that you unload here. Besides, you'll be sailing into waters and calling into various places that know of your ships original shape, so you're to strip off your petticoats and get cleaned up for your own patrols in two days time. We have plenty of fuel, we eat fresh food, already have a good supply of ammo but what we need is the tinned fish and the eggs, plus several items of spares. What have you brought?"

"As much as I could carry for you and myself."

"As I've said, we've got a whole ship load of ammo, 4.5 inch shells including amongst it. We, shall we say, rescued them from the Yanks last month. There's the ship over there. The one next to it is a cold store, also borrowed. It's like shopping in a giant store. The only thing you use for money is hot lead and cold steel." Freiburgh laughed, taking another glass of whiskey from a passing steward's tray.

"What about the passengers and crew of the ships commander?"

"We're still using them to work on this base and another one further up river. We need new prisoners now, as most of the current ones are ready for pot."

Meir looked inquisitively at the commander, when he heard the word pot.

139

The Black Rose

"Captain, it's POT as in cooking. The natives around here, and at our second place are cannibaleros, and are partial to white meat. They have one pot every two days, which means that they have 1 human in for supper that night. Pregnant women and children are their favourites. They guard our port from the land, so we oblige them by giving them one pot every two days as their payment."

"How many people were used to build this place then commander. You seem to know the locals pretty well." Luchens enquired as he joined the small circle of officers.

"I've been here for 6 months now, building this place for my U-boats. From the original 100 captives, only about 4 are left mostly due to river or jungle animals. But your lot has a special rota system involving the processing of the so-called enemies of the state. All Polish men are worked to death then given over for the pot. The Jewish men are also worked but given over as live pot. Also the women and girls, but they are used for the men's pleasure first. All those I've just described are called POT PEOPLE. But if we find any captive deemed friendly or amenable to our Fuhrer's cause, they are used as harbour defence. This is where Commodore Becks gets his gunners and other crewmen from."

"So that's why I was sent over here." Luchens cooed.

"Yes Captain Luchens. We need someone like you to sort the human traffic out. We also need the gallant sailors like Captain Meir for the captured ships. We get to sort out the cargoes." the Dutch delegate stated, as he offered a large box of captured Cuban cigars around.

"This is just a sample of one such private cargo." he bragged.

Meir looked at Freiburgh with his disgust thinly veiled.

"Commander Freiburgh and I have some tactics to discuss. So if you'll excuse us both, we'll see you before you leave." Meir said, as he ushered Freiburgh towards the lounge doorway.

"It seems, Meir, that we've got a set of greedy men in there.

I wonder if our Fuhrer knows about it. He'd go daft if he found out that his officers were plotting to deprive the Fatherland of such goods, instead of rendering it all for the cause."

"I have got a complete cabin full of personal effects, but don't know what to do with them now the owners have disappeared. It seems that we take the risks for the Gestapo to take the spoils. This is what I propose to do." Meir whispered, then went on to explain to Freiburgh a special plan, one even Luchens would envy.

"If the Yanks do decide to join the British, then we can kiss goodbye to the happy times we're enjoying now. So it would be prudent to conduct such contingency plans now, and I have just the very place in mind.

"I'll take you on a base inspection tomorrow, and show you it then." Freiburgh whispered back as they made their way into the lounge again, to find Luchens and the delegates had left.

"Captain. Luchens said he'll be back in the morning." Kirkmeister informed Meir, as he handed Meir and the Commander a fresh drink.

"Thank you 3rd Mate, but no thanks. I must be going. I have a shopping list to prepare." Freiburgh said politely as he refused the offered glass.

"I shall have my dockyard workers here at 0700 to off-load the cargo you want to leave behind. I shall come back to see you less formally for a base inspection at 1100 hours, Captain. Your officers will be teamed up with my spare crew officers and men to get anything else sorted out." Freiburgh announced and went to leave the ship.

Meir and Schenk followed Freiburgh to the gangway and saluted as Freiburgh stepped into the sleek limousine.

"You heard what the man said, First Mate. Lets get some shut eye, before we get 'potted' too." Meir muttered as the noise of the departing car gave way to the noises of the night in a jungle only yards away from where they stood.

Meir was woken early by Winkler and had his shower whilst Winkler provided his breakfast.

"This place is giving us all the creeps, captain. One stoker went for a walk along the jetty and has not returned. When are we going to find a place for us to have a run ashore, only some of us hasn't had one since leaving Wilhelmshaven."

He looked at his trusted steward, as he remembered sailing from Wilhelmshaven, which somehow seemed a lifetime ago.

"Steward. Is it such a long time since we've left our Fatherland? I must confess that it seems just like yesterday."

"Yes captain. The men enjoyed their barbeque in the 'Spanish Drum' but it's not the same as having female company around, even though it might just be your mother in law."

Meir chuckled at the very thought, but remembered Freiburgh's distraction plan so that they could do their 'inspection'.

"Tell your friends that I will organise a reception to be laid on for you all at 1300 when you secure for the day. There'll be enough cold beer to swim in, plenty of good food, and a room full of European women and girls, or little boys, depending on your bent that is, enough to sate all your lusts. I have a special base inspection and meeting to attend, but the rest of the officers will be there to see that you all enjoy yourselves. How's that steward?"

Winkler looked pleased and thanked his captain for letting him know of this secret first hand.

Meir stood on his bridge, looking out at the scenery and enjoying the cool of the morning, before the sun had risen fully out of the murky waters of the slow moving Orinoco and the deep ocean beyond its delta.

The sounds of the jungle were muted as the prowlers of the night were replaced by the predators of the day. He heard a faint tramping sound and crossed the bridge to the dockside of the ship.

He was taken aback by the sight of human misery as he saw a long single file of gaunt looking workers, who had dejection and total submission written all over their faces, dressed in tattered rags, trudging wearily over the gangway.

In contrast, were the smartly dressed guards lashing out with long whips and striking any person that dared stop or speak. With much shouting and whip lashing, these people were goaded into unloading of the crates of torpedoes onto the jetty. The derricks were in full swing to lift the cargo out of the holds for these poor wretches, who sweated and toiled in the rising heat of the morning

Looking at them through his binoculars, Meir saw some were just women and children, and realised that these were the so-called 'Pot people.' He turned his head away and started to scan the base and its facilities, to discover that the pilot had taken his ship through a gap in a sandbank, around a small hillock and into this lozenge shaped pool. The place was totally surrounded by jungle, with a small clearing between the high perimeter fence and the huts that were built on stilts on the bank of the river. He counted several wooden huts along the side opposite him. The two ships that were mentioned he saw were aground in a little creek further up past the huts.

His binocular inspection was interrupted as he heard a scream and a splash. Crossing over to the outboard side of the ship he saw somebody trying to swim across the narrow waterway, but within the blink of an eye, the person was ripped to shreds and eaten by several very large alligators. He realized that it was no wonder there was no attempt to escape by swimming for it, or through the jungle. The choice was Cannibal or alligator.

Luchens arrived back on board and disrupted Meir's little bit of peace and quiet, to tell him of the arrangements and visits

The Black Rose

the ship wiould be making during his patrols. Meir listened quietly, making notes and let Luchens complete his so called orders.

"It appears Captain Luchens, that you have a different agenda for this ship than the one I've been told. We must try and dovetail in both requirements, otherwise our beloved Fuhrer will be having us both shot for not doing his express wishes."

Luchens just grinned and said magnanimously.

"Captain. We both have aspirations of greatness. You as a highly decorated war hero, and be an Admiral with your own fleet. Me the governor of some real estate here in the Caribbean, once we've taken it off the British as war reparations. So let's try and get on."

Meir looked at Luchens and realised that much of what he said was pretty near the truth for both of them, but decided he'd endured enough for now and dismissing Luchens got on with some work.

Freiburgh arrived and invited Meir to take a walk with him around the base. Meir had already seen most by binoculars, but at least Freiburgh was explaining everything he saw. They walked slowly around the inside of the perimeter fence before coming to the main gate to the base compound, where they met an old man dressed in western style clothing.

"This is an old friend of the family, who works for the government but also owns the land around these parts." Freiburgh said as he introduced the man.

Meir just nodded his head and shook hands with the man, whose smile revealed a mouthful of rotten teeth, and breath like a sewer.

The three men walked slowly outside of the base and down the jungle encroached pathway that was the main roadway, until the man pointed to a small pathway leading to an outcrop of rocks overlooking the northern entrance of the base.

The Black Rose

The man pulled back the shrubbery to reveal a disused narrow gauge rail track that disappeared into a small black hole in the side of what appeared to be a disused quarry.

"Here we are Meir!" Freiburgh declared quietly, as he told Meir that this was an old silver mine his Mother's Grandfather used to own.

"Do you mean that nobody but us three knows the existence of this place?" Meir asked, feeling very suspicious.

"Senor Meir! I am the last of my family who helped mine this place, and the only one alive that knows its secrets. Please, I show you!" the man said as he walked slowly to the entrance of the cave.

They walked into the dank smelling cavern, which was freezing cold compared to the jungle outside, and the man found a discarded torch made from shrubbery.

He lit it with his matches and held it up aloft for them to see as they went further into the cave.

They reached a much bigger chamber, where the man pointed to a large blackened hole in the side of the rock.

"That is where the furnace is to smelt the ore. See that puddle over there? It is pure silver, as is the lining of the tools you see around you."

Freiburgh smiled at Meir and said.

"We're rich already. There's enough silver to buy your ship just for yourself Meir! Think about the potential this place has."

Meir nodded slowly in recognition of the statement that Freiburgh had just made.

After a little while exploring the disused mine, the three men walked back to the main roadway, where the man left them to go home, and the two officers made their way back to the base.

Meir noticed several movements in the bushes as they walked back, but was not alarmed, as Freiburgh had explained

The Black Rose

that what he'd seen were in fact the natives of the local villages and who were the guards to the base.

"Once they get to know who you are, even by association with me or our man, you'll be very safe. That dear Meir is something that most of the people in the base and especially our Gestapo friends do not share. So consider yourself privileged. Any unwelcome move, then the culprit gets eaten, or his head shrunk and nailed to a tree. Big Ju Ju's around here if you like."

Meir grinned as he thought of the shrunken skull of Luchens nailed to his cabin door.

"Well Meir. That's the end of my inspection. You will have your ship ready for sailing tomorrow night, as I need the space for two of my friends due in around then. They know of you and your ship, so that will be a bonus for you when you go on patrol. I'll leave you now to get on."

Meir nodded and saluted as he left to prepare his ship for sailing from his new base he designated the Jungle Drum, in keeping with Kildrum and the Spanish Drum.

The Black Rose

Chapter XI
Tanned Skin

The ship was now looking more like its former self as the false bits were taken away, but kept the material in its cargo holds in case it had to perform a metamorphosis to be able to escape in its new disguise.

Meir waved goodbye to Freiburg and his officers as the ship stole into the night and beyond the safety of the base.

"Navigator. Have you plotted a course from the base to our new patrol area on the new set of charts, yet? I want you to superimpose the grid our friends operate in to include both British Cruiser Squadrons demarcation lines." Meir asked Klinshoff as he walked over to the chart table.

"I've done all that captain, including the major shipping routes."

Meir looked at the different coloured markings and shaded areas of the chart with the **Black Rose** flower stencilled in the middle of it.

"Just as I thought. The British northern cruiser squadron does not in fact meet up with its southern counterpart. We have a nice little gap to use as an escape route for when we have to cross over to the Spanish Drum. We have our full speed back now so we can transit an area quicker than our enemies realise." Meir said delightedly pointing to the unshaded areas with his pen.

"OOW! Set patrol routine. Steer 210 speed 30 knots. We're heading straight towards our first main shipping lane. Tell the engine room to clean and clear the funnel whilst its dark. I don't want any dirty smoke to give me away in the morning, when we arrive. Call me then." Meir ordered as he left for his day cabin and a decent nights sleep.

"Captain, we have several columns of smoke appearing

The Black Rose

ahead of us, range about 30 kilometres. The lookout spotted them from our crows nest."

"Very good Voss." Meir said quietly as he opened his eyes and peering into his watch dial noted the time.

"Have hands to early breakfast, and go to action stations in 30 minutes. Has the engine room finished smoking yet?"

"They finished about two hours ago, and I've had the deck watch sluice the decks down afterwards." Voss responded as he left the cabin.

Meir ate his breakfast and got dressed into his steaming gear then stepped out of his bridge cabin and went straight over to his high chair.

He saw that everything on the bridge was as it should be, quiet and efficiently manned, as he picked up his powerful binoculars to scan the horizon ahead of him.

Meir saw a couple of slow moving ships ahead of him to his left going the same way as him. And a couple away to his right coming towards him, but still far away. Just like a predator choosing its next victim, so did Meir, until he decided which ship he was to assault.

"OOW! Get the men to action stations. Helmsman! Starboard 10. Tell the engine room I want revs for 30 knots." He ordered.

He studied the ships through his binoculars for a little while, assessing his plan of action.

"Midships! Stop together." Meir countermanded as he finally decided on his tactics.

"Crew at action stations captain." Beiderman advised.

"Very good Guns! See that ship on our starboard bow coming towards us, bearing green 5. That is our target. I want you to get two boarding parties ready to swing over from the main derricks when we get alongside her. Keep all the men hidden. Use the bofors to knock out their radio masts, and have the 50mm cannons ready to strafe in case we get some opposition. Wait for my signal." he ordered quickly rattling off another string of orders to the bridge crew.

Meir had his ship stopped and the signalman to hoist 2 black balls up the signal halyard, which indicates that the ship was not under power and in difficulty.

He watched the oncoming target ship and held his breath, and was relieved when the ship altered course towards them, and appeared to slow down to render assistance.

Meir called Brantz to verify the target ships particulars, and was satisfied that it was just the type of freighter he needed to start his shopping list.

A lookout reported that the ship was now flashing its aldis at them, which the signalman read out.

"She's the SS *Tacoma Star*, out of New Orleans, bound for Buenos Aries, and asks if they can help you."

"Tell him that we're the SS *Killarney Castle* out of Cartagena bound for Cadiz. Have put a fire out in my engine room but still need assistance in getting started again."

The large freighter came slowly towards Meir's diminutive ship, like a whale about to nurse its calf.

Meir noticed how low the ship was in the water.

"Hello captain. I'm Captain Holliwell. I'll throw some ropes over to secure you against us. We have a medical officer on board as well. How many engineers do you need?" came an American voice from the lofty bridge wing.

"Hello Captain Holliwell, I'm Captain Merson. No medical assistance required, just a chaplain. How many of your crew can you spare to get me under way again?" Meir replied in fluent English.

Meir kept Holliwell talking until the ships were close enough to tie up alongside each other.

"We had better be quick, Captain Holliwell! There are U-boats operating in these waters. Give me as many as you can so we can leave quicker."

The Black Rose

Holliwell thanked him for the warning and ordered his men to climb down onto the ship.

Meir watched as the other ships crew came on board, and noticed that they had an audience of several inquisitive passengers from it.

He asked Holliwell to come over to see the damage for himself, which the man did.

As soon as Holliwell arrived onto the bridge, Meir gave an order, taking everybody from the freighter by total surprise.

"Captain Holliwell. You will tell your crew not to offer any resistance and you will surrender your ship to me. Now if you please!" Meir said coldly as he held his pistol to Holliwells forehead, even though Holliwell stood several inches taller.

"Jeez Christ! I'm being fucking well ambushed by short-arsed pirates." Holliwell stuttered, turning pale and urinating himself.

"Tut tut captain. Where are your manners? You should know not to urinate on another Captains' bridge!" Meir hissed as he slashed Holliwell across the face with his pistol.

"Now give the order to have every person on board up on deck where I can see them. Any tricks and I'll have my machine gunners kill everybody."

Holliwell held his bloodstained handkerchief to his cheek and screamed Meir's ultimatum to his men, as they came on deck with their hands up.

Meir saw that the passengers had been lined up on the passenger deck, with Luchens pushing and shoving some of them into line.

He had all the passengers transferred over to his ship, and the ships safe delivered to the bridge.

He went down to the passengers with two men with guns, and told them to relieve the passengers of all valuables. He also sent four men across to search the passengers' cabins and bring all the valuables over to him

The Black Rose

"The reason why I'm doing this, is just in case some of you get killed. I would then be able to send all your effects back to your families." Meir said convincingly, as the passengers started to put their jewellery and wallets into the bags the armed men were carrying.

It took half an hour for the 4 searchers to come back with several bags loaded with the passengers' effects, and for Meir to have the freighters crew bound and put below into the cargo hold.

"First Mate! Get our prize crew on board the *Tacoma* and have it follow me. Get me the 3rd and 6th mate."

Kirkmeister and Voss arrived and were given their orders and charts. After a short discussion, the officers climbed onto the *Tacoma* and started to untie the two ships.

"You will follow me Captain Holliwell!" Meir ordered as he went down to look at the passengers.

Luchens met Meir on the passenger deck, looking quite pleased with himself.

"We have 45 passengers, and half of them are Jews. There are several Jews among the crewmen too. I demand that I exercise my duty now Captain." Luchens gloated.

"You may proceed when I've got us out of these waters and secured from action stations. But whatever you've planned, you've only got until we arrive in the Spanish Drum, about seven days from now." Meir replied as he pushed Holliwell roughly towards Luchens.

"Here's another one to your list."

Meir had the freighter steam full speed, with his own acting as escort. In the meantime, he finally discovered just what Luchen's orders were:

'Sort out the passengers by nationality, then by creed. Any Jews, Gypsies, cripples or those with outward signs of problems such as Down syndrome, are to be singled out for

extinction. Any Polish or Black people are to be used as slave labour.'

Of the passengers Meir had captured, 27 were Jewish, and of those 13 were women and 9 children.

The Jewish men were blindfolded and made to 'walk the plank' overboard. As for the women, each female was stripped naked and given a cabin to use and had to sexually satisfy every *Killarney* crewman on board. If they did not, then they got thrown overboard as well.

"I've told them that the first woman or girl to complete her task will get a special prize. That should keep our 60 eligible crewmen happy and the women from fretting whether or not I'll just throw them and their brats overboard anyway." Luchens said nonchalantly.

"What about the others?" Meir demanded angrily.

"As it happens. Captain. We have a few German sympathizers whom we can press into service. These can be used for what Kaufman would call our spare crew. Besides, we need new recruits to help keep the locals pacified when we get to our base."

"Very well then. But I don't want a shoal of sharks following my ship. It's bad luck for one thing, and lets other people know what we are doing, for another." Meir concluded as he walked back up to his bridge.

"OOW! What speed are we doing?"

"Barely 20 knots Captain." was the reply.

"20 knots? Very well, ask Lt Brantz to see me in my day cabin."

Brantz came into the cabin with a signal just as he was summoned.

"Message from Kirkmeister, Captain. Ship has more cargo than on manifest. If separated, will r/v on Black Rose co-ordinates." Brantz stated as he read out the position.

Meir looked over his chart and saw where it was, and nodded.

The Black Rose

"Tell Kirkmeister that is approved. We'll move on ahead and prepare for your reception, then come back for you."

Meir handed the signal back to Brantz and mulled over the fate of those Jewish females had to endure. Killing troops and sinking enemy ships for a living was one thing, but what Luchens did was not for him.

During the next few days, Meir had all the looted valuables listed and locked away, ready for off loading when he got back to the Jungle drum, and Freiburg.

The *Tacoma* safe yielded several gold bars, thousands of American dollars and other currency, and several pouches of gemstones, which he had stowed in the same place.

He knew that this action against the *Tacoma Star* had now branded him an outcast among the rest of the international maritime fraternity, even though he had built himself up as a brilliant sea Captain. He felt depressed at the thought that Luchens prediction and statement was coming true.

"Smoke from several ships coming fine off our starboard bow." Klinshoff reported as Meir stalked up onto the bridge to try and clear his foul mood.

The report offered Meir that opportunity with the prospect of proper sea action, as he ordered the crew to action stations.

"Ship closed up at action stations." Flens reported.

"5th mate, you will take over the gunnery control as well. I want all guns ready for action but not uncovered until we get closer and find out just what we're dealing with. I also want you to get the senior rate in charge of the mine ramp up here to me."

Flens left to supervise his added duties and came back with the senior rate.

"Chief Stukker reporting!"

"Stukker. I want to lay a pattern of mines across the path of those ships coming our way. Set their float depth of 3 metres so that they cannot be seen. The targets are in a loose convoy and about 7 kilometres wide. Use a double ramp but on an alternative drop, so that each one is about 500metres apart. I also need you to have a batch of smoke canisters ready, but only drop them on my command." Meir explained.

Stukker repeated his orders, saluted and went swiftly off the bridge.

"Navigator. We have about 20 minutes before we close the convoy, so start your plot. Pilot this is your first action so just obey my helm orders."

Meir waited until he calculated the distance from the several lines of ships before he gave the order to start dropping mines. He managed to get across and around the convoy long before they reached his line of mines.

"I intend to carry out the *Dalmatian* tactic and pass 800 metres down the flank of the convoy, so you will fire each torpedo when the critical angle is reached.

"Set depth to 2.5 metres. We have about 10 kilometres to reach the end of the convoy before I come around again on the outer flank for my second pass. There are two escort frigates with them, so make sure your main weapon systems are locked onto their targets when they appear."

Flens acknowledged the plan and spoke swiftly down his telephone command, then stood by Meir waiting for further orders.

"Stand by to fire the starboard torpedoes. Full ahead together! Midships, steer 179. Signalman, keep a sharp lookout for those escorts. Let me know what type " Meir ordered swiftly but calmly.

He made a final check on his angle to the lead ship then ordered Flens to commence the torpedo attack.

The ship fired its torpedoes in salvoes as it raced down the side of the convoy. She reached the third one down the line before the convoy hit the mines and the torpedoes started to hit

The Black Rose

their targets. Like a shoal of startled fish, the convoy seemed to split up and go every which way, with the escorts trying hard to track down the U-boat menace.

"Captain! We have a Hunt class frigate, bearing green 10, coming through the convoy. I don't think he's seen us." The signalman shouted

Meir looked out towards the direction given and ordered more mines to be dropped.

The warship came through the swirl of smoke the stricken merchant ships were giving off, and met a hail of bullets and torpedoes as Meir did yet another classic naval manoeuvre by 'Crossing the T' of your enemy column.

The warship exploded like a firework cracker and disappeared in a cloud of debris.

Meir looked desperately around to see if he could spot the second one and decided to cut through the convoy and get down wind of the smoke to hide himself.

"Starboard 20. Slow ahead together. Set off 2 smoke candles on deck."

Meir dodged his ship between the fleeing but slow moving ships, firing torpedoes and his mortars as he passed close by any of them, until he got out of the lanes of ships.

"Z class destroyer. Green 15, range about 5 kilometres." The signalman reported excitedly.

"Slow ahead together. Make more smoke on deck. Stand by for a port side broadside. I'll get within about 1kilometre of him. Load with AP and HE for the mortars."

Meir was at his fighting best now and his orders flew thick and fast from his lips. The Z class went the same way as the other escort, with a loud bang and sank within seconds, which left Meir to sink the crippled merchant ships at leisure. His bag of ships sunk by direct action were; 2 warships, 4 tankers, 6 freighters, and a further 6 with his mines.

A total of over 100,000 tons of much needed supplies for

The Black Rose

Britain and 2 valuable warships were lost in only 2 hours of action, by one small ship commanded by a medium sized man in a very large ocean.

Meir had his ship return to its base course to continue its way towards the Spanish Drum, as the crew celebrated their victory. Even the American captors who witnessed the action were reluctantly impressed with Meir's tactics and daring actions. But stated that their navy would make mincemeat of him if he dared to do the same in American waters.

The ship arrived into the base and disembarked its captors as Horstenitz and Becks met Meir again in his day cabin, and listened to Meir's account of his recent actions, which his written documents and logbooks substantiated.

"Your records show that you are now one of our top commanders at sea. It's about time you got promoted Lt. Cdr Meir." Horstenitz said with satisfaction as he glanced at the ship's 'ATTACK' log.

Meir just smiled and offered Horstenitz and Becks another glass of schnapps.

"Yes, I concur with your remark." Becks said amiably as he raised his glass to salute Meir.

"In that case. As it takes two officers of flag rank to promote an officer to a higher order of rank, it gives me great pleasure in promoting you up to a rank deserving of a heavy cruiser captain.

By the authority invested in me and on orders from the Fuhrer himself, I do promote you to a full 4 ring captain. Congratulations Captain von Meir!" Horstenitz proclaimed as he handed Meir his new 4 gold ring badges, gold-rimmed cap and a letter with the German eagle emblem denoting it came from Hitler himself. Becks stood and clapping his hands offered his own congratulations.

"If this war keeps up the way its going, you'll reach Grand Admiral in no time, Otto." Horstenitz reminded him.

The Black Rose

Meir smiled and basked in his triumph and glory for a while, before he announced that he had a freighter full of cargo that was high on their shopping list, due to arrive tomorrow.

The three officers discussed what the plan was for the cargo and the passengers, and for Meir to retrieve his crew again before he went back into the Caribbean and his base that side of the Atlantic.

He loaded his ship with more torpedoes and mines whilst he waited for his prize crewmen to come back on board.

Once more the ship sailed under darkness and headed back towards their jungle hideaway.

It only took them seven days to reach the base, as they met no ships to distract them. Those peaceful days were greatly appreciated by the crew, who were trying to gather their strength again after the previous six days of their enforced four times daily sexual encounters with the Jewish women.

Freiburgh congratulated Meir on his promotion before discussing Meirs next patrol.

"So I'm to bring the next ship here. What about Horstenitz on the other side, he needs supplies too? What about the ones up the creek?"

"He's already got his orders and besides he's got the Marigold assigned as the Daffodil has been sunk by the British cruiser squadron from Bermuda. You will have to put a skeleton crew on board and sail them down to another special place on the Amazon delta.

It appears that our Brazilian friends want paying for their groceries and someone in Berlin has failed to do so. Those ships plus another four will be used to honour the payments. You will not need to supply any crew, as we'll get them from your captured men. Just bring the ships here that's all."

Meir wrote down the particulars but knew he'd get them in his next batch of typed orders.

The Black Rose

"I have our first batch of groceries on board, to be taken ashore tonight. Here is your copy of the list. I also have one of my crew who had been a jeweller before the war, and a metallurgist who will smelt our metal for us. I had a special stamp made in the onboard workshop, that will be used to mark our ingots." Meir said softly, handing Freiburgh the list and metal stamp.

Freiburgh looked quickly down the list and noted the bullion.

"It seems that we've just started our business in style. I'll have the gold and silver coins melted and the gems put into special cases just like these." Freiburgh replied as he tossed two brown leathery looking bags, each with a button effect on the end of them.

Meir looked at the strange bag and asked what the material was and what the strange button was.

"Our local tribesmen are excellent tanners. Those pouches are made from the breasts of our female pot people.

"They tan and oil the skin to keep it lovely and soft just like a breast should be, the button by the way is the nipple. We'll use them for the diamonds, emeralds and the other small stuff. Any ivory etc will be put into wooden crates. All will be weighed and valued and properly catalogued so we can keep tabs on it all. Anyway, leave all that to me."

"As an idle curiosity. If the ships are sold off for scrap, what happens to the clothing, dishes, cutlery, mirrors, and all the other ships' furnishings, what about all the useful machinery, pumps and the like?"

Freiburgh explained the set up and Meir's eyes widened at the thought of Luchens double scam.

"Anyway dear Meir. Its time you got your ship turned round and back out to sea. I will expect you back within about four days as these ships are about to sail from those ports." Freiburgh announced as he gave Meir a neatly typed list of ships and ports.

The Black Rose

Meir started to enquire about the information.

"We have good friends in this part of the world, and another ship doing the same job, although the captain is not as successful as you. Besides, our silent friends will be able to come and go as and when it pleases them, thanks to your fresh supply of torpedoes."

Freiburgh finally left the ship, taking the special crewmen with him, as Meir returned the customary departure salute.

Meir went to his secret stash of valuables, and taking several large diamonds, emeralds, rubies and pearls wrapped them into the velvety bags Freiburgh gave him. These were not on the list, so Meir had them secreted in a special place that nobody knew about, except him. It was a secret compartment in his bridge cabin that his Uncle Heinz kept for just such occasions, so as to evade the stringent customs checks every time he came into any British colonial waters.

He was starting to think of a long-term strategy and was planning these events as they arose, on a 'what if' basis.

Chapter XII
Little Children

The early morning was cool, with a clear starry sky as the ship sailed out of their jungle hideout, with Meir issuing his orders before going back to his bridge cabin for a brief nap.

Before long he was woken by the OOW telling him that they had arrived on their patrol area.

He looked at his watch and feeling bone weary, lifted himself off his bunk and stumbled out onto the bridge.

"OOW! What is our ship status?" Meir asked sleepily, and got a long reply from Voss.

Meir was still thinking of the first few statements before he snapped at Voss and told him to slow down and repeat slowly what he had to report.

Voss repeated slowly every detail to his captain and waited for any comeback orders. There were none, so Voss carried on with his duties on the bridge.

Shortly, a lookout reported a ship sighting off the port bow, prompting Meir to sit in his chair and look through his binoculars at the ship. He decided that this was to be his first 'bag' of the day, even though he spotted another column of smoke over the horizon to starboard. Make that two to take back, was his calculation as he called for the navigator.

"Navigator. Take a true bearing of those ships ahead of us, work out a reciprocal course and given that each have an average speed of 15 knots. I want to engage both ships."

Klinshoff worked furiously at the calculations, and reported by showing Meir exactly what he needed to know.

Meir rubbed his chin thoughtfully, before he gave his order to action stations.

"1st Mate, what are you doing on the bridge? You're my damage control officer."

Schenk told Meir what the problem was, which made him to

The Black Rose

send for Emst immediately.

"Chief Engineer!" Meir started loudly but decided that Emst and Schenk should accompany him to his bridge cabin for a more private discussion.

"We have a so-called German Sympathiser who is starting to sabotage our engineering systems.

He was taken off the *Tacoma Star*, but is a Scottish National, by the name of Cresswell. He was one of the *Tacoma Star's* engineer officers that I had to use in place of my 4th engineer, who somehow disappeared yesterday. A good swap I thought, as Creswell seems to be more qualified than he pretends."

The three officers discussed the problem, not wishing to kill the man as he was proving to be a good engineer, but in a way that would persuade him to stop.

Meir decided that any thing that remotely tells the purpose of the piping and electrical systems on board would be removed. But only the three of them were to know about each system, and that the system drawings be kept locked up in the bridge cabin at all times.[2]

This closed the matter, and each officer returned to his post again, but it was a subsequent return signal from Kildrum that did the trick, stopping any further antics from Cresswell and giving Meir peace of mind.

"OOW! Get the crew to action stations. Boarding parties at the ready! Full ahead together."

Beiderman reported that the ship was ready as Klinshoff reported that he started his plot.

Meir looked intently at his target in front of him, and decided that he'd take the ship against the rule of the road. That way the ship would panic and veer right into him, allowing him to grapple it before anyone knew what happened to them.

---

[2] See *A Fatal Encounter*.

The Black Rose

"Listen up attack team. Keep your heads down. I want it to seem as if nobody is on the bridge and we're steering on a general course. Watch your steering pilot, as I shall be coming up next to him about 800metres to his starboard. As soon as he alters towards us, you get ready to turn with him."

Meir looked at his target again and decided to slow down to the same speed, in case he over shot the ship.

"Stop together." Meir ordered and counted the seconds until he felt the ship had almost stopped.

"Slow ahead together, make revs for 8 knots. Steer 015. Guns, get your mortars ready. The first one is to land on their aerials and the next to land onto their fore deck. Have your heavy machine guns ready to strafe the decks."

Meir saw that he had managed to creep up behind the ship and had almost overtaken her when someone on it waved frantically to him.

Waiting until the target was set up to his liking he ordered the mortars to fire. The result was as he predicted.

When the ship started to veer towards them, Meir spoke through his megaphone to the astonished men on the bridge, some still wearing their pyjamas.

"Heave to, or I'll shoot the lot of you." Meir threatened, and got his rewards as the ship slowed down to a stop, with his own adjacent to it.

Meir had his ship tied securely alongside the large freighter and got his crew onto it quickly. He arrived onto the bridge with Beiderman and spoke for several minutes with the freighter captain.

"I'll have your ships logs, charts and manifest, Captain. Your passengers and crew will come to no harm providing you do exactly what I tell you." Meir said coldly as he looked around the bridge then went down to the Pursers office.

Meir had the ships safe opened and the contents, along with all the personal valuables of the crew transferred, before

The Black Rose

Luchens arrived on board to process the crewmen.

"Luchens! This is another American freighter, with a few more passengers. I suggest that you go lightly with the Jewish women, because they could fetch good money in the Arab slave markets." Meir hinted, which drew a glint into Luchens eyes as he recognized the truth behind it.

"Good thinking captain. But as the morale officer for our crew, I deem it necessary for the Jewish whores to perform well and service our crew before I decide to kill them."

The American captain heard the conversation and started to protest, quoting the Geneva Convention and the fact that his ship was a neutral and therefore not allowed to be touched by any warlike nations.

Luchens simply turned round, drew his pistol and shot the man between the eyes.

"Is there anyone else wishing to argue with me?" Luchens hissed as he waved his pistol around the other officers on the bridge. There was complete silence from them, which gave Luchens the prompt to go and see his 'captive audience'.

Meir went with him to see the same scene he had witnessed on the *Tacoma Star*.

"Luchens. I shall be putting a prize crew to take the ship back to Jungle drum. Leave these passengers, as you will be needed for my next one tomorrow. Incidentally, I'm curious to know what was the prize you offered to those other women?"

"The prize winner was a 13 year old who was given the day off. But I decided as she was so good at it she got to do it all over again." Luchens smiled as he rubbed his groin.

"Anyway. I need to process all of them captain, especially the Jew whores and their little sluts." Luchens protested.

"Can't I just have the passengers? They can be put with the others surely?"

Meir looked at his watch and decided that because this boarding raid had taken too long and he had missed getting the

The Black Rose

second ship, finally but reluctantly gave into Luchens request.

"Guns. Here are your orders. This ship is a good one and capable of getting you back within 18 hours. I'll see you when I get back. In the meantime I request you do me a favour." Meir ordered, then leaned over and whispered into Beidermans ear.

"Aye Aye captain" Beiderman responded and took control of the freighters bridge while Meir and Luchens returned to their ship again.

Meir waved them off, as he veered his ship sharply away from the freighter, with the Stars and Stripes still fluttering at its stern flagpole. He realised that this must have been a sister ship to the *Tacoma* as it seemed pretty similar with the same house flag flying from its mast atop of the bridge. He decided that the ship was still too big for him to use as a guise, as he needed something a little smaller in height for the superstructure, which presented him with yet one more problem to solve before it got too late.

Two days passed without further incident as the ship went further north then west through the Lesser Antillies chain of islands until he came to the crossing point for the main shipping routes. That way he could have the pick of any full tankers coming out of Venezuela or other merchant ships making their voyage to any point on the compass.

The added bonus would be the ships coming or going via the Panama, and now as it was the tourist season, big fat liners dodging around the Caribbean at will.

Again Meir was woken up in the early morning to see the sun rising from its sleep out of the black waters of the Caribbean. Better still, and to his delight, several small ships lazily steaming along, showing all their lights, like a Christmas tree.

"OOW! It appears that the war in our part of the world has still not reached this side of the ocean. The Americans are still pretending to be neutral and don't know how to darken their ships against our silent friends below them. Come think of it, they are not even aware of the surface danger we pose them." Meir chuckled as he looked through his binoculars at the brightly lit ships around him.

"Let's give them a little surprise. Close up torpedo firing stations. Get a few more lights on, so we'll not be too suspicious. Oh, and get the false funnel rigged with lots of smoke coming from it."

Once again Meir pretended to be just one more tramp steamer, swimming along merrily without a care in the world. He had his ship go that little bit faster than the one in front, but when he passed them firing his torpedoes at them, he called for full speed ahead to catch up with the next one in line, just to do the same. He managed to torpedo and sink three of them before the other ships started to panic and rush around trying to get away from their unseen attackers.

Brantz came onto the bridge to report that there were several mayday calls warning of submarines in the area. He also reported that he had intercepted an encoded signal that came from the west of them and suspected it would be the Royal Navy on its way.

Meir looked at his chart and guessed from it, that it was the Southern Cruiser squadron coming to the rescue. He called off the attacks, reduced his speed and went back into pretend mode again, as he went to his day cabin and read his special instructions, orders and intelligence reports.

Meir came back onto the bridge and called for Klinshoff, who helped him go through the captured charts.

"The corridor is on the eastern side of the Dominican Islands. But according to the sea-lanes, there is a diamond shaped area without any marked traffic. That is where our friends go and hide, and as it happens that's where we'll go instead of using the corridor. Lay on a course for that." Meir

The Black Rose

ordered as he pointed to the area he had marked on the chart.

Klinshoff nodded in agreement as he made his calculations then reported the course to Meir.

"OOW! Full ahead together. Make speed 30 knots. Make your course 070." Meir ordered as he looked around the horizon for any sign of ships. He saw none and felt disappointed as he wanted to have a look at these warships that was spoiling his fun.

The ship took less than 12 hours to reach their point on the chart, where Meir had the ship stop, and prepared it for transformation. Soon the ship had lots more superstructure to match a second fake funnel, and a missing rear derrick, which was in actual fact lowered down onto the cargo deck.

In the meantime, Luchens was 'doing his orders' whilst the Jewish women were forced to perform his sexual marathons again, with the Jewish men shot and thrown overboard to the ever waiting sharks.

Meir decided that Luchens had to go, and devised a plan that should do the trick. But he had to wait until the following morning when a lookout reported a medium sized cruise ship coming their way.

Meir did his 2 black balls trick again, which brought it close alongside him.

"I'm Captain Tindall. My ship is the *Lorraine*. How may I help?"

"I'm Captain Dermot of the *Killarney Castle*, bound for Barcelona. I've had a fire, but put it out. Need a doctor and some engineers to help me get underway again Captain. Suggest you come alongside and secure to me."

Meir went through the same tactic of having Tindall come onto his bridge before the trap was sprung.

"But Captain Dermot, I am only a small cruise liner with 200 school children, their parents and the school teachers.

The Black Rose

What do you want off me? I have nothing to give you!" the elderly captain asked almost unruffled.

Meir had Luchens brought to the bridge and told him of the *Lorraine's* passengers. He was to transfer the ones off the *Killarney* onto it, and transfer some of their crew on board to replace them. He told Luchens that he was to stay on the bridge with Tindall until he came back.

"Captain Tindall. You are to get all your crew on deck and all your passengers too but with their passports. I am a German Naval Officer who is out to catch a gang of spies. So I need to see each person immediately. Once done, you can go." Meir lied, as he gave Luchens a sly wink.

Meir arrived on the *Lorraine* with his boarding party, and went straight onto the bridge where he met the First mate.

"First Mate. Bring me your ships log, Charts and passenger list right now if you please. If you don't, you and your other officers will be shot in front of all these children. So keep it nice and quiet, and very simple." he barked.

The officer went to the back of the bridge where Tindalls bridge cabin was, and brought out the required documents.

Meir looked through them then told the officer to take him to the purser's office. He had two of his crewmen with him when he opened the ships safe, and took all the contents from it.

"Now First mate. I want all adults to hand over their valuables and passports to these men. Nice and gentle, remember."

"But you can't be serious. That is piracy!"

Meir told him the same story as he did before, which seemed to pacify the man.

It took about an hour to fleece everybody of their valuables and without mishap, before Meir was ready to hand the ship over to his prize crew and Luchens.

Meir called his prize crew together, and told them that they were to sail the ship over to the Spanish Drum, drop the passengers and Luchens off and return back to the Jungle drum. He gave Schenk the chart with all the courses and positions and told him that he would meet up with them again in about 18 days, given the ship could sail at 25 knots. They were to stay out of trouble and any problems they were to contact Admiral Horstenitz. Remembering to quote food shopping for your list of requirements each end.

"See you up jungle, Captain." Schenk said brightly but lost his smile when Luchens came on board.

"Well lookee here, a ship full of little children! Captain, how did you know it was my birthday today? What a lovely present I shall be able to buy." Luchens cooed, then started to cackle like an old witch, as he saw all the children sitting down quietly by their parents.

"Luchens. No antics this time, or I won't give you any more." Meir growled but it seemed as if he was talking to himself.

Meir turned to Tindall and told him that he was to remain here, but to bring his best 2 engineers and 6 sailors with him.

The ships disentangled themselves and went their separate ways as Meir had his ship revert back to their patrol routine.

"Captain Tindall. You will be kept as a hostage for a while, but you will be able to return to your ship once it comes back again in about 3 weeks. In the meantime, you will be given a passenger cabin for yourself, and feel free to enjoy the luxury of the passenger saloon where your meals will be served. I trust that you and your men will behave themselves whilst on this cruise, if not then you'll be fed to the sharks. Do I make myself clear Captain?"

"Perfectly clear. I am a neutral, and your ship is dressed up as one. Which one of us will survive Captain Dermot?"

Meir smiled and whispered coarsely.

"I don't fuckin' give a damn. You fuckin' Yanks are a load of fuckin' wind and piss, just like a fuckin' barber's cat, bejasus."

The Black Rose

Tindall looked wide-eyed in amazement at Meir's tirade, as he was ushered off the bridge and down into the passengers quarters.

"OOW! Tell the chief chef to cook a special meal for everybody. And issue an extra ration of beer. I feel lucky tonight." Meir said happily as he went down the ladder to his day cabin.

Meir was taking his customary evening stroll on deck and noticed that the ship seemed to glide easier through the water, as if a great weight and stench had been lifted right off her decks.

He was even told by Winkler that the men were feeling much happier and safer and were looking to regain their name as fighting men, not whore hunters.

"Yes Steward, we can put it all down to the fact that our friend Luchens is now off the ship, God willing, for the last time." Meir agreed with a satisfied smile.

The ship had arrived at another sea-lane crossroads, where Meir ordered the ship to stop, to beautify herself. The captives off the *Lorraine* were put to task and he saw that they worked just as hard as the rest of the crewmen. Even Tindall was required to do his share of chores that befitted an ancient mariner.

"Come over here Captain Tindall!" Meir ordered as he showed Tindall his very own chart, but with extra coloured lines added onto it.

"Here is your transit course, and your ports of call. What I need to know is how you managed to squeeze yourself through the little hole in the Leeward Islands?"

Tindall just looked and refused to answer, which annoyed Meir.

"Captain. You will not be giving any state secrets out by telling me, it's just that when I ask you, mariner to mariner, I expect some sort of an answer even if your answers were totally crap."

Tindall still refused to answer, and screwed his cap tighter down onto his head.

"Okay Captain have it your way. OOW! I have no use for this man, so have him taken onto the after deck and lashed to the ramp. Action stations in 15 minutes."

"Aye aye sir." Flens responded and had Tindall removed off the bridge protesting and asking for a second chance.

It was evening time and the sun was setting, as Meir had his ship darkened and ready for action, to take on the ship coming over the horizon.

"We have two ships, not one. The first one appears to be moving faster than the one behind it, which is about 10 kilometres astern of it.

"We shall sink the first one by mines, and torpedo the other one. I want a staggered pattern of mines. Set depth of 3 metres. Set torpedo depths to same." Meir ordered.

"Captain, we still have a man lashed to the mine ramp!" Flens reported.

"Let's see if he can swim then." Meir growled, as he could have done with Tindalls help in and around the countless and uncharted islands the Caribbean seems to contain.

"Mines dropped Captain." Flens informed Meir.

"Very good. Flens!" Meir acknowledged peering into the blue-lit chart table.

"Navigator. We'll stay on this course and follow it to pass the Jamaica Islands and on through the Windward Passage to the other side where we'll stop. Our friends are operating to the northwest of us in the Straits of Florida. Lay on a course for me so that I boomerang back behind that island ahead of the Passage."

Klinshoff muttered his response and worked fiercely to comply with his orders.

The Black Rose

"Starboard 10. Make speed 15 knots. Tell engine room to stop making smoke. Switch off all navigation lights. Make sure all deadlights are used. We are going down the wrong side of both ships so they will not be expecting us." Meir stated as his orders were repeated, who was told when the orders were carried out.

Meir had his torpedoes fired at close range, which struck the tanker almost at the same time as the front ship hit the mines.
Both ships lit up the sky around them as flames reached up to the stars, then quickly sank without any reported signs of survivors. The signalman handed Meir their names and their particulars, which angered him when he realised he sunk two empty ships, instead of full ones. But still 25,000 tonnes more to add to his list was his only consolation.

Meir heard two more explosions before the ship arrived into the Windward passage, and guessed that his mines were doing their work just as the ones off the coast of the Spanish Drum.

He decided that as this was only one out of the three bottlenecks for the ships to pass through the Greater Antilles islands, he would leave the Windward Passage clear of mines but would sow a minefield in each of the two shipping routes. To do this they would have to pass either side of the smaller islands of the Great Inagua islands and the two larger masses of Cuba and Haiti.

The ship finally arrived at the eastern end of the small islands of Great Inagua, where Meir decided that it was time to alter the ship's silhouette again for the return leg.

He did this in full daylight, but several miles away from the islands, so that nobody could see him. Once done, he searched for a suitable island that had a beach so his men could enjoy a barbeque and a swim for a few hours before he took them back into action.

The crew enjoyed their brief interlude and were ready to do

The Black Rose

their captain's bidding, without question. Such was the popularity Meir had with his men. The only blip on board had now gone. Luchens!

"OOW! Weigh anchor! Navigator! I want to transit through the gap on the Cuban side, and turn right to go between it and Jamaica. I want to transit that stretch and come around behind the Cayman Islands join the sea-lanes up as far as Cape Catoche. Use the special grid and lay those courses for me. Use a mean speed of 35 knots to the Caymans, and 15 knots up to Catoche."

Meir still had a lot of fighting to do, and wanted to get right into the Mexican Gulf to sink as many American ships as possible before turning back for supplies.

Meir made his return through the Windward Passage late at night and at full speed. If it was a motor vehicle on the road turning a tight corner, then the ship would have made skidding noises as it turned right and sped through the Jamaica Cuban gap before the morning light.

"Half ahead together. Speed 15 knots. Port 20 steer 240. Tell the engine room to make as much smoke as they want." Meir ordered, scanning the empty horizon that shimmered in the morning sunlight. He went out onto the bridge wing and breathed deeply the fresh morning air.

He was never a romantic, but the balmy Caribbean climate and the calm seas made him wish he was somewhere elsewhere, doing something constructive and generally enjoying life. Instead, he was embroiled in a vicious unforgiving war with his enemy, the British.

He sauntered down the steep steel ladder and went to his cabin for his breakfast, and a good shower to freshen up, before any more events took over his mind.

Meir finished his coffee and hadstarted to read his next set of orders when Brantz knocked and entered his cabin.

"Captain! We've got a signal from Admiral Horstenitz, and

The Black Rose

Commander Freiburgh." He exclaimed as he handed them to Meir, who read them out:

'From Jungle Drum. Need several crates of tinned fish and boxes of fresh meat. Please supply a.s.a.p.

'From Spanish Drum. Have crates of tinned fish, boxes of hens and duck eggs. Swap for boxes of fresh meat.'

"That dear Brantz, means that Admiral Horstenitz has a new supply of torpedoes, and mines for Commander Freiburgh. But both want volunteers to man their bases. Let's see what we can do, so here's my reply."

Brantz wrote down the reply signal, making sure he had it word perfect before leaving the cabin.

"Oh and by the way Brantz, our ships new name is the *'Ballymuffin Bay'* so make certain we've got it written on our stern and the appropriate national flag from the aft flagpole. Tell the pilot to make his own little house flag to be put up as well." Meir smiled as he said it, which drew an equally appreciative smile from Brantz.

"Aye aye captain. Our Irish fisherman will be thrilled when he finds out." Brantz answered as he shut the cabin door behind him.

Meir went up onto the bridge at noon and saw Klinshoff on watch, which meant that he was to take his midday sunlight to plot his position. It only took a few minutes before he had it worked out and marked onto the chart.

"Navigator. It appears that we're several kilometres off track, and instead of the Caymans ahead on our port side, they will appear to or starboard. Have you got the almanac on local currents and tidal influences here?"

"Yes captain. It's under the chart in a side locker."

Meir looked in it and found it to be empty and said so.

Klinshoff came over and looked for himself, and even searched the entire chart table area for it, before he stopped and turned to Meir.

The Black Rose

"So that's what that old fool Tindall was up to. He's nicked our almanac too, captain." He said apologetically.

"Not to worry navigator, he's had his punishment for it. He went overboard with the first mine. Maybe he'll use it to work out his tidal positions as he washes up and down the Windward Passage." he chuckled, and shaking his head slowly turned to the helmsman.

"Port 20. Slow ahead both. Tell the engine room to stop making smoke. Navigator, I have the conn. Set a reverse course to take us back through the Windward Passage and over to the Spanish Drum. We have been ordered to get some prisoners for them and to take a load of torpedoes back to the Jungle drum."

He stopped his ship for a while, waiting for sight of a ship going his way, and didn't have to wait long.

He had his ship take a parallel course and only 8kilometres away and astern from a large freighter that was about to enter the Windward Passage. He got the signalman to find out what ship it was, and call it up with his aldis.

"She's the *Houston Ranger*, out of Houston bound for Barcelona. She's listed as a 17,000 ton general cargo ship." The signalman shouted as he completed reading the flashing light.

"Tell him we're the *Ballymuffin Bay*. Out of the Caymans bound for Dublin. I've started to come back the wrong way and can't remember the route through these waters. Request he lead the way for us until we reach the open Atlantic." Meir said as the signalman wrote the reply message down then started to flash back to the other ship.

"Be my guest. I shall be increasing speed to 15 knots though, due to U-boat activities in this area, just keep astern and follow my course."

"Signalman, make to him. Am able to match that speed and thanks for the U-boat warning. I'll follow your wake." Meir responded quickly.

"OOW! Keep 5,000 metres astern of her. Speed for about

The Black Rose

15 knots. If she turns so do we. In other words, stick to her like glue." Meir stated as he left the bridge ready to plan his next move.

He now had a target, but didn't know what the cargo was, and he was short of crewmen to make another prize crew. If trouble came their way he'd be undermanned to fight back.

They followed the larger ship all the way through the Windward Passage and even found that several other ships had formed up behind them in a single file, as if to stick together for safety through this possible U-boat shooting range.

As he was in a loose convoy, he felt safe from any warship that might just pass them, for they would steam full speed past these slower moving merchantmen. Bluff it out was his tactic until he got out far enough to start taking a few more scalps.

That time came, when the ship in front started to slow down again, and the other ships behind him in turn.

He saw another ship astern heading the same way as him, and decided to tag along until they were nearly at the end of the long southerly loop across the Atlantic to pass by the Canary Islands.

This meant that all he had to do was bag both of them and take them just a short distance to the Spanish Drum under the watchful eyes of his U-boat friends in that area.

Therefore, his crewmen could enjoy a leisurely cruise across in company with their victims. He described them as 'wolves among a flock of nice fat sheep, to be able to eat any one of them as they wished.

Meir encouraged the crew to enjoy some upper deck time and even got a few 'jezebels' back into costume again to add to the deception. The ships kept in touch via the aldis lamp and even held brief newsy chats with the short-range radio.

This idyll lasted for almost eight days before the Canary Islands were sighted. During that time, Meir had his ship work

The Black Rose

its way slowly towards the rear of the small convoy. It happened as a natural course of events due to a slightly slower speed, so nobody took much notice.

Meir also found out during the lazy passage, what each ship was carrying, and how many passengers each carried. The *Houston Ranger* had 100, and the other ship, the *Oregon,* had 75. More than enough to satisfy both sides of the Atlantic, providing Luchens and his cronies didn't get to them.

Meir checked his chart and saw that the Canary Islands were now 4 hours steaming away to the south of them. As it was a dark and overcast evening with no shining moon to light up the sea, he decided to go to action stations.

"Ship closed up. All deadlights fused, captain." Flens reported.

"Port 15. Full ahead together. Make speed for 30 knots. Stop making smoke."

Meir had his ship veer to the left and race off around the 2 ships to get ahead of them.

Before he disappeared from view, he had a mine thrown overboard with a 30minute fuse that would blow it up, thus giving the impression that his ship was in the process of being attacked by a U-boat.

Whilst the ship was making headway he got the crew to alter certain parts of the ship making it look different for when he came back to his prey.

When the crew finished, the front part looked just like the *Lorraine*. The ship sailed for about 2 hours before Meir turned her around and stopped her to wait for the other 2 to catch up. He noticed that he was up wind, so set off a couple of smoke canisters to keep the area dark for his attack. He even had all his lights off.

"The *Houston Ranger* is on Green 5 about 8 kilometres, the *Oregon* behind that again at Red 5 and about 25 kilometres" the signalman reported.

176

The Black Rose

"Stand by bofors and machine gun action. I will need 2 sets of boarding parties of 20 each, once I've destroyed their radio aerials and bridges, and get them stopped." Meir explained swiftly to his officers and urged them to be quick about things, as they only had about 30 minutes in between each ship.

He wanted as many people alive as possible and as little damage as possible so they'd better be spot on with their gunnery.

Meir waited until he was in a good range for maximum effect then gave swift gunnery instructions to suit the target, before they opened fire.

Meir used his loudhailer to tell the captain to stop his ship or it would be sunk with all passengers. This did the trick as the ship slowed down until it finally stopped.

Soon the boarding party was safely on board using the front derrick to swing them up onto the damaged and bloody bridge. As soon as he was given the signal that all was under control, he raced his ship towards and caught the other ship that was almost on top of them. The same tactic was used and the same response was received. Meir had stopped and captured 2 ships within 1 hour of each other.

On both ships, he found that most of the bridge crew had been killed, and both captains were totally surprised to find just who their attacker was. They just couldn't believe that a tramp steamer could turn out to be a Q ship of the highest quality.

Meir had the 2 captured ships sail at full speed and escorted them directly to the Spanish Drum, where they were met with open arms.

Admiral Horstenitz saluted Meir this time, in recognition of what he had just performed, as he read Meir's accounts of his last few weeks and his recent action. Meir's debriefing took slightly longer to conduct, but in the end everything was as it should have been.

Total success to the U-boats and the Kriegsmarine, as Meir found out that Britain was now alone and becoming a besieged fortress. They were winning the Battle of the Atlantic, and Meir was helping to persuade the Americans to stay at home.

Meir saw that the *Lorraine* was lying alongside its berth when he entered the Spanish Drum. He explained to Horstenitz that he was going to use the *Lorraine* as a support ship and a scout for him during his patrols, and in fact wouldl take all his prisoners back to whatever Drum needed them.

He asked about Luchens and was told that Luchens was now a Colonel and had somehow got himself roped into taking charge of some sort of bullion delivery, which would take him across the entire North African desert to Persia. Also that he was a very rich man now, with his own little army of SS troops to get his way with.[3]

Meir was glad at the news and said so. And took great delight in telling Beiderman, Voss and co.

Horstenitz split the prisoners equally among the two bases, but told Meir that Becks was a couple of thousand miles further south, building another base and needed a lot more to complete the constructions. He had taken several bulldozers and material but few workers, so Meir would have to send his prison ship down there as and when it was convenient.

Meir was shown the area, and made a mental note of the corresponding bases he might need to set up on the South American side, to be able to go from base to base without having to dodge awkward questions in any neutral port that he might have to call into.

"Your ship and the *Lorraine* will have silhouette changes completed and loaded up with the necessary supplies by 0500 tomorrow. I want you to get back over there to Freiburgh a.s.a.p. His squadron has been re-enforced as mine has, so take as much as you can safely carry. I'll see you before you sail." Horstenitz said as he handed Meir a small package.

Meir opened it to reveal a solid gold, jewel encrusted

---

[3] See *The Lost Legion*.

The Black Rose

Submariners badge, with a black and gold sash that had a 'Kaiser' medal on it.

Horstenitz looked at them and smiled as he shook Meir's hand.

"You have been recognized by the Officer Core and the submariners of your country, which means that you can now join the elite few such as myself. Even our Fuhrer wants to see you soon. Once more I congratulate you Otto."

Meir slipped the package into his inside pocket and accepted the accolade Horstenitz was bestowing upon him.

"You will carry on sewing your mine fields as and where you wish, Otto. According to my friends, your mines have accounted for 6 more ships off this coast, and several more around the shipping lanes in the Caribbean. Therefore, you will have an extra supply stowed on the *Lorraine*, who will also carry all your paint and props that you need. Make sure she gives them to you before you part company." Horstenitz stated as he gave Meir another stores list to take with him.

Meir took his batch of orders and stores documents, saluted Horstenitz as he left the ship, then went into the passenger lounge to join in among his officers again.

There was an impromptu party on the go, which Meir let himself get fully involved in.

He also discovered that most of the *Lorraine's* crew had volunteered to stick with their ship no matter what, but that each one was offered a lucrative pay deal, which not even their former employers could have matched. Lots of pay, women to enjoy, plenty of free booze and a grand pension to enjoy once the war was over.

Meir was told that he had to keep some of his trained crew on the *Lorraine* as it was now lightly armed, with a small cannon on its bow.

He was given good replacements from the captured ships crewmen, almost like for like as this was to be the policy and the trend from that moment on. Meir would get them suitably trained up to fit in with the rest of his ships company as and when he needed them. His own crew, were moulded by him into a highly efficient fighting unit, which was why he needed quality replacements.

He allocated Schenk, Beiderman, the Bosun, a few senior ratings, a few gunners, and one of his best Radio telegaphists to stay on the *Lorraine*, as he needed a reliable team on board that he could trust. That done he saluted them goodbye and signalled them to follow him out of harbour. Destination Jungle Drum.

Chapter XIII
A New Dress

The two ships sailed back across the Atlantic in the shipping lanes enjoying the few days of peace and good weather and each other's company. They met a couple of ships on the way towards the Caribbean, but as they were in ballast, Meir simply noted their names and particulars for him to look out for on their loaded voyage home again. They arrived at the Jungle drum without incident, with much excitement from the base occupants.

"Welcome back Captain, I see you've started to expand your operations." Freiburgh said happily as he nodded to the *Lorraine* anchored up stream.

"I have lots of goodies for you Commander." Meir said as he pointed to the 4 gold rings of a Captain, whereas Freiburgh's rank would only have 3.

Freiburgh smiled and clapped Meir's back gently.

"We both have been very busy dear Otto!" Freiburgh laughed as he showed Meir his thick gold band indicating that he was now of Flag rank, and a commodore the same as Becks. Meir smiled back and returned the gesture, as both men went to Meir's day cabin, where Winkler had a chilled bottle of wine ready for them.

Both men toasted their new ranks and talked briefly about the events of the next few days. They both knew that the real conversation should be of the special cargo Meir had for them, when Freiburgh told him about another inspection of the new additions to the base that was recently completed.

"Tomorrow morning at 1100hours again Otto! In the meantime, I'll have both of your ships unloaded starting with the other one. I have a succession of friends visiting me during the next few days. Your cargo will be offloaded directly into them as they come alongside, and you'll be able to entertain them as they arrive."

The Black Rose

"That's fine by me. See you then Commodore." Meir replied but got mildly rebuked "Come now, Otto! You know my name is Sam, but nobody else knows about it, so keep it that way."

Meir nodded and smiled and repeated the name before both men left the cabin for their individual duties, as Meir escorted Freiburgh to the gangway and off the ship.

Meir got his cabin load of valuables and passports brought ashore and stashed away in the hidden cave. It took two days to render the precious metals down into gold and silver bars. The jewels were put into the small bags according to size and value, with the most valuable ones kept to one side and put into a special box. Both were surprised how much gold and silver bars were made, as they stood nearly 3ft tall and square.

"Enough to start another little war Otto! Each bar has our **BLACK ROSE** stamp on them, and each of a specific size that no other gold bar is made to. Look at what we've done to some of them." Freiburgh stated as he broke open a gold bar.

"We have made them in a special way so that they can be snapped open in the middle and put back together again. That's because we've hidden the diamonds, emeralds and rubies in them, so that each special bar, with the double **BLACK ROSE** stamped on them, has more than its value than in its weight value. All these special one in that pile over there are ours."

"But we are supposed to send all this back to Germany for the war effort, including all the passports and stock bonds whatever, Sam."

"Ah yes dear Otto! Our Fuhrer will get the ordinary bars and all the other stuff. We'll keep the special ones for ourselves 'for a rainy day', as the English would say. Besides, nobody knows how much we've collected for them to determine how much they'd get."

"I suppose you're right." Meir agreed as he looked at the large pile of bars earmarked for him.

The Black Rose

"We'd better get back Otto, but remember. We'll have to change our workers so that nobody but us knows about our cave. Our friend who showed us this place has already met his maker. A sad case of ivory poisoning."

"Ivory poisoning?"

"Yes Otto. Our friend got eaten by alligators when he, accidentally, fell into the harbour." Freiburgh smiled wickedly, as he ushered Meir out into the open and the bright sunlight of the day.

Over the next week, the base was a hive of activity unloading all cargo of the *Lorraine*. It was given a new 'dress' with fresh paint and embellishments added to it, ready to lure unsuspecting ships into its deadly trap.

They re-created the shape of the *Schlezwig* alias the *Ballymuffin Bay*, alias the *Kilkenny Castle*, alias the *Killarney Castle* and any other aliases Meir cared to give her. But for command or operational code name purposes she was given, and her emblem on her charts, she was still known as *THE BLACK ROSE*, no matter where she went or what the name was painted on its stern.

The *Schlezwig* played host to the grey wolves that sneaked in and out of the base, and each U-boat crew were treated to a good welcome or send off as they came and went. Each U-boat captain making themselves known to Meir and the officers of the *Lorraine*, who openly admired the daring deeds Meir had done, and were gratified to know that Meir was entitled to wear their highest honour, the twin golden dolphins of the Submariners Badge.

Chapter XIV
Chipolatas

Meir had his ship cleaned and dolled up again just like the *Lorraine*. Then after both ships were loaded up with mines and an extra supply of ammunition, they too slipped out of the base and out to their new patrol areas.

Both ships turned right at the mouth of the Orinoco and made their way slowly towards Georgetown and the British naval base only a mere 300 kilometres from theirs.

They arrived late in the evening, before the moon came out, so Meir had both ships darkened, then laid a minefield off the mouth of the river where the base was known to be. It took them a couple of hours but they managed to get away again before a distant ship was reported coming their way.

Meir decided that they would return the way they came before and joined the local shipping lanes to make their way out and between the gap between Trinidad and Grenada. This was a very fortuitous decision for him as he had stumbled onto a shipping lane that only had ships bound for the European countries. All sailed from ports along the Venezuelan and Guiana coastlines laden with those countries bounties, that the Europeans needed to support their life styles and national ideas. Each ship filled with gold, silver, diamonds, oil, iron, tin, copper, manganese ore and all the other element needed by a warring nation to sustain its belligerent stance aginst its neighbours.

In four days, Meir had three such bullion ship sent directly to Cadiz for onward route to Germany, one to Freiburgh to cover their own private needs and that of the bases, and a further one plus four ordinary freighters over to Horstenitz, to cover his shopping list.

By the time he was finished, he only had a quarter of his original crewmen on board to maintain his fighting ability.

The Black Rose

But he was somehow rewarded bu the abundance of conscripts who were keen to fight to replace them, especially when each one had a gold bar in their hands to keep for themselves, plus the added knowledge that there was more to come.

Meir had his two ships sail to a 500 square kilometre lumpy bit of ocean where several shipping routes crossed over from most points of the compass, and only a few hundred kilometrers south of Puerto Rica. This was where he would strike the American ships taking their cargoes of oil, and various ores to keep their countries war machinery going.

It was like their life's umbilical cord, just like the one the British had over the North Atlantic to sustain its life. Meir knew if he severed that, the Americans would think twice about entering the war with Germany, who was so far, winning it all hands down.

"Captain. We've arrived and stopped at the centre of our patrol area, just as you've ordered. *Lorraine* is 3kilometres on our starboard bow." Klinshoff informed, as Meir climbed out of his bridge cabin bunk.

"Very good. Who's the OOW?" he asked wearily as he stretched and put his sea boots on. This was the cabin where he slept fully dressed, whereas his day cabin was for harbour, and a full nights sleep.

"Speaking!"

"Good. Have the *Lorraine* face the opposite way and about 3 kilometres astern of us. Any oncoming ship would think that we've just passed each other. Have the crew to early breakfast then to action stations within 1 hour from now. Get the steward up here with my breakfast."

KlinsHoff nodded and left Meir to prepare himself for yet another lonely day in command. The officers and men had each other to laugh and joke, and share confidences with, but Meir had nobody, even though he was revered and loved by his crew. His life as Captain was a lonely one, and he kept it that way as the tradition of every ship's captain.

They were 'God' on a ship, and every person on it did as he desired or commanded, or suffered the consequences as prescribed in the age-old tradition of life at sea.

Meir ate his breakfast in silence, as Winkler hovered and fussed around him.

"Winkler, you're one of the last of the original crew. Tell me, how are the new recruits fitting in?"

"Captain. The men are all right behind you. Most of them, including the British ones, have more than enough ability to carry out their duties, even though some of them can't read the German language signs they're supposed to follow. Mind you, the promise of gold as their pay seems to be doing the trick, as none of them have been paid in ages."

"That is good, Steward. It means that Cresswell and his likes cannot sabotage my ship in the middle of an action."

"The down side of that Captain, is that even some of our original stokers have forgotten the layout of the pipe systems. Especially when pipes keep getting re-routed or used for other than what they were designed for. At least that is what my stoker friends tell me. No doubt our Chief Engineer will prove me wrong, but it's best to speak to him not me."

Meir stared momentarily at Winkler, taken aback at the sudden but very useful inside knowledge he had not been aware of before.

"I will certainly do that steward. Now please clear this mess and have my civvy tropical uniform ready for me in case I need it."

"Aye captain." Winkler said dutifully as he carried away the remains of Meir's breakfast.

"Smoke of two ships bearing Green 10." Came a loud voice from a bridge wing.

The Black Rose

Meir was in his seat with his binoculars and looked over at the direction given, but had to put his eyeglass filters on as the sun was coming up directly into his line of sight.

"More smoke bearing Green 15." Came the same voice.

Meir looked at the new sighting, but was interrupted by Brantz who stood before him with his signal pad in his hand.

"Captain. I've just intercepted a coded signal, which was loud and clear, coming from the DF bearing of Green 15. It's from a British warship."

He looked again at the three smoke columns over the horizon and gave his binoculars to Brantz to take a look.

"You're spot on Brantz. Those sightings just reported by the lookout are exactly what you've just reported. It appears that we're about to be inspected by the British Caribbean squadron."

Brantz had a quick look and smiled at Meir with satisfaction as he handed back the binoculars.

"Tell the *Lorraine* to go to Action Delta, but remain within 2 kilometres off my starboard bow. Make plenty of smoke."

Brantz wrote down the signal, repeated it back for concurring, and then went off down the hatchway towards the wireless office.

"OOW! Hands to action stations, assume Action Delta."

Meir had the helmsman manoeuvre his ship so that it was not pointing directly into the sunlight, but also so that he could see the ships more clearly.

"Ship ready for Action Delta." Flens reported breathlessly.

"Get a second lookout up into the crows nest. I want a running commentary of both sets of smoke."

Meir had the *Lorraine* between him and the three little dots on the horizon, which would increase into bigger ones and a load of grief for them. He was going to hide behind the *Lorraine* and attack if necessary, but for the moment, would act naturally as a merchantman would do anyway.

The Black Rose

"Torpedo officer, we still have time to launch a few mines into their transit course. Set their depth to 3metres. Go when ready."

Flens repeated the order then reported back that the mines had been slipped overboard.

The signalman identified the two sightings nearest them were in fact 4 ships. 2 British V class destroyers and 2 Hunt type frigates, these were ahead of the other sighting, which he could identify as a 6inch County Class cruiser.

Meir was about to meet the Southern Squadron on its way home off patrol, and was prepared to fight them all. But decided to act peacefully and pretend he was what everybody took him for, a simple merchantman plying his trade.

The escorting destroyers sailed in a V formation in front of the cruiser only some 10 kilometres off Meir's starboard side as they passed the two merchantmen swiftly and went harmlessly away.

Meir held his breath as the ships passed, but he also took time to have a good look at his enemy. He realised that he could out gun the escorts but had to get under the guns of the cruiser to do any damage.

It had several centimetres of armour plating all over the place, whereas he only had a few around his guns and his bridge. A tough nut to crack even for an armed merchantman was the decision, so Meir had his two ships act out their charade by having the jezebels perform for the eagle-eyed British.

His ruse worked as the squadron disappeared well behind them, with enough time for Meir to order full speed ahead for themselves to disappear before the warships met the minefield.

Meir had his two ships turn around slowly in the evening light, to follow the warships, just to see if they had met the small mine field in their path.

The Black Rose

Meir gave a whoop of joy when he saw a flash of light, followed by a loud explosion heard several seconds later, from the direction of the warships, and looked intently through his binoculars to see which got hit. Before he could discern what was what, another explosion sounded followed closely by a third.

The two ships moved slowly towards the sinking warships and discovered that the others had left the stricken ones behind. He went into his own minefield and collected some special souvenirs from those warships, to prove that it was he that sunk them and nobody else.

"Signalman. Scratch 2 warships. 1 'U or V' class destroyers and a Type 1 Hunt class frigate. But I'm after the cruiser, whoever she is."

"She is the light cruiser Yorkshire." the signalman informed his captain as he stencilled yet two more images onto the place where he kept his tally of warship sinkings. Meir wanted to follow the cruiser to see if it struck the minefield at the entrance to its base, but declined the urge, with the hope that his friends the grey wolves would eventually tell him when he got back to the Jungle drum.

Meir signalled the *Lorraine* to reverse course and return back into their little hiding area within their patrol area, with the view of having a day off from their activities.

This was not to be, as several juicy targets presented themselves almost in succession, so Meir took advantage of his good fortune, and attacked them at will.

But he made sure that there were no survivors from those ships other than those he had taken on board, or kept to be sent to the new base that Becks was making some several thousand miles away on the other side of the ocean.

As he was getting short of crew, he decided to return to the Jungle drum to get them back, but sent the *Lorraine* over to the Spanish Drum with the captors.

The Black Rose

"Welcome back Otto! You've done well. All the new prisoners have also been busy as you can see from our latest edition to our base." Freiburgh said pointing to a new compound that was full with the captured cargoes.

"We have enough ammunition and diesel fuel in that compound, and enough frozen food in the container ship up that new creek there, to supply our friends for another 6 months or so."

Meir looked at the vast amount of crates and containers stacked up as high as his ship's bridge as it seemed a lot more on land than on ship.

"What about our other shopping list?" he asked quietly.

"All ready crated up and ready for storing somewhere else. I say that because it's getting too bulky for us to handle. Anyway, leave that to me."

"It's nearly Christmas time, Sam. Do you intend having the entire squadron and my two ships in port for it?"

"The squadron and your support vessel yes. You dear Otto, will be sailing to a new set of co-ordinates on the African coast to hide most of our special cargo. You'll be back in time for the New Year."

Meir nodded his agreement to the plan, but insisted that he had his original crew back, which Freiburgh agreed in return.

"There is one thing you must do for me, and that is to stick to orders, Otto. When you left last time, you went down to the British Port of Georgetown for a while before you decided to go onto your agreed patrol area." Meir looked surprised at this declaration, which made Freiburgh chuckle.

"I have coast watchers all along these shores, so don't be too surprised, Otto. It was a good idea, and in case you didn't know, one of your mines severely crippled the cruiser as it entered its base area. However, I shall not tolerate you disobeying direct orders again, in case your crazy ideas jeopardise our base here if the British decide to put a shadow on you. Do you get my drift Otto."

The Black Rose

Meir just smiled at the news and nodded his acceptance to due military orders. His little minefields were now coming into full play, which meant that he could now implement more tactical plans as he needed them.

Meir had his men back from the prize ships and sailed again fully loaded with his support ship, ready for another round of shopping.

In the ensuing months, the capture of, or the total destruction of merchant ships in that part of the world, and purely by Meir's actions were now being reported by the world press, which was good for Germany but totally dismal for the British and their allies.

Meir was told by special signal that the Fuhrer knew it was his doing and was delighted.

But the British and their allies decided that whomever it was committing such atrocities against neutrals would be sought out and destroyed. They did not know who was doing it, but the allies would bring the perpetrators to justice, which meant that Meir and ships like his were now public enemy No. 1, and everybody was alerted to try and capture these despicable people.

Meir laughed and scoffed at the feeble attempts to capture him, and his tally of sunken ships mounted by the week. The year ended on a high for the German Navy, and a very profitable one for Meir and Freiburg, as he landed his special cargo on a very forbidding African coastline but seemingly in the middle of nowhere.[4]

Meir arrived back into his Jungle drum base, where his ship was given a week off for R&R, whereby the female prisoners were required to perform all over again for the crewmen, whilst several lakes of ale were quaffed and mountains of food consumed in the meantime.

---

[4] See *Fresh Water*.

The Black Rose

Meir's crew were more than glad to get back to sea again, if only to escape the sexual Olympics they had to endure each night they stayed there, let alone to the relief of the female prisoners.

'Totally shagged out' would be the expression Meir had in mind, as his crew slowly recovered their strength again and found the usual crop of VD victims to cure.

He never took part in such antics, but decided that for the subsequent R&R periods, the sexual needs of his crew would only be on demand as opposed to by command. He needed a fully fit crew at all times.

The next several months were spent creating havoc with the merchant shipping again, with only the return to base for refuelling and re- arming, to punctuate the routine Meir had set up.

The Americans sent a few warships to look for him, but lost them to Meir's tactical genius, as he established himself as the invincible and uncatchable.

On one of his return visits to refuel, even the local newspapers accorded him with the accolade of being the Unknown, Unseen Terror, more dangerous than a squadron of U-boats. That the price on that Pirate's head was growing by the month, to value over 1 million US dollars but in gold.

Meir was the toast of his crew and all those who relied upon him to keep their supplies coming in. More so when he met up with Luchens again, who was waiting for him in his new bolthole on the West African coast.

"Captain Meir. We have unfinished business to attend to. You will see to it that I get these supplies on your next return to base." Luchens demanded.

"Colonel Luchens! You have a whole regiment at your disposal, why can't you do your own dirty work!" Meir said coldly as he waved Luchens away.

The Black Rose

Luchens went pale, drew his machine pistol from its holster and levelled it at Meir's head

"Don't you dare dismiss me like that again Meir! I'll have you skinned alive then shoot you like a dog." Luchens hissed, and signalled two of his henchmen to grab hold of Meir.

"It appears that you've forgotten your manners Luchens. Unless you have your baboons release me this instant then you'll –" Meir started to say.

"Or what little boy? I'm the Gestapo Commandant here now, not your namby pamby sailor boy Becks. From now on, I'm calling the shots." Luchens said menacingly, as he leaned into Meir's face and gave a sneer.

"I have come to relieve you of all the gold you've decided to keep instead of handing it over to our Fuhrer. Where have you hidden it Meir?"

"I don't know what you're talking about." Meir said nonchalantly, but got a slap across his face by Luchens.

"It appears that you need a little lesson on how to remind yourself on such matters." Luchens responded then clicked his fingers.

"Hello sailor boy! Remember me?" A soft-spoken voice said from behind him.

Meir turned and saw a tall female dressed in a white fur coat, as she came slowly up to him blowing several smoke rings into his face. He recognised her as the woman he had thrown off his ship, and remembered her last words.

"Strip him! I want to see just how manly this so-called National hero is." she shouted, as the men holding him started to rip off his uniform.

Meir was spread-eagled and bound by his wrists and feet in a 'star' fashion, as the woman looked at his naked body.

"Hmmm! I was expecting a nice big juicy saveloy but instead all I see is a puny looking little thing for such a big hero. To call it a chipolata would be an insult to the chiplata."

The Black Rose

she said, as she cupped his genitals gently, trying to tease him into an erection, but was unsuccessful.

"Just as I thought sailor boy. You've found no use for it in the past so it would be no loss to you now. If I taste your sap after you plead forgiveness for throwing me off your ship, then I shall cut it off for you and stuff it in your mouth as you scream."

Meir saw the woman wield a large curved dagger and hold it close to him, but he didn't say a word nor did he flinch as the cold steel pressed against his body.

"Now then sailor boy. Where have you got your gold kept? My colonel and I have need of it." she said softly as she fondled his genitals again more purposefully this time.

Meir did not move, nor did he say anything, just held his breath waiting for the woman to slice him up.

"No man can resist my technique like Luchens, or at least last longer than 5 minutes. Most men spend themselves within seconds. Let's see how long you last, to see just how good you are." She said seductively as she manipulated his genitals almost lovingly.

"I've told you before sailor boy, if I taste your sap and find that you're really good, and you tell me that you're really sorry, I'll only cut one of your balls off. If not then I'll cut them both off then your pathetic little prick, not even a little girl could get any pleasure from it." she said aloud as she performed oral sex on him.

Meir tried to concentrate on a hypothetical tactical problem, which seemed to last ages before the woman cried out in triumph.

"Hah, a typical man! A couple of sucks and a few rubs and you squirt all over the place." she said as she sneered into his face and wiped her mouth with her hand then dried it on his body.

"See! You only lasted 10 minutes before your disgusting little squirt wet my face and hands. That means I can have at least 1 ball off you. Which one do you like the most, little man?"

The Black Rose

Meir looked around to see Luchens sitting in Meir's chair and smiling, obviously enjoying the spectacle as he was urging her on.

"Come now Meir! You're not going to refuse me just for the sake of one little chipolata? Tell us where the gold is hidden. You've had your ten minutes of fun now you've got just 10 seconds to tell me before I use this very sharp knife." she threatened as she stood up and drew the blade across his lower abdomen, drawing a trickle of blood.

Meir winced in pain as he saw his blood oozing out of its cut, but saw a reflection in the highly polished brass work over his bridge chart table as the woman then reached for his genitals to cut them off, and started to count.

"You do realise that, in hurting or killing me you'll never know where I've hidden the tons of gold, diamonds, emeralds, rubies and other such valuable items. I'm the only one with this knowledge. You have a choice. Kill me before your get that information, which proves that both of you are stupid as well as greedy, or keep me alive and well so I can lead you to it. " Meir said slowly, trying to stall the moment.

The woman poked her leering face in Meir's as she licked her lips.

"You might be a national hero to sink all those ships, but to me you're just a stupid little boy with no taste to you. I have others that will give me the information we need, so as I've told you earlier, your balls are now mine, captain Meir. Open your mouth wide now like a good little boy, ready for when I stuff them into it. You've had your pleasure, now have your pain."

As her face was so close to Meirs, he managed to head butt her so hard that he heard and felt her nose break and heard the knife drop from her hands and clatter onto the steel deck, as she clutched her face and screamed in pain.

The reflection he saw was Voss who appeared swiftly from the bridge cabin, and in that moment of confusion shot Luchens

The Black Rose

in the head with his luger, then the two henchmen, before he clubbed the woman unconscious onto the deck.

"You all right Captain?" Voss asked gently, as he reached over and cut the ropes from Meir.

"This particular female is the one who murdered my brother and sister before my family was taken away to that so-called holiday camp. In fact it's a death camp for all who go there." Voss said angrily.

Meir was helped to get dressed and had his stomach wound bandaged up, as the woman still moaned and writhed on the floor at his feet.

"Get that piece of shit off my bridge, and put somewhere where I will deal with her later. I want Luchens baboons disarmed and tied up, and have us ready for sea in 30 minutes.

"Once at sea, throw these dead men to the sharks." Meir ordered as he donned the last piece of his uniform, his cap.

The ship sailed under the cover of darkness to make its way back up the coast to the Spanish Drum.

The following day was bright and the sea calm, as Meir had the SS soldiers lined up on the after cargo deck. He also had the woman tied to the cargo hold covers.

Voss had the crewmen armed and lined up facing the SS soldiers, who were looking seasick or sick with the knowledge that they were about to face execution.

"Each prisoner will strip naked. See to it that the woman is held up to see what I'm about to do." Meir commanded, as the 40 prisoners stripped and stood naked in a long line, facing the crewmen.

Meir walked down the line of men and saw that each one had a blank stare on their faces, and found that each one was turned into a eunuch, where that woman had brutally hacked off their testicles for them.

Meir called for Winkler, and when he appeared, whispered a

message to him. Within five minutes, Winkler re-appeared, panting and struggling with a heavy wooden chest.

"Now then men. It is obvious to me that each of you have been deprived of a possession, no doubt at the hands of this pathetic female in front of us. Whilst I cannot do it myself, there is a doctor employed by her boss, the Deputy Fuhrer, who just might be able to put back that which was cut off from you. Get yourselves dressed again." Meir stated loudly, as he handed each prisoner a gold bar. His own crewmen just smiled sympathetically at each man as they looked at the solid gold bar they had been given.

When Meir had finished handing out the gold bars, the look on each prisoners face told him, that they wanted to seek vengeance on that woman in front of them.

"It seems Madam, judging by the demeanour of these men, you've got quite a collection of their balls that you seem to take great delight in possessing. Just maybe you were hoping to add mine to them, no matter if you were told all that you wanted to know. I feel sure that each one would like to get their personal retribution on you and the rest of your lesbian kind. However, I have a better idea, and I'm sure that you'll appreciate my subtleties, now it's my turn to show you exaxtly what is what." He said aloud and with much vehemenence.

Meir turned round to his ships company and ordered them all to strip naked and stand in line in front of the woman's spread-eagled body.

"You obviously like the feel of power when you've got a man's pulsating penis in your hand as you cut his balls off. Let's see how you get on with men that still have them."

The woman started to wail and plead for mercy, but Meir slapped her face and told her to keep quiet.

"Now for your punishment. You've had your way all along with shall we say a 'captive audience' to demonstrate how weak we men are. Now that the role is in reverse, let's just see

The Black Rose

how you are at being a woman." Meir whispered in her ear as he ripped off her once very expensive clothes.

"Hmmm! A skinny bag of bones with one pair of standard sized scrawny tits! A thick black pelt between your legs that's covering a piss-hole that's probably been stitched up several years ago. Maybe that's why you prefer the taste of men rather than a belly full of arms and legs." Meir teased as he started to rub her pelvic area with a large belaying pin.

"Maybe you are of the lesbian type and prefer little girls piss-holes. Let's see how you do with real men with balls that you seem to like cutting off. I've seen a ten-year-old Jew girl manage to take on five big men all at once. How many men can you take, or to satisfy you?"

Meir had reversed the role he experienced on the bridge and told the woman that she was about to be destroyed by a famous pair of aviators, All Cock and Balls.

The woman looked at Meir in sheer terror begging to be let go, then started to threaten them all by quoting what her famous Uncle would do to them if they didn't.

Meir just laughed in her face and reminded her that there were over 100 men on board still with their balls intact and that she would get to know each one of them. That as they were now at sea, not even all the powers commanded by the Fuhrer himself could stop them.

"6th Mate. See to it that all crewmen on board that is able to do so, enter this woman's orifices in batches of three at any one time, and as many times as they desire. When the last man is done, you will see to it that these poor eunuchs have the privilege of throwing her overboard." Meir commanded, as the woman started screaming afresh, begging his forgiveness saying she didn't really mean it.

He went over to the woman slapped her face hard again, and whispered in her ear.

"Your orifices will be opened so wide that not even a

The Black Rose

saveloy will touch the sides by the time the crew have finished with you. Just think of all those balls you've cut off, as they come bouncing back to you to avenge their cruel severance. However, just to make you feel at home shall we say, I shall instruct my torpedo men to concentrate on their favourite firing position called 'down the throat' shot. But then how fitting it is for you as this is was your favourite pleasure and pain torture system. This is your fate and so shall it be, but don't bother to thank me afterwards."

"6th Mate! Carry out the prescribed punishment." Meir commanded, then left to return to the bridge.

Voss smiled at his captain, and told him that he would take great pleasure in carrying out his orders.

The woman was brutally gang-raped by the entire crew, as they satiated their sexual needs to whichever orifice they fancied, but mostly concentrated on ramming themselves down her throat. At the end of her ordeal some hours later, she laid there barely concious with a fixed glazed look, babbling incoherently, whilst violently vomiting up mouthfuls of semen. Voss finally came over to her and had her badly bruised, blood and semen-stained body, dragged over to the ships side, and with great relish and a loud cheer, she was thrown unceremoniously overboard by the eunuchs. He came back onto the bridge to tell Meir that the punishment was now completed and that the last piece of trash had now been ditched.

The prisoners had been reclothed and were standing ready for Meir to speak to them again.

"Each of you are now part of my crew and it is for me to decide where you end up. You'll keep the gold I've given you, and for you to get yourselves integrated into life on board my ship. It will be up to you if you live long enough to spend your wealth, and there's a lot more to come, I might add.

"I hope that you'll put it all to good use and get yourselves back to as normal as you can, and at the same time serve me to the best of your ability." Meir paused to let the men think on what he said.

"I need men to do their duty, without question or without complaint. I do not keep passengers on board my ship. Any person among you who does not want to sail with me, are at liberty to say now, without punishment." Meir paused again to gauge the reaction of the prisoners, but there was not a murmur, nor a sign of discontent.

"Then I can take it that each of you will succumb to a bullet in his ear if he refuses or disobeys an order?"

Meir waited again for any response, and yet again all he got was a sea of impassive faces and blank stares, and realised he was wasting his breath.

"6th Mate. Sort out their skill factors and assign them to whatever they are good at."

"Aye aye sir." Voss said quietly, as he saluted his captain, then turned and started despatching the docile men to whatever part of the ship that was most suited for them.

Chapter XV
Crabs

Meir arrived back to his Jungle Drum hideout to see Freiburgh, and to get new orders where he was told that the Spanish Drum was found and had been destroyed by a massive landing of American forces on the western tip of North Africa. Also that the Kildrum operations were now winding down and although they were ordered to continue their operations, they had to be self-sufficient in providing their own supplies and bases from then on.

"We need a new base roughly around the Amazon delta, and that new one opposite, but you'll need to set up at least 1 more each side and further down the Atlantic to sustain your operations, Otto." Freiburgh explained then went on to show Meir the new bases and the approximate areas his new operations were to be carried out.

"But Sam. Each transit across the Atlantic takes a good week, even at full speed. How do I get back again without fuel and other supplies?"

"You will have to continue as you've been doing, by pirating and looting any ship that has your cargo on board. The thing is, you need to have everything set up to stop the flow of troops and other major supplies coming around the Cape.

"We also have reason to suspect that the Allies may have broken our cypher code, which means that we'll just have to continue in plain language and use our shopping list code to fuller effect. That dear Otto also means that if the former is true, then we're out for a hiding, and will sustain heavy losses amongst our grey wolves. If that's the case, then any wolf pack not discovered, will in future, be on their own unless you're there to support them, from your new, and special supply port of L'Orient.

"They have special new U-boat pens there, and is the place

The Black Rose

where you'll need to return to from time to time. That is why you'll need to be extra active and vigilant towards our cause."

"Whose orders will I be under, and who will I be asking for my own support and supplies, Sam?"

"You'll be on your own as soon as you sail from here, I'm ordered back to Germany for redeployment, which is the naval term of being replaced and put behind some stupid desk somewhere.

"But realistically, I've been recalled to, shall we say, explain the creative accountancy in regard to the gold we sent, which supposed to be used as payment to the Arabs for the oil that they've supplied us with. Something to do with a missing gold shipment that we've been accused of, shall we say, waylaying."

"But what of our own Sam?"

"I've got a piece of paper here with certain map references to tell you where some of it will be found in Brazil, Argentina, Chile and certain African countries, but basically, at each of your little bolt holes.

"But when you get to add to those quantities, make sure you've got an inventory just like I've given you. The rest is already crated up for you, to take with you to hide in your new bolthole over on the African coast. I have the co-ordinates for that, but you might decide to have it moved to a newer location. The reason behind that is because we have a special covert operation, involving several senior-ranking officers to collect this bullion for when the war is over. Although its your share, we might have to use it to re-invent ourselves in a new life, or even to come back and help the Fatherland get itself back onto its own feet once the Allies have finished with us. Luchens is nowhere to be seen or can be accounted for, so he can whistle for his share. Remember, it's the *Black Rose* emblem that distincts our gold from any other gold that you might encounter."

"In case you didn't know, Luchens is dead Sam. So is that tart of his." Meir volunteered.

The Black Rose

"You mean that you've killed that bitch? If that is so, then we can all look out, because she was a relative of the Deputy Fuhrer and was on such special orders that only he knew where she'd be. Unless you can keep yourself hidden, then every last Gestapo agent will be on your tail."

"She was just as bent as her relative then. Luchens and she weren't interested in prisoners anymore, only the valuables and other such riches they could purloin for themselves. They had a go at me, but it was me that disposed of them."

"Well done Otto, but that's strictly academic now. Get yourself fully prepared with all your spare equipment and hide yourself. The local district governors are getting wise to our operations and are now getting too greedy. They are threatening me that if we don't cough up almost three times as much as we've been giving them, they'll have us shut down and reported to the Allies for operating uninvited, or supposedly, unknowingly on their coastline.

"By the way, and before I forget, there's a special cargo on board for you, mind that you use it on the enemy, and that's on the High Admirals orders. The instructions are with the cargo but be careful as its highly deadly stuff."

Meir saw the look Freigburgh gave him, and realised that the game in this little haven was about to end.

"Very well Sam. I'll take all that I can carry, and you can put as much onto the other two ships as possible. We'll set up a base lower down on the Amazon, just like this place, for you to find us."

Freiburgh and Meir shook hands on the deal and set about loading as much equipment and supplies as Meir's ships could carry. This lasted for several frenetic days, with the local politicians kept at bay as to what was happening.

When Meir sailed his little armada, now three ships, out of the now deserted base, he knew that he was on his own, as nobody in the neutral world would officially help him.

He would now be operating covertly and in a clandestine manner with whoever decided to help him, but the price to pay would be extortionate even for Meir.

He sailed his ships down the S American coast to the Amazon delta where they sailed up the mighty river, a day's sailing inland, to a spot where Meir once visited with his Uncle Heinz.

"Pilot. Pull into this deep channel to starboard, and steer us up this little tributary." Meir said as he pointed to a small opening in the dense jungle.

"Signalman. Tell the other ships to follow our wake, and be careful of the sandbars. Navigator, start plotting our course as I tell you each bearing and speeds." Meir said calmly, as the ship neared the almost impenetrable jungle along the riverbank.

The ship twisted and turned for several hours, through a series of sandbars and ended up in an oxbow of the river, followed closely by the other 2 ships.

Everybody was surprised about how perfectly this oxbow of the river suited their purposes, as each dropped their anchors into the clear waters of the lagoon.

Meir had everybody ashore chopping down the vegetation to create a clearing for the supplies the ships had, and even had a little jetty made for the ships to secure alongside, rather than anchoring out in the lagoon.

It took a full two weeks to have their new base functional and ready to receive further supplies and materials for their usage. But it took a further four weeks and just two captured ships to provide the prisoners as workers and other machinery to run this base just like Freiburghs. All of which made Meir very satisfied with his new impregnable fortress, and the knowledge that at last he had somewhere where only he knew what was what.

He even had some of his cache of gold taken ashore and buried in a secret place nobody else knew about, because he

The Black Rose

killed the workers who lugged his gold for him. A pirates treasure of the modern world.

Meir decided that he'd take one ship from his little armada out for their first Atlantic patrol, to see if he could furnish his African site. He left the other one to scavenge on the ships using the deep Amazon River channels until he got back.

The patrol lasted several days and only yielded one victim for him to bring over to the African coast. Fortunately for him it was a tanker full of diesel. His own tanks could take several hundred tons, but his other two ships were getting very low and starting to become a drag on his own resources.

Meir went first into the newly constructed harbour, followed by the captured tanker and the *Lorraine*, and discovered with delight that it was almost like the Spanish Drum.

Except that there was a clean, steep sloping beach up to a row of several sand dunes, in the middle of two large mounds at each end. He recognised the ships he'd left several months ago which were now almost covered in sand. Yet again, just like the Spanish Drum, there were two islets hiding this beach from seaward, and only one true entrance to it. Meir guessed correctly that Becks must have copied the Spanish Drum for him in case Becks wasn't around anymore to see him to enter this new place.

"Secure from harbour stations. Finished with engines. Get the ship ready for unloading." Meir commanded.

Meir and Schenks walked over the gangway and across to a place carved out of the sandstone cliffs, which looked appropriate for him to set up his office.

"This will do us for now First mate." Meir said as he opened a door that led into a cool but well-lit room that had the furnishings of an office. He noticed a large but dusty envelope on the table that was addressed to him:

The Black Rose

'*Dear Otto. As you can see, I've re-created the Spanish Drum. But the segregated prisoners compound is in a specially constructed area amongst the sand dunes, as you'll see from the drawings. There is a 3 mile perimeter fence made of barbed wire around the base, with another inner one of steel about 2 feet high. You will notice that the beach has several lumps in it. These are not mines, but something more deadly, and something that absolutely everybody must be aware of if they want to live. They are nocturnal crabs as big as a British Tommies' steel helmet, but move at great speed only a few inches under the sand during the day. They don't like water, especially salt water, and the only way to kill them is to flip them upside down to bake in the sun, or be thrown into the sea. Beware of the area between the 2 and 5-fathom line, as there are strong off-shore currents. We had several local Arabs brought here to trade for the prisoners, who disappeared quickly and in a great hurry, rather than come near this place. Not even the local animals dare venture within a kilometre from this particular beach. These crabs have a poisonous spit that they use to stupefy their prey, and can strip a human body down to a skeleton within minutes. I witnessed an elephant coming off the desert to eat some of the grass on the dunes. It was eaten alive and only the bones were left in less than 3 hours. I am the only one alive now so I leave this letter as my last journal to you, all the rest, including the plans to this base are in my safe behind this desk.*

'*Lastly, there is no fresh water for 600 kilometres either side of the beach, and 400 kilometres inland. You will have to make your own water from your ships' evaps, and store them in as many sealed, watertight containers as you can make, as any fresh water here has a habit of evaporating right before your very eyes. Regards Becks!*'

Meir handed the letter over to Schenks, as he looked around

The Black Rose

the room as if expecting Becks to come through some doorway or another.

Schenks read the letter and turned to Meir.

"Bloody hell Captain. We've certainly got ourselves into a bit of a hellhole. Poor Becks, I wonder what happened to him. Mind you, that explains why there's a lot of bones littered on the beach."

"We'll name this place, in his memory. Becks Bay. And to start off, we'll have to convert the tanker into a floating water barrel once we've cleaned out its tanks. If Becks is right, we won't be using any base perimeter guards to keep the prisoners in. Once they've been shown the crabs, they won't want to wander outside their steel enclosures." Meir said glumly.

Again it took Meir and his men several days to get the base ready for operations, but not before several disbelieving prisoners tried to escape over the sand dunes during the dark period between sunset and moonrise.

The cries of terror and pain and the piteous begging to be rescued rang out over the sand dunes. But within minutes the only sound to be heard, was the clicking of giant claws accompanied by a hissing sound, which soon lapsed into total silence. Everybody heard it, which emphasised the fact that the only way off this part of the coast was by sea in a sturdy vessel.

Chapter XVI
In the Meantime

Due to the German success in finally cracking the British Naval codes, Meir was able to be in the right place to intercept the cargo ships he needed to maintain his special operations, without making the long voyages to the French Atlantic coastal ports designated to receive him. He enjoyed several months in a productive period of capturing ships for their cargoes, and especially the prisoners who were needed to keep his two new bases going. He was proving to be a veritable thorn in the sides of the allies on both sides of the Atlantic. So much so, that a special task force was set up by the Americans, and backed by a British cruiser squadron to search and destroy any rogue ship designated as a 'Q' ship. All enemy 'Q' ships were to be sought out and destroyed, or captured and their crew held for any war crimes that could be attributed to them.

One such signal was sent to Meir, telling him that the *Tulip, Marigold, Pansy* and the *Thistle,* had already been destroyed, but that the allies were still in the dark as to which was which, when it came to the call signs or designated code words, and needed to capture a live Q ship captain to provide the answers.

Meir looked at his calendar and at the growing list of ships' names, who became his victims, and decided that the only way to do his duty was to have his ship revamped and made as powerful as can be to be able to withstand these unknown stalkers. He knew that he could more than match the average frigate, destroyer and probably the odd light cruiser such as the Americans were sending out to catch him. He needed a more potent punch, or at least more of the same. So decided that he'd take a swift transit up to L'Orient to get himself prepared.

"As you know, we have got two support vessels running a shuttle service to and from the L'Orient, supplying our friends

The Black Rose

operating to the south and west of us.

"We also have a further three ships in use as store ships at each base, and we're proving to be getting very fat off these merchantmen. The thing is gentlemen, I will need a full compliment of officers and men to sail the ***Black Rose*** back to L'Orient for its overhaul and much needed refit.

"Most of you have been re-assigned to your own duties on your own vessels, but I intend to take back the original crew save for a few of the number kept for their, shall we say, own protection." Meir stated to his officers as they listened respectfully whilst relaxing in the passenger lounge.

Meir demanded total obedience from his crew, but he was also a man who let them talk among themselves openly, to discuss his plans or ideas. It was his way of keeping the loyalty of his men, and even promoted their contributions to the thought process. He commanded not by fear, but by respect and reverence.

"Most of us have not seen home since the Jungle Drum flight, and naturally we'd all wish to make the trip with you. But as our company has swollen to such a large number, and all those who equally deserve a trip home, we have to name the lucky men, or keep the status quo and maybe have a second trip for the benefit of those who didn't go the first time. For this we offer you the following list." Schenk said politely as he gave Meir a list of men.

Meir looked down the list and noted that there were several crewmembers amongst them that included the Luchens band of eunuchs.

"Why have these men be given favour over our own crewmen?"

"To preserve our integrity as a whole unit Captain. These men are good and know their jobs, which would leave some of our own men out, for the more important duties in case you need them at a later date. I for one, need no reminder as to why

The Black Rose

I remain behind, neither do Lt Beiderman and the others of the ships' company that you'll find are missing off the list. Moreover, should you sink or meet an overwhelming foe, we can carry on in your tradition with the rest of the original crew, that's all." Voss said stoically.

Meir looked at his officers then down at the list before he decided to comment.

"Your logic touches me, gentlemen. But fortunately I have no plans either now, nor any time in the future, which involves losing my ship or my brave crew. At least not this side of a peace declaration." Meir commented, which drew a loud cheer from the officers.

"I am happy with the list. See to it that each of our ships are manned the same First Mate."

This comment drew a standing ovation from the officers, as Meir left the officers to celebrate the news.

Meir had his ship prepare for its first trip homeward and sailed in company with one of the prize ships to ensure his safe passage northwards.

His philosophy was that two ships in loose company would receive less notice than one solitary ship, which proved his point when they both arrived off the coast of L'Orient, and a squadron of E boats sped past as they entered into the harbour.

Meir gave his last bridge orders and went down the bridge ladder towards the gangway to meet several officers who were the welcoming committee on such occasions.

There was a band playing, and several cameras recording the events, as Meir was heralded and welcomed as the hero returns. Even several of the U-boat crews lined the jetty as spectators to cheer him ashore. The welcome was tumultuous and every man-jack on board was treated in the same way as Meir. Such was the mixture of emotions that it took several days for the euphoria to settle down enough for the men to get

The Black Rose

back to their normal duties.

Unbeknown to anybody around, there were a few spies to take advantage of the situation, by taking several photographs of Meir and his ship, and even several anecdotes from the drunken crew men, enough to put a dossier together and send to the British Admiralty post-haste.

Whilst the German High Command paraded their heroes to feed the propaganda machines of Germany, the Allies were slowly and quietly plotting the downfall and eventual collapse of the Nazi war machine, and their world-renowned band of people who committed such horrific atrocities not previously endured by mankind. Even more than those at the hands of their Axis allies, the Japanese. But in the meantime, Meir and his ship still lived on.

Meir and his crew enjoyed two glorious weeks leave at home with their families, as the ship was given a good overhaul.

When he retuned, he found the ships main guns were altered. He still had his 105mm turrets, but was given two extra gun turrets that mounted a twin 160mm gun on each cargo deck, with the forward one just below the bridge. These special guns had inserts to adapt the barrels to take a multitude of calibre shells. Although they had shortened gun barrels, which gave them a shorter range than normal, they could give a much bigger and more powerful punch, once up close to its target.

The hull and decks were reinforced for protection, and her workshops replaced by extra storage space for the ammunition needed for those extra guns.

The ship's hull was scraped clean and given a new coat of paint, as was the rest of it.

Meir looked at the transformation of his ship and realised that as a merchantman, it would survive any close scrutiny that the allies might give as they passed within close range. But he was relieved to know that he had been given a few catapults to launch a new type of smoke canister already nestling in their crates as deck cargo, which to him looked like the special crates he left behind in Becks Bay. His special fuel tanks were enlarged, and his engines had also been refurbished and given new parts so that he could sail much further, and at a much higher speed. The passengers' quarters were reduced to allow the ship's fridges to be enlarged to carry more food.

The fresh water tanks capacity was greatly reduced and turned over for the new ammunition magazines. Instead there was an extra evaporator installed so that the ship could make their fresh water as and when they needed it.

It had several types and calibres of guns, with mortars, torpedoes, mines, and although Meir didn't know at the time, deadly Chemical Warfare weapons, in the shape of those smoke canisters.

He also discovered that there was an abundance of wood, thin sheets of metal, canvas and paint. This was his 'jezebel' uniform that he was to use from time to time. In short, his medium sized merchant ship was turned into a disguised, pocket battle cruiser.

His ship was now armed and he was instructed to do a more specific job other than supplying the hundreds of U-boats. As they were now operating at will in most parts of the North and Mid Atlantic, and all the way across from the European and North African coastlines to the Pan American coastlines; he was to concentrate on the shipping lanes and supply routes coming north from the African Cape. He was also required to make occasional raids on the routes coming up from around the Cape Horn and the Pacific.

"In effect Captain, you are a fast, specially armed surface raider, that can sail 25,000 kilometres without refuelling. If you're successful then we'll build a whole fleet of such ships.

"Am I covering the entire South Atlantic on my own, Admiral Feldsbusch?"

The Black Rose

"No Captain. We have two squadrons of our latest type of U-boats that will be in a double string, from the Brazilian Rocos Islands across to the Liberian coast that will be supplied by your base up the Orinoco. And by the way, that base is now strictly off limits to you. You've got to find another one further south, say aprox 50 degrees lat."

"I've got one on lat 30 degrees south on the African side and another one at 40 degrees latitude 10 degrees longitude. Maybe if I can operate just in those waters I wouldn't have to steam too far. Anyway what about my supply vessels?"

"The alternative is to create a rectangle from those bases, down to the Bouvet Island and then across to some offshore island in the Chilean area of Tierra del Fuego." the admiral stated as he traced a large rectangle across the large oceanic chart.

Meir was still quite adamant on the area of his patrol stating that his supply vessels would only be able to traverse the perimeter just the once before they needed refuelling, let alone provisions and pyrotechnics. Then he raised the spectre of an ambush by a much superior force and having to dodge into a neutral port to get out of trouble.

"It appears Captain Meirs, that you have doubts on your own ability. I'm beginning to wonder just how you won your medals for bravery, if this is how you moan at a simple task of sailing a couple of ships around the ocean." the admiral said in a condescending voice.

"I'm only a mere mortal Admiral, whilst you're supposed to be Jesus Christ and can walk across the ocean in your special boots." Feldsbusch continued.

Meir sneered at the Admiral, grabbed his briefcase and cap and left the Admiral gasping at the cheek of a subordinate leaving without permission.

"Captain Meir! You might be the darling of the German people, but you're still only a captain. Come back here and

213

The Black Rose

finish your briefings." Feldsbusch stammered as Meir slammed the door so hard, several pictures on the wall near it fell down, smashing the glass coverings.

Meir returned to his ship and called his officers together to get them organised for a very long patrol. One from which they might never return, given the immensity of the area and the heavy seas they were to cover.

He was standing on the bridge wing, when Feldsbusch burst onto the bridge demanding that Meir present himself in front of a superior officer.

Meir took no notice, but signalled the gangway be taken off, and gave the bridge crew his orders for moving off the jetty. Feldsbusch looked in amazement as he saw himself stranded on a ship that was rapidly leaving the dock and with no way that he was able to get back off it.

The pilot was singing his Irish shanties that had several expletives dotted through them as he manoeuvred the ship out into the harbour and out to the open sea.

"Admiral. I have exactly 100 specialist crewmen as extra passengers on board this ship, you now make it 101. Under the Mercantile marine law I am carrying one passenger too many to comply with the shipping Insurance deeds. To you, that means that you now represent an uninvited passenger, commonly known as a stowaway on this vessel. In view of the fact that I have a non-stop voyage to undertake, I suggest that you get below somewhere out of my sight, and stay off my bridge." Meir said icily, as he pointed towards the hatchway the admiral was to take.

"If you're good, I'll let you get off in my next port of call some 10 days steaming from here. And by the way, Admiral." Meir paused as he nonchalantly brushed his 4 gold rings with his gloved hand.

"I hope to make this as crystal clear as I can and I shall say

The Black Rose

this only the one time. I am the captain on board this vessel therefore your rank means nothing. These are my men, so do not try to interfere or throw your weight around. If you are found to do so or interfere with my orders, you will be shot. Do you understand?"

Feldsbusch huffed and puffed at the notion of being treated like this by a junior officer, but nodded his head meekly and muttered his revenge as he slowly descended through the hatchway and into the officers quarters.

"OOW! Our companion is keeping station 5 kilometres astern of us, keep on this course and speed for more than two hours then come and get me. Ask the Chief Telegraphist to come and see me." Meir ordered quietly as he entered his bridge cabin, and did not wait too long for the person to arrive.

"Chief Sparks. Set up a special link between our companion and us. In case someone should be listening, tell them that we have an uninvited guest on board who was keen to try a trip around the harbour, but unfortunately someone forgot to tell him we weren't coming back for supper. Also tell them that they are to commence their new orders on receipt of your signal. You will tell them to maintain radio silence on all frequencies except the coded one you have and where they will contact only if and when in difficulty. Got that chief?"

The Chief Telegraphist read back the message and when Meir was satisfied he left Meir to muse over his new set of charts.

"OOW?" Meir asked aloud from his bridge cabin.

"Aye Captain?" Kirkmeister responded.

"Alter course to starboard, steer 175. Set a cruising speed of 20 knots. See that our companion follows our wake. Get the signalman to flash them up and tell them to blow their smoke when it's dark. Inform our engine room too."

Kirkmeister repeated his orders and reported when they were carried out.

The Black Rose

"Captain. What are we going to do with the admiral? He's becoming a nuisance in the mess, and is trying to undermine your authority." Kirkmeister asked quietly so as not for the helmsman to overhear.

"Send the messenger down and ask the admiral to come to the bridge."

"Very well captain."

Feldsbusch arrived all pompous and full of self-importance, swaggering across the bridge towards Meir, who was leaning over the bridge's chart-table.

"Let me guess Captain. You've sent for me so that I can forgive you, is that it? Or you've lost your way and can't read a chart and need me to show you the way?" Feldsbusch asked cockily.

Meir saw that Feldsbusch was less than a couple of feet away, and planted a well aimed boot into his genitals, making him howl and double up in agony.

"Now then Admiral, stand up like a good officer. No sense letting the men know that one of their admirals cannot take a bit of pain now and again, is there?" Meir hissed, as he grabbed Feldsbusch's lapels and dragged him up onto his feet.

Feldsbusch was gasping for breath, moaning, and holding his genitals, and at the same time trying to speak, but could only gasp and groan.

"OOW! It appears that our admiral here has somehow hurt himself. How did he manage that? Did anyone of you hit him in any way?" Meir asked loudly to all on the bridge.

"No captain. We saw nothing. He must have hit himself on the corner of the chart table when we turned to starboard." Kirkmeister said quickly, as everybody shook their heads in denial of any knowledge of the incident, yet all saw what had happened.

"Admiral, you are a menace to yourself and my ship, unless you can control your body and especially your mouth when

The Black Rose

you're in the officers mess, then I'll shall have to take steps to restrain you. Do I make myself clear?" Meir shouted into Feldsbusch's ear.

Feldsbusch nodded his head and scuttled below again still holding his genitals, as Meir signalled the messenger to accompany him below to his cabin.

What had happened on the bridge got around the ship in no time, and even twice around the officers mess, Feldsbusch never spoke another word to anybody, keeping to his cabin for most of the time.

When the two ships passed down the coast of Morocco to the location where their old Spanish Drum hideout was situated, Meir stopped his ship and had a dinghy lowered over the side.

"Admiral Feldsbusch! This is where you get off. You will take off your jacket and wear this merchant navy one for your own safety. You have enough water and supplies to last you a few days once you get ashore. Keep moving north, you should reach a small town there to give yourself up." Meir said sternly as he took the admirals coat from him and threw a tattered old one to him instead.

Feldsbusch looked over the side at the small dinghy and back at Meir.

Meir looked over the side to the small dinghy and laughed dryly.

"Sorry about not being able to provide you with a handsome Admirals barge, nor a suitably sized ferry to take you ashore, but at least it's safe and seaworthy. Just think, admiral! You can be your own captain and crew all at once. Your very own special navy if you like."

Feldsbusch glowered at Meir and started to climb down the Jacobs ladder to the dinghy.

"You'll all hang for your mutinous behaviour, you especially Meir, see if you don't. I'll be waiting for you when you get back."

The Black Rose

"Now, now then admiral. You'd better save your breath for all that rowing you're about to do. You've only got about 3 kilometres to the beach, mind you don't capsize in the shore breakers. Remember about the little town north of here." Meir said as he gave Feldsbusch a mock salute before walking back up to his bridge again. Meir waited and watched with his binoculars to see that Feldsbusch was almost ashore before he got his ship underway again and back to his patrol routine.

"Captain. If the admiral goes to that town, he'll get taken as a hostage by the locals, or even be sold off as a slave." Kirkmeister said absentmindedly, but with a grin on his face.

"Now he tells me! Why didn't you remind me OOW!" Meir replied in mock horror, but smiled and said.

"The Americans are still trapped on the desert there, so they'll recognise his jacket as it's a British Officer's, complete with a passport and photo that looks like the admiral. That should keep him alive until he gets to whoever is in charge. By that time, we're long gone from these waters." Kirkmeister whistled softly and scratched his head.

"You've certainly cooked his goose. They'll think he's a spy with poor English vocabulary, or even a deserter. Either way, he gets shot no matter which side of the trench finds him."

"Exactly. Besides, I need his jacket for my own subterfuge when we get south again." Meir grinned then left the bridge.

Meir's two ship convoy sailed ever downwards to their new HQ, Becks Bay, alternating their position and even sailing close beside each other, keeping each other company. When they finally arrived at their Namib Desert coastline hideout, they secured alongside their respective jetties. Everybody at the base seemed very happy and joyous to see them return, there was even a small band and guard of honour paraded at each berth. Meir saw his welcome party waving, as they waited for him to come ashore.

The Black Rose

"Welcome back captain. As you can see, we've been very busy making our base much more habitable." Beiderman greeted as he saluted his captain.

"Good to see you Beiderman, and you Voss. Yes there certainly has been a big and much needed improvement around here. Commodore Becks would have been pleased and I am very impressed, well done. I've brought everybody lots of presents and a ton of mail for you all. But first I have a pleasant duty to perform." Meir smiled as he pulled out a small black box.

"By command from the Fuhrer himself, it gives me great pleasure to give you, Lt Cdr Beiderman and you Lt Voss the Distinguished War medal." he said as he garlanded both men with their honours, then handed them their new gold rings of promotion.

"I have a citation for each man and volunteer who remained at this base, which both of you will be giving out this evening. Make sure you're properly dressed for the occasion, as I shall be looking on." Meir said with a smile as he tapped his own 4 gold stripes on his epaulette.

The welcome back party went on all night without incident, as each man toasted their captain and themselves for the citations that were given out. Meir left the party with Winkler following along behind, and went into his new office. He saw photographs of the 3 admirals and Becks adorning the walls each side of a large photo of Hitler. But the item that surprised him most was a picture that took pride of place behind his desk. It was an oil painting of himself, in full uniform showing his 4 gold rings and all his war medals.

"Winkler, what do you know of this life sized painting! Who is the artist, as I can't read the signature?" Meir asked after a moment to get over his pleasant surprise.

"Me captain? I know nothing." Winkler said innocently but wearing a large grin, almost from one ear to the other.

The Black Rose

"You old scoundrel, you're the only one who knows precisely when I was presented my Knights Cross with gold oak leaves. The furniture behind me in that picture comes from only one room. That's the investiture room where our Fuhrer gives such awards. And that I've just had my hair cut for the occasion." Meir chuckled as he peered more closely at his painting.

"Not guilty captain, but I know a man who is, and he's not here in person." Winkler said as he looked at Admiral Meir's photograph.

"Hmmm! My father has a lot to answer for, including this portrait of me. However, I like it too much to take it down, so it shall remain there until we leave for home again." Meir said affably as he sat down in a large leather-bound chair captured off one of the prize ships.

"I would like a model made of our ship, and that of our prize ship companion.

"I also want a large, suitably framed mural on one of these walls that depicts all the ships we've captured or sunk, since we left Wilhelmshaven."

Winkler nodded his head and told Meir that he was going to get turned in whilst it was still dark.

"Mind out for those crabs steward. They love human flesh, if the skeletons along the perimeter fencing are anything to go by. It's a wonder we've got any workers left, Jews or not."

The sun rose early as did Meir, who went for a quiet stroll along the duckboards placed as a pathway along the beach, that protected the walker from the ever-shifting miniature sand dunes, which marked the killer crabs whereabouts. He noticed that the man-made islands opposite him that formed the protective barrier between the open sea and the harbour; were starting to show some life, and he saw the gun emplacements built in strategic places, being camouflaged for the day.

The Black Rose

He stood for a while witnessing such activity, and he was in wonder at the simplicity of what those men were doing. It was yet another instance, when an idea or plan began forming in his mind, to be formalised and agreed by his officers. He finished his walk with a swim in the cool seawater, before he made his way back to prepare for his day's desk job.

Becks had mysteriously disappeared, which left Meir to take up those duties normally done by him. He also had a fleet of 4 prize ships to manage and protect, let alone going off to fight a war. It was time for him to inspect his new base.

"Lt Cdr Beiderman, according to this layout of the base and the details of the buildings, we have a good stronghold. I will inspect this place now and again tonight, see to it in 30 minutes."

"Harbour and installation inspection captain? Aye aye sir." Beiderman responded to the surprise orders.

Meir was taken around the base by land then by sea across to the 2 offshore man made islands.

He saw the different gun positions, the boom defence, the areas with ground and sea mines, the machine gun posts and the manned outposts that were dotted a couple of miles away from the base. Meir looked at all and everything that was or was not mentioned in the plans, and told Beiderman to ensure that they were.

"Right then guns. I've seen enough. I want a night inspection and an exercise drill to see if your security system works. I will have Lt Voss with me. 2100 hours will be just right, make it so."

"2100! Aye aye captain!" Beiderman said as he saluted Meir who turned away and entered his office.

Meir had Beiderman take him and Voss by launch several miles off shore from the base.

"Lt Voss. I can see certain items that do not fit in with normal security procedures. Can you tell Guns here what you can see?" Meir asked as he handed Voss his binoculars.

The Black Rose

"I don't need them thank you captain." Voss stated as he declined Meirs offer of the binoculars.

"It appears that there are several lights showing along this area. I can even see smoke coming from behind that central island." Voss said as he pointed out the areas he observed.

"Please explain these lights, Guns!" Meir snapped.

"The smoke is coming from the shore galleys, but I can't explain the lights." Beiderman said truculently.

"Take me to within 1000 yards off shore on the northern side. There's supposed to be a howitzer battery there." Meir commanded.

When the launch was near the spot he had the launch engines stopped then rigged a mortar gun on the deck.

"I will fire 1 round at that gun position and another towards the cluster of lights I can see." Meir said as he pointed towards the land.

He fired his round at the gun position, which, after a few minutes, drew return fire but at a different spot to where the launch was. He fired the second round, which exploded and doused the lights from that area.

"What do you deduce from that drill Lt Voss?" Meir asked

"It appears that in the first instance, the gunners are either firing blind or can't discern where our fire is coming from. And in the case of the second firing, you've shot those lights out, captain" Voss said authoritatively.

"You see Guns. Your gunners are not keeping a watch out, and your night patrols are not keeping those lights off. I need a total black-out all along this section of coast, and a set of gunners who can hit their target. See to it. Next I want to inspect your boom defences. I don't want the British to do a 'Scapa Flow' on us. I want to keep my squadron of ships afloat." Meir snarled.

Beiderman had the launch take them to each of the 3 entrances to the base, but in fact only one was the main channel for use, as the others were strategically mined.

Meir climbed over the side of the launch and swam to a little float marker that a fisherman would normally use for his lobster pots. When he came back he told Beiderman that he'd need to speak to the only true fisherman in their midst, to get the proper idea on how to locate such items.

"Never mind his swearing or his manners, he's a good man who will take great pride in showing you." Meir concluded, as he dried himself and got dressed while the launch was making its way back through one of the openings.

"Your night inspection failed miserably, Guns. You have until tomorrow night to remedy everything I've written down. I shall do another inspection to see that my base is secure and ready for proper action."

"What time is your next inspection captain?"

"I'm not telling you, Guns. But I'll want a full inspection of the defence team at 1300 hours tomorrow." Meir replied as he and Voss stepped off the launch and strolled over the duckboards to the main office block.

Meir went to his office and worked through the night, preparing for his scheduled meeting with his officers.

Again Meir had his early morning stroll and swim before his day in the office began.

"Victor, kindly have all officers meet here in the large anteroom in half an hour. Dress not important, just be here." Meir said to Schenk who was sitting at a nearby desk.

"Aye aye captain." Was the civil reply.

Meir called for the steward and had a large dixie of iced lemonade prepared for the officers when they arrived.

"I've called you all here to re-assign some of you to other duties. I shall deal with the regular officers first then the volunteer officers. In the meantime, smoke if you wish, and there's a dixie of lemonade over there in the corner for those of

The Black Rose

you who are thirsty."

Meir drank his own lemonade then picked up a ream of papers that he started to read through.

"Commander Schenk, you will remain in command of the *Lorraine*

"Commander Emst, you will remain ashore and become our Ship Repair and Plant Manager.

"Lt Cdr Beiderman, you will become our Base Commander. You will be in charge of all prisoners, the base defences and its security.

"Special Officer Liebers, you will become the Base Supply and Logistics Officer.

"Lt Voss, you will remain ashore and become the Harbourmaster.

"Lt Brantz, you will remain ashore and become the Base Communications and Intelligence Officer. You will set up a radio and monitoring station, also an integrated telephone system for our needs.

"Special Officer Wagner, you will become the Base Medical Officer and set up a suitable sickbay.

"My ships' crew is exempted for this, but each of you will pick your men including those suitable from the prisoners that you feel are trustworthy enough to do the job." he stated, and continued to read on through the list of officers with similar tasks, that also included some of the captured merchantmen.

Meir's meeting lasted until noon, but he gave his officers time to question or offer any other alternatives to his plan.

"Right then gentlemen. We will have all of this week to get ourselves sorted out before I go hunting again. Just one last thing! In future, no prisoner will be killed out of hand unless caught in the act of sabotage or escape. The latter is highly unlikely, so be extra vigilant from now on. I shall try and get as many captives to help with the labouring jobs as possible, but I cannot guarantee that, as you all well know. There is a

The Black Rose

war on you know."

The officers filed out of the room and went their separate ways, except for Schenk and Emst.

"Richard, I'm glad you've stayed behind with Victor, as I have another thing just for you two. My real business if you like. Victor, you will take charge of the prize ships and see that they've got a suitable mix of crewmen. Both of you will be responsible for training in your own departments, as I need quality crewmen to man my ship at all times. If we come across suitable conscripts then you see to them before handing them over to me.

"For you both to realise the situation, thanks to lax security back at L'Orient, I have been identified and am now a marked man for any glory hunters to track me down and kill me or my ship. So when I sail on patrol, I might not be able to come back for a while, if at all. Therefore, I shall make a special signal to let you know where I am, or I'm on my way back. If the ship returns and I'm severely wounded, or in fact dead, the world must keep on believing that I'm still around, and still on patrol. If the latter is the case, then both of you will have to take joint charge of my operations.

"You will find special instructions to that effect in my office safe, but only to be opened when we've reached that point and at no other time." Meir said sombrely, as he swept his long black hair back off his forehead.

His two officers looked at him then at each other, before Schenk spoke.

"We will do our duty for as long as its necessary to win this war. But I will not be able to match your seamanship and tactical skills, so I'll just have to make the best I can. Besides, we're winning this war and there's nobody afloat to harm you, Otto." he said with a touch of bravado.

"Yes, Otto. You wreck them and I'll fix them better than new, you watch." Emst avowed.

The Black Rose

Meir looked at his two friends with a faint smile on his lips and reminded them that their other friend Lt Cdr Kirkmeister would also become part of this equation, as he would in fact, be taking over the command of the Black Rose in that eventuality. The slow nod and a brief silence from the two officers, was enough for Meir to conclude his real business.

Meir had his lunch and prepared for his inspection of the gunners.

He walked around their ranks, speaking to one or two of them before he came back out in front of them.

"Last night I found our defence gunners were not performing their jobs as trained. They were firing blindly, and at any old place their guns were pointed at. From now on, each gun position will keep a double look out. Specifically, one in the gun position as target ranger, and the second nearby. I want a coastal watch, and any sign of a ship is to be reported immediately to the gun captain, and onwards to the base commander. I also want extra patrols along the beaches, and any light found shining will be put out and the offender dealt with. No lights of any kind to be visible seaward, that includes smoking.

"I want each position and in fact the entire base totally blacked out. Further to this, no weapon or firearm will be discharged unless under specific command to do so.

"Gun captains take special note of this. We have to pretend that there's nobody here except for those infernal crabs." Meir said as he completed his tirade on the men.

"Lt Cdr Beiderman. You have your duty, see to it. Make sure the galley does not make smoke after dark, nor are any other fires to be lit between sunset and sunrise. Don't forget the harbour and perimeter defence patrols, I want them properly manned at all times. This base must be defended at all costs." Meir said as he returned Beiderman salute when he left the parade.

Meir was having a typical day where he felt he was doing everything and everybody else doing nothing.

"Steward! Get me my bathers and towel. Tell the pilot to get the launch ready, I want to go for a swim off the base." Meir said as he finished off a cool glass of wine.

He decided that it was time he started to enjoy himself even though he lived a Spartan life away from his officers and men.

"Launch ready, captain. Where do you want to be taken today?" the Irishman asked jovially.

"Surprise me pilot. Maybe the French Riviera or the Spanish Costas would do." Meir retorted in good spirit.

"Right ye be cap'n. Plenty of sand and sea it is! Mind you the local natives aren't very friendly today." the Irishman said as he sped the launch across the harbour and out of the base.

"Here's a quiet spot that I like coming to Cap'n. Plenty of date palms to shade under, with a nice delicate pink coral beach to relax on." the Irishman said as he slowed down and turned into a little cove not very far from the base.

Meir looked around at this peaceful little haven and smiled at the ingenuity of this so- called thick Irishman.

"Before we go ashore cap'n, we've got several juicy pieces of steak and a crate of beer to take with us. Care to handle a few items?"

Meir smiled at the cheeky invitation and grabbed a large crate of beer as he splashed into the shallow water and waded onto the beach.

"Surprise surprise!" Came a chorus of voices, making Meir reach automatically to his ever-present pistol holster strapped on his waist, just like a cowboy did.

He looked around and saw a few of his officers dressed in swimming trunks who were coming running down the beach accompanied by several very beautiful but naked women.

"Its picnic time Cap'n." the Irishman said jumping

The Black Rose

overboard and catching hold of a long-legged woman, as she jumped up into his arms and started to kiss him.

Meir just stood there for a moment, totally dumbfounded as he saw the jollity and the absolutely perfect means to enjoy his so-called private picnic.

"Welcome to Becks Cove, captain!" Kirkmeister laughed as he arrived, and saw his captain trying to take in this sudden rush of jolly activity.

Meir realised that he'd been tricked, but let it flow over him as he started to join in the fun with his officers. He was always up for parties, but this was the very first one since he couldn't remember when, it was that long ago.

The fun of the barbeque and especially the attentions of two nubile girl prisoners towards him, made him forget his past and present, as the day wore on into the evening.

"It's time we got back now cap'n. Don't want to break the blackout curfew, otherwise Guns would be on our backs. His boss is a strict one for such things." the Irishman whispered and gave a mischievous wink.

Meir searched and finding his watch and was alarmed at the time of day, but was politely reminded by his fellow officers that these things were just like a good wine, better sipped not swigged.

Meir was among his friends who'd protect him with their lives, and felt cocooned against the outside world, so he merely shrugged his shoulders in a happy surrender to their wishes. He was still enjoying the close intimate attentions of the two young women, and laughed at the idea, but agreed that just for this once, all would be okay. In the meantime, they should beware of any consequences that the morning might bring. This also led to hilarity and sensuous laughs from his happy band of people who seemingly had no care in the world other than to just enjoy the party whilst it lasted.

Chapter XVII
Single Again

The daily routine at the base quickly settled down into a slow pace of life, and was such that everybody worked from early morning to midday, then everybody had the time to their selves, apart from those on duty or supervising the prisoners. Even they had the evening off and 1 day a week to relax. The swimming and beach parties took on a new meaning as the barriers between the prisoners and their captors reached an understanding that everybody had a job to do. A lax jail but everybody knew what was what, and kept to their roles in the base. Fortunately for them, as nobody knew they existed, therefore nobody from the outside world came near them to be disturbed.

It was during this time that Meir had his and his escort ship altered into their jezebel outfits ready for their next patrol, even a little pretend launching ceremony as they renamed the ships. The **Black Rose** got the *Becks Bay* written on her stern and the *Lorraine* got the *Becks Cove* on hers. But each ships crew were drilled both in daytime and at night, in the art of changing the ships outfits. Meir explained that these drills were the subterfuge and camouflage necessary to gain extra space or time to get away from some perilous or tricky situation they might find themselves in.

A full month passed by before Meir had his base and his ships ready to resume the war, which was marked by a big party for everybody on the base.

The prisoners were gathered together and were told the truth cum propaganda that Germany was winning the war and it will all be over shortly. Of how the entire American Battle Fleet was sunk at Pearl Harbour by the Japanese Air force. How the cowardly 58,000 British troops in Singapore surrendered to a mere 9,000 Japanese soldiers, and other such great victories.

The Black Rose

Meir finished his speech to the prisoners, who were left to ponder over their fate, before he went to meet his officers for his final briefing before sailing on his first patrol from this new base, as his third theatre of war and operations.

"Pilot take us out on a steady westerly course, to our first hunting ground. Navigator, set your grid pattern on the chart and give Irish his course. OOW! Set patrol routine, procedure Bravo. Darken ship but tell the engine room to blow smoke if they want." Meir ordered and waited for the 3 men to repeat their orders before he left the bridge.

Meir left the *Becks Cove* behind as his ship sailed at full speed out into the shipping lanes of the South West African coast. The ship stopped at its pre-determined spot in the vast empty ocean and waited for its victims to approach him. They didn't wait long, as in the early morning light, a lookout spotted a column of smoke over the horizon.

Meir had his crew to early breakfast, and ready at action stations before the ship could be distinguished as to what it was.

"Lower the 2 black balls! Slow ahead port!" Meir ordered as he watched a large tanker becoming even larger in his binoculars.

"Signalman. She's a shell tanker, of some considerable size. Get me her details, by speaking to him with your aldis. Tell him I am having engine trouble and need assistance. 5thMate, have the engine room give a few blows of soot up the funnel, to make it look as if we're stopping and starting all the time."

The puffs of smoke coming out of the funnel looked like a Red Indian smoke signal, as the tanker veered towards them.

"She's the *Shell Capri* from Durban. According to the registry she's a new one, and of 20,000 tons. She asks what is it we require." the signalman said loudly.

"Tell him that we're the *Becks Bay* from Dublin. Fuel contaminated, need a top up if its possible." Meir responded.

The Black Rose

The signalman sent and received the reply.

"He says that he'll heave to and send over a launch with a couple of engineers. Would supply 30 drums of fuel oil if your hoists can reach over on his port side."

Meir grinned at the invitation and had Flens ready with his bofors ready to blast the wireless office off the ship.

The tanker dwarfed the *Becks Bay* as both ships came within a few yards of each other. If the sea was rough then both would hit each other, but fortunately for Meir it was calm, and mainly due to being in the lee of the much larger ship.

The two engineering officers appeared on the bridge to speak to Meir, but found themselves looking down the barrel of a machine gun that was levelled at them. The grappling hooks and ropes were snaking across the gap, as men came swinging over onto the tanker from the after derrick hoist, whilst a bofor gun shot the wireless aerials and a machine gun made bullet holes into the bridgework.

"Captain! You and your men are advised to stay just where you are. You are now a prize ship of the German Navy." Meir shouted over using is megaphone.

The tanker captain was brought over to Meir, who cursed him angrily, not for the piracy, but for killing his bridge crew.

"I'm Captain Cousins. We thought your kind had all been sunk, as this is my second voyage in these waters and there was no sign of you lot, except for the U-boats some 500 miles south of here." Cousins said in a broad Somerset accent.

The information about the U-boats operating to the south of him was news, but he kept his face straight not to show Cousins of his surprise.

"My apologies for the death of your bridge crew Captain Cousins. But needs must, as you certainly would not have stopped for me otherwise." Meir said mildly but snapped a question to Cousins.

The Black Rose

"It says here that your manifest is 15,000 tons of diesel. How were you able to give me barrels of oil, if in fact that I needed it?"

"My deck cargo is an extra 4,000 tons of furnace oil ready for transferring over at Tristan De Cunha, but I didn't have time to have it entered onto the manifest." Cousins replied offhandedly.

Again that piece of information was highly significant, as it meant that there were warships to the northwest of him.

"Lucky for you, we need diesel then Captain, as this ship loves the stuff. Your men will become my prisoners and your ship will be taken to a special place. For you the war is over Captain Cousins. The only way you and your crew can survive now is to just do as you're told. Your men just might be able to keep working on their vessel as volunteers. The German navy are good payers for such good seamen." Meir explained quietly.

"I'll do no such thing Captain, whoever you are. Geneva Convention and all that!" Cousins snarled, but hastily shut his mouth when Meir held a pistol to it.

"One more word from you Captain, and you'll be swimming back to Durban on your own. Do I make myself clear?" Meir said menacingly.

"5th Mate, stand down all guns. Make ready for our prisoners."

Meir went along the single line of prisoners telling them that some of them would be spared if they were prepared to accept the pay of the German navy as opposed to the usual penny-pinching company misers that they were working for.

He held up a gold bar for them all to see, which was like holding a bag of sweets in front of a child. He laughed at the greed some seamen showed and he told them to stand aside from the ones who refused to join them.

Meir looked at the few men still in the same line and told

The Black Rose

them that they would now be tied up and would eventually end up in a labour camp that nobody has ever escaped from and lived to tell the tale. Nobody moved as Cousins was shoved past them to join his other ships officers.

"It seems that you have less crew now than what you sailed with, Captain. I have several of your good men willing to earn their crust, doing just what they've been trained to do. It's a pity you and your officers are so stubborn." Meir sighed as he beckoned Flens to set an armed guard on them until Schenk took them.

He had the volunteer captors return to their ship and sail it back to the base, under the eagle eyes of his own men.

This was Meir's first prize ship on this patrol, and he even managed another one before he went to lunch. The rest of the day produced nothing except the odd smoke column too far away to chase after.

He decided to reshape his vessel overnight, and moved his hunting area further out into the Atlantic, where the other shipping lane comes across from the South American continent.

Meir's tactic was that Schenk's support ship would stay just over the horizon, about one hours steaming away, and come to get the prisoners when he received his signal to do so. This worked well for several days, before Meir decided that he would return to base, along with the over-full *Becks Cove*.

His crew was only at half strength due to the prize ships he captured, so he decided to press-gang some of the prisoners to help out. It was a torrid time for him as the pressed men were reluctant to do anything and even attempted several little sabotage stunts.

"OOW! Get the pressed men and prisoners on the after deck cargo." Meir ordered, and waited until the order was carried out.

Meir strode onto the after deck and saw that his own men were pointing guns at the prisoners, who were sitting in a huddle on the cargo cover. He went over to one of the men he knew was a troublemaker, grabbed hold of him by his lapels and dragged him to his feet.

The man started to shout about the Geneva conventions and prisoners rights, when Meir drew his pistol and shot him in his ear.

The man's brains splattered all over the other seated prisoners, who looked absolutely dumbstruck at what they'd just witnessed.

Meir got hold of another prisoner and did the same to him, and was about to reach for the third one, when a loud voice shouted at him to stop.

Meir looked at the man who stood up among the others, and asked him if he was their spokesman. When he admitted that he was their ringleader, Meir shot him dead too.

"Now then my brave men. How many more of you wish to join your dead friends here?" Meir growled at the prisoners, who just sat there totally silent. There was not a movement, nor a word from them.

"Now that I've got your undivided attention, the next man to try my patience or misbehave in anyway will be thrown overboard with a bullet in his ear, just like your dead friends here." Meir said loudly as he pointed to the small pile of dead men.

"Do I make myself clear?" He shouted. But got no response.

"I said, do I make myself clear?" Meir shouted but very angrily.

The men just nodded and offered a muffled reply, which Meir shouted at them to repeat just as loudly as he.

When he was satisfied, he turned to them and said in a quiet voice, "You have now accepted what my crew did the day they sailed. One mistake or one time that you're found shirking your duty, you'll be shot on the spot."

Meir turned to Flens and told him to dump the bodies

overboard, but make certain they were weighed down, as he didn't want another ship coming across them just yet.

He left the after cargo deck and went back onto the bridge, where he met Klinshoff at the chart table.

"You've certainly stopped them in their tracks captain. I don't think we'll have any more incidents on board. Pity you didn't think of it before." He said jovially.

"Amen to that Navigator. Perhaps we can make a move back to base now, so make a direct course to it. Tell Schenk to close up on me, and follow me home as there are possibly a few warships to our northwest. Procedure Charlie."

The three ships sailed back to base without meeting any others, and arrived to see their handiwork almost choking the harbour. He looked at the ships rafted together, and saw two sleek grey wolves tied up at the end of his own ships jetty.

"We've got company. Probably from the squadron Cousins was telling me about." Meir said with surprise, as he continued to look around the harbour.

"I had forgotten how many we captured. We'll send two of them over to the Amazon drum with some of the supplies." Meir said to Kirkmeister who was acting as First mate.

"The ships are easy to sort out, we'd better send another two up to L'Orient with the next supply ship. It's the prisoners who are overcrowding the place. Captain."

Meir looked around the base and saw what Kirkmeister spoke about.

"We'll convert that freighter over there into an accommodation ship." Meir said pointing to a rusty ship almost aground on the sandy beach.

When Meir got ashore, he was met by Beiderman and Emst and accompanied by two other naval officers that he did not recognise at first.

"Welcome back captain. We have two guests that have just

The Black Rose

arrived and will be staying with us for a couple of days." Beiderman stated.

Meir looked over his officers shoulders and saw two scruffy looking officers standing waiting to be introduced, and recognised them instantly.

"Welcome to Becks Bay Captain Kaufman and you too Hilsinger." he smiled as they saluted him smartly.

"What brings you to our neck of the woods. I thought that by now you boys were ruling the British waves for them?"

Kaufman explained that the British brought out a new weapon called sonar, and that the wolf packs were starting to get annihilated because of it. We have brand new U-boats now that can travel much faster and further, so are deployed here to destroy the African shipping routes. At present we have four more on patrol to the south of here, and they will be coming in here for their supplies. We've ran out of absolutely everything and lucky to arrive here, and need re-supplying a.s.a.p. Kaufman explained.

Meir turned to Beiderman and Voss, and told them to see that these U-boats had a special deep-water jetty of their own, and have a special supply area built up for them to draw from as and when they arrived.

"Basically gentlemen. You'll have your own little base within this one. Just let the Base Supply Officer know what your needs are in the way of quarters, etc. We cannot offer you spare crew anymore unless you specifically request some brought down on the next supply run. Our Base Comms officer will help you with your radio set ups etc."

Kaufman thanked Meir for the information as the officers arrived into the main office where a table of food was waiting for them.

Meir showed the 2 U-boat commanders a few detailed maps and charts of the base for them to study, then offered them temporary accommodation until such times as their own little area was to be constructed.

The Black Rose

Meir was eventually told of the story about the so-called Battle of the Atlantic, which the U-boats nearly won, if it hadn't been for that little gadget that can detect metal objects some way off that the British invented. Whereas before the British had relied solely on listening devices which the U-boat commanders successfully countered with their own special tactics to dodge it. He was told also, of a new type of aircraft the British were using that had an even more deadly device on board.

It was a special aircraft that took off and landed at sea, and the British were using it to spot and kill any U-boat not recognised as a friend, and could even dectect them from a great distance.

Kaufman told about many of his good friends being sunk without even knowing that they had been spotted in the first place. Also and more importantly, they were losing the North African Desert war. Such were the tides of war.

Meir listened well into the night about these new developments and the spine chilling tales Hilsinger and Kaufman related to him and his officers.

"It appears that I will only capture ships for supplies from now on. Any troopship or war supplies on their way north of here will not get past me." Meir avowed as he pointed to the growing list of ships he'd captured or sunk.

"I need one of your boats to act as a forward unit to keep me informed of any such vessels coming along this coast. You will be given a special radio network to report these ship movements. The rest will be able to concentrate on the warship escorts and all the slower ships in the convoys. I will deal with the individual ships too fast for you, providing you keep me informed. As in a game of football, you'll be my wing men and central players, and I'll be the goalie to stop anybody getting past."

All agreed on this terminology and gave a toast to the new coin of phrases.

The Black Rose

"To the wing! To the Goalie!"

After the new instructions were completed, Meir had the ships despatched and waited until the return of his supply vessel. The *Shell Capri* was kept for their own fuel storage and usage, but they also had another one that they used to distil and keep their fresh water in. They had a small freighter kept for its freezers to store their frozen stuff. The bunkers storage areas were getting full of booty taken from the ships, so Meir had it all crated up and sent up to Cadiz for onward shipping to Germany. All these utility ships were interred in sand just like the 'hotel' forming the outer perimeter of the harbour, but they had to sink two of their prizes to supplement the two islets off their beach. The prisoners spent more time shifting sand, and making cement blocks to improve the docks and other buildings, than they did handling cargoes. Meir even had two extra offices excavated out from the sand stone cliff where his own offices were.

"We've got a signal for Goalie from Winger 9. There's a convoy being assembled off Cape Town, and should arrive your end in 5 days. Consists of 8 large and 10 smaller merchantmen and 2 converted liners, probably troopships. The escort looks like a British Colony class cruiser and 4 destroyers. We'll get them and leave the troopships to you." Brantz stated as he read the signal out to Meir who was planning his next sea routes with Klinshoff.

Meir took the signal and read it for himself, and looked at the map to see what areas were involved.

"No need for reply Brantz. I'll be expecting another one in about two days. Navigator. Get the officers together for a meeting in 30 minutes. I also want to speak to the guest U-boat Captains."

Klinshoff went over to the phone on Meir's desk and phoned around the base, getting all the officers together. When they were all sat down in the cool and spacious anteroom, Meir came in and held up the signal.

"It appears gentlemen that a nice juicy convoy is about to enter our waters." he announced as he read out the signal, receiving a cheer from his officers who shouted

"Tallyho!"

"I shall take the *Becks Bay* and *Cove* out and pretend we're going the other way. The *Cove* will be in the lead, but double back once I've completed my runs. You Captain Kaufman will position your boat between us, and the base. I have full torpedo capability but need you as back up in case some foolhardy escort tries to follow us back."

He went on to explain his operational plans which had two options and a conclusion, and gave them their procedure codes accordingly.

The meeting broke up and everybody went their own separate ways, as Meir called for his steward.

"Winkler. You won't be coming on this trip, as its only half a day. Have everything laid on for when we come back." he said quietly to his elderly steward, who looked crest-fallen at the prospect of not joining his captain.

"Very well then captain. Don't ask any other sailor to do a British 'Hardy' on you, as you're flaking out on the deck." Winkler stated as he left the room, slamming the door behind him.

Meir sighed and shook his head at the petulance of his trusted man, but turned to his charts and plans to finalise them.

The two ships sailed out in the early morning with the U-boat creeping along behind them and then dived to let the ships carry out their well-worked charade.

Meir saw and counted the columns of smoke showing over the horizon and realised that there were a lot less than the signal had stated.

The chief telegraphist arrived on the bridge and gave a signal to Meir who read it quickly, then dismissed the man.

The Black Rose

"OOW! We have two fast runners and two with crutches on their way. Get the crew to action stations."

The klaxon gave out its raucous noise, turning the ship into a hive of scurrying bodies everywhere getting to their appropriate stations.

"Ship at action stations captain." Flens announced, as he stood by Meir's high chair.

Meir sat in his lofty seat looking at the tell-tale smoke of an oncoming ship although she was still just out of sight and just over the horizon.

"Start Operation Jezebel, and tactic *Windermere*. You have 30 minutes to get the Jezebels on deck. Navigator start your plot." He ordered.

Flens passed the orders on before he continued his own preparations whilst issuing strings of orders down his telephone link to the gunners and the torpedo men.

The minutes ticked by as the crew waited calmly at their weapons. Meir had most of his old crew back again, and it showed, as every one of them sensed what their captain was about to do. So much so that they anticipated each order as it was given.

"It looks like the old *Zambezi* sir. Listed as 18,000 tons and has a single 105mm gun on its foc'sle." the signalman said loudly into the bridge.

"Very good! Now concentrate on the smoke behind it. 5th Mate, I make her speed of 20 knot. Range at 15,000 yards and closing. We're 7 degrees on her starboard bow, so stand by starboard tubes. Have the main guns turned to starboard. I'll close to within 2 kilometres down on that side. Fire when the angles are critical. Stand by for a full broadside and throw all we've got at her." Meir said coldly as he kept looking at his stopwatch and counting to himself.

"Stand by 5th Mate. First torpedo should now be." Meirs started to say, but Flens shouted the order to fire down his telephone link.

The Black Rose

Meir counted after the bow torpedoes were fired, before the two side torpedoes were launched and another 10 seconds before the mortars were fired, followed closely by the main armament.

Yet another ship was stopped almost in its tracks as 3 torpedoes struck her in succession. The decks were pulverised by the hail of mortars and machine guns, whilst the main guns punched large holes into the ships superstructure. Men were jumping overboard trying to escape, but the machine gunners strafed them too. The ship sunk within 5 minutes, leaving a large black spot of oil where it died.

Meir turned his ship around and went out towards the second ship starting to show itself above the horizon.

"Clear away the debris. Get those empty shells off the deck, and prepare for the next action." Meir ordered.

He had his ship do exactly the same routine as before, but found that instead of it being a troopship, it was a large freighter full of weapons with tanks and artillery pieces lashed to its upper decks.

"Stand by port action, 5th Mate." Meir said eagerly as the freighter came into the firing set up.

The ship lasted less than the troop ship blowing up like a volcano when one of his shells must have hit the magazine for the tanks and guns. He did not bother to stop and shoot survivors, as the blast of the explosion would have killed every living thing on it anyway. It was so fierce it even seared the paint and camouflage on his ship.

He had the camouflage removed quickly before he turned his attentions to a crippled liner trying to make its way with a large hole in its bow.

When the ship arrived, the liner flashed him up to tell him that there was a U-boat pack south of them that attacked and sank almost everybody. But he had managed to get away. He

The Black Rose

advised Meir to take a wide loop seaward before attempting to round the Cape.

Meir saw that the ship could only make about 8 knots and sailed past him pretending to do what was suggested. He did make a loop, but back towards the ship, and at full speed. They did not know it was the same one that passed them because Meir had re-altered his looks again.

Before they knew what hit them, the troop ship also sunk in a bath of blood and oil.

Meir was after the 4th escapee, when the chief telegraphist told him that the *Becks Cove* had reported a large warship had just passed them and gave its position and speed.

Meir looked at the direction to which he expected this warship, and saw to his amazement that it really was a big warship appearing quite rapidly into his binocular vision.

"Tell our friend below what to expect. I will keep on this course and bluff it out, and carry on down to the bottom edge of our patrol area."

The chief telegraphist repeated the signal wording then went below.

"5th Mate. Have the action station teams stand down and help to clean the ship. I want a few well-placed jezebels on view when this enemy warship passes us. You've got 30 minutes before I want full action stations again. On the double." Meir ordered swiftly, as he went over to the chart and Klinshoff.

"Keep your plot going. Don't forget to mark on the chart the exact position of each ship sunk. Here are their names and details." Meir said softly, as Klinshoff was in the middle of marking out courses and ships speeds.

Klinshoff looked at the details and swiftly marked them onto his chart, before he returned to his primary duty of keeping his navigational plot going. This plot kept exact records of each turn of the rudder; the course run; and the speed of the ship. This was so that he would be able to reckon his position on the chart to alter to a course back to the original track, thus being able to steer directly back to base if necessary, with little or no error.

He had his ship prepared to look like a tramp steamer, with a few 'female' passengers enjoying their voyage down the African coast. He had his bridge crew hide, and for those who remained on deck, to be in civilian clothes. He even put on a scruffy outfit taken from one of his prize ships so that he took part in the disguise.

As the cruiser came closer, it flashed the *Becks Bay*, challenging its presence.

Meir had the signalman tell them that he was on his way from Boston to Durban, and that he was trying to race his pal the *Becks Cove*, who had an eight-hour start over him.

The signalman read the reply wishing him good luck as he'd just passed it only two hours ago. But that there was a U-boat pack some 100 kilometres south of here, and suggesting that they take a wide loop around the area and come in from the south. The cruiser asked Meir if he'd seen two troopships and two large merchant men making their way north.

Meir replied that he did see two smoke signs way off to his port some hours ago, before he came onto this course, but could not tell who they were. His own crossing was clear apart from a storm they went through.

The cruiser flashed back her thanks and continued to plough her way through the sea, but unbeknown to her there was a U-boat waiting for her, only two hours away.

Meir waited until the heavy cruiser had almost disappeared then he stepped down his action stations, and onto patrol routine.

By that time, the jezebels were too far into their routine for Meir to call a halt, instead he let the rest of the off-watch crew join in, as a calm down from their very uptight encounter with

The Black Rose

that very dangerous leviathan. It could have blasted them out of the water just as quickly as he had the troopships.

It was the first time he had seen such a new and powerful armament array as on the cruiser, which made him anxious. His hunch paid off yet again in not trying to slug it out with his enemy. Picking on someone your own size sprang to his mind, as he dismissed the near bloodbath and his own death.

The chief telegraphist re-appeared into Meirs bridge cabin telling him that the cruiser had been destroyed by the U-boat, and that it was safe to return to base.

Meir told him to tell the *Cove* to return to base, as he wanted to continue to the end of the patrol area and maybe sneak into the Indian Ocean to see what was cooking.

They met the *Becks Cove* coming back just as it was getting dark, so Meir had to transfer some fuel and ammunition over, for him to continue the patrol. Once the transfer was completed they parted company to go their own separate ways. Meir and his ship were now a single unit again, except for the friends he'd pass on the way around the Cape.

Meir sailed his ship some 1500 kilometres around the stormy cape where the colder, higher waters of the Atlantic met the lower but warmer waters of the Indian Ocean.

Where the oceans met, they created the mayhem of stormy and turbulent waters that most ships had better be on their merit to endure and survive the voyage, otherwise they'd flounder and sink in the confusion.

It took slightly longer going around the Cape than predicted, but when the ship finally got through the maelstrom they found that there were calm warm waters waiting for them to continue their voyage.

Meir saw a ship pass him several hours before he received a message from base. He was to prepare to intercept a large UK bound convoy coming down and around the Cape from

Madagascar. The intelligence reported that there were at least 5 warships as escort for the 30 strong convoy, but that there may be another 5 waiting on the Atlantic side to take them north to Gibraltar.

What surprised Meir was that there was a suggestion of at least 3 troopships and 5 ammunition ships in it that needed to be singled out and sunk, hence the inordinate number of escorts.

He decided that he'd get as far into the Indian Ocean as possible to intercept this convoy, but had the hunch that some of these troopships were too fast for the much slower tramp steamers. They would simply rely on their speed to run through the gauntlet and to get themselves past any U-boat threat that was known to be waiting for them just off Cape Town.

This was his plan of attack and he decided to sink every ship that tried to pass him, excluding those who'd have a warship as a close friend to look over them.

So his tactic was drawn up, and telling his fellow officers what to expect, settled down to a night's peace and quiet, just floating along at slow speed to the vicinity where the convoy was supposed to be gathering.

It was a long, humid, but peaceful night for the crew to enjoy as the ship waited like a spider, for the first ship to enter its 'parlour'.

The chief telegraphist knocked urgently on Meirs bridge cabin door telling him that he had a contact to the east of them and according to its call sign it was a very large liner, the SS Southern Star, probably some 30 kilometres away, judging by its radio transmissions. He explained that it was at least 20,000 tons and probably full of troops.

Meir sat bolt upright in his little cabin, bumping his head on

The Black Rose

an overhead strut, and cursing the chief for disturbing him so suddenly. He took the signal from the chief as he climbed out of his bunk and went out onto the bridge, where he saw the sun rising out of the inky blue waters of the ocean. He scratched his face and stretched before he bent over the bridge chart table and plotted the contacts' bearing.

"OOW! Have the lookouts concentrate on our port side for a while. We've got a juicy target coming our way, and I want time to get prepared."

The OOW acknowledged his orders as Meir dismissed the telegraphist, then turned to issue his next orders.

"OOW, have hands to breakfast. Action stations in 1 hour! Jezebel not required this time, but tactic *Windermere*. I'm going below to my day cabin for a while. Tell the Chief Engineer to see me in half an hour."

He had just finished his breakfast when he heard a polite knock on his cabin door, and commanded the visitor to enter

"You sent for me Captain?"

"Morning, Chief! Hope you've had your breakfast?" Meir asked politely, which was returned with a smile and a thank you from the engineer.

He went on to explain what he wanted done and for the engineer to make sure it was done exactly as and when it was required.

The meeting only took a few minutes, before the engineer went on his way back down into the bowels of the ship to do his duty.

"Ship at *Windermere* stations captain!" Flens stated, as Meir came onto the bridge and sat in his high chair with his binoculars around his neck.

"Very good! Navigator, start your plot." Meir commenced as he gave out a string of orders to the helmsman and others in the bridge team.

The Black Rose

"Captain, the ship ahead of us has just said hello. Asked us to identify ourselves and if we've seen any signs of a reported Q ship or any U-boat activity in the area" the signalman said loudly as he operated his bridge aldis.

"Tell him we're on our way to Bombay, and no sign of any enemy to port of us."

"Range now 10,000 metres. We'll pass him starboard side and at 2 kilometres distance. Stand by." Meir said calmly to Flens, who relayed the tactical information down his command telephone line.

As the ship got nearer it started to dwarf Meir's ship, as he looked through his binoculars to find the ships name written on its bow.

"Captain, I recognise it as the old liner SS Southern Star. Me brother was a deck officer on it a while ago before he changed over to warships." the Irishman volunteered.

Meir thanked him and told Flens to start the attack in precisely 30 seconds.

"Slow ahead together but keep on the same course". He ordered.

"Guns! I'm slowing right down so that I can manoeuvre around her once we've stopped her."

Flens nodded and rechecked his calculatons for his firing sequence.

Meir looked at his stopwatch and started a count down, but was overtaken by Flens, who ordered the sequence of firing.

The ship shuddered and shook as each shell or torpedo left it, but continued to make its straight line of wake through the water. The ship sank within minutes to the 7kilometres deep floor of the Indian Ocean, with only a few bits of flotsam to mark its own grave. Meir was pleased with his latest action, until 3 half drowned men were dragged onto the bridge and thrown down onto the deck at his feet.

"Who the bloody hell are these?" Meir said in surprise more

The Black Rose

than in anger.

The three men coughed and spluttered for a while, before the tallest and largest of them started to call Meir all the names going and promised to get his revenge.

"Who have I the pleasure of addressing, if that's not too difficult for you to answer without spouting your mouth off?" Meir asked coldly.

"I'm Deck officer Trewarthy. Who the fuckin' hell are you?" Trewarthy growled and went to grab hold of Meir, but was knocked down to the deck with a savage blow by Klinshoff.

"Show some respect to the person who saved your life." Klinshoff snarled, as Trewarthy sat on the deck rubbing his neck and glowering at him.

The other two men were asked to identify themselves, but refused, until the Irishman recognised one of them.

"He's a leading donkey man by the name of Barnes. How are ye Barney? Still into your old tricks of nicking from your fuckin' shipmates are you? You owe my brother for that 45 gallon drum of diesel you fuckin' pinched off him in Belfast." the Irishman said sardonically.

"Why you fuckin' dirty thieving traitor. Go back to your bog and fuck your spuds." the man said as he tried to take a swing at the Irishman, but met the same punishment as Trewarthy.

Meir smiled and told Flens to secure from action stations, but to get these wretches off his bridge and into some secure place where they can't do any damage.

He looked at his position on the chart and decided that it was time to return to base rather than reach a point where he'd run out of fuel before getting back again. So he turned his ship around and hoped that, with a bit of luck to sink a few more ships on his way.

Meir had also made an opportunity to take a nice

The Black Rose

photograph of the captured men sitting under the 150mm (6inch) guns. He had Flens make a list of names of the ships he sunk, and their tonnage, and a further list of the warships he had sunk or damaged. It would make a good picture in the passengers' lounge, and remind anybody visiting the ship how heroic the ship and its crew were.

The Black Rose

Chapter XVIII
Confusion

"Several columns of smoke over the horizon, bearings from red 10 to green 5." the lookout reported to the OOW.

Meir was in his bridge cabin to hear the report, and came out with his binoculars to take a look for himself. He went over to the chart and made some quick calculations before making any conclusions.

"Full speed ahead. Tell the engine room, make revs for 40 knots. Start making smoke. Action stations in 40 minutes." Meir ordered in quick succession. His bridge crew had heard these quick fire orders so often, that they knew these orders meant they'd see action very soon. He had the men conditioned and tuned so well into his way of command that he really did not need to prompt them any further. Such a well-oiled team of men they werere compared to the green sailors he was sinking left right and centre.

"Operation Jezebel and *Dalmatian*. But I want a double lookout to keep an eye on the escorts. They are too near their home base for us and they could be re-enforced by any number and at any time." Meir said to Flens as he reported the ship cleared for action stations.

"Half ahead together. Make speed 14 knots. Stand by for snooping warships." he ordered, as the ship was met and challenged by a warship. After a brief discussion by megaphone, his ship was allowed to join the convoy and given a convoy position number, but at the head of it as he was moving a bit faster than the others.

Meir complied with his orders as he saw several other warships rushing around like sheep dogs controlling their wayward flock.

After getting into position, he slowed his ship down even

The Black Rose

further to conform with the rest of them. But decided to wait until dark before he made his move.

"Stand down from action stations and bridge attack team. It's going to be a long day otherwise." He ordered calmly, then left the bridge to the oncoming OOW.

As evening fell with the convoy settling down for a long night hoping that no U-boat would come near it, Meir had his attack team and action stations resumed.

"Signalman, get yourself a friend to help you as I want you to keep a small plot going where you'll be marking the different positions and any alterations of the escorts around us. I will be wanting to know just what type it is that's coming my way." Meir said evenly as he showed the signalman a sketch he had made of the ships in the convoy.

"This is the position of the merchantmen in the convoy block. You simply put an X and a number for each warship, and follow its track along the board. I want relative bearings and approx range. Here's a rangefinder to help you."

The signalman asked if he could do the looking, and his friend the marking. Meir agreed to this and left him to his duty.

"5th Mate. Have the minelayer set delayed fuses of 30 minutes before laying a pattern of 6. Do not launch until I veer off course."

Meir waited until the order had been obeyed, before he looked at his watch. He waited until the sky was at its darkest and before the moon began to shine over the convoy, to start his attack.

"Start the attack. Full ahead together. Starboard 15. Tell the engine room to make thick smoke. 5th Mate! Fire your torpedoes on critical angles. Gunnery teams to stand by. Mortars to fire those special canisters in between shrapnel rounds."

Meir had his ship make lots of smoke before he ran ahead of his column of ships and swung his ship round so that he could

The Black Rose

bisect the column as per his *Dalmatian* tactic. As his ship started to re-enter half way down the convoy, a warship came towards him and began to open fire at him.

Meir heard the signalman's report of the warship just as the first salvo splashed into the sea either side of his bows.

He started to weave his ship to dodge the shots of the warship, when he was told of another coming from behind them.

"Roll a pattern of mines. Make more smoke. Stand by both 150mm turrets. Make range 3,000, fire when ready." Meir said calmly as he heard the whistling of shells passing over him and making large splashes either side of him.

Both warships had him boxed in, but due to his evasive tactics they kept missing, almost hitting each other. The moon was out but almost obscured by the smoke given off by the burning ships and his own.

Meir heard both 150mm turrets fire at the same time as both front and rear torpedo tubes were fired, the ship staggered and shook at the recoil. The warship behind got hit on the bridge with the 6inch salvoes, and had its bow blown off by a mine.

The warship in front of them got hit by both of his forward torpedoes, and had its for'ard main armament blown off its mountings, before Meir had his 104mm (4. inch) guns in action to blast into the side of it. There were merchantmen blowing up as they met the mines, and torpedoes, but what made them all swerve and almost collide into each other were the special smoke canisters.

They contained a very deadly and dangerous mixture of Zyklon B, and Mustard gas.

Meir already had his crew protected as he went through this smoke, and was able to take advantage of the situation firing at one more warship that was seemingly out of control. He had the mortars drop shrapnel into the open bridges of the warships, with the bofors and machine gunners raking their decks to prevent any of their torpedoes being fired at him.

The Black Rose

As his ship came around one large sinking freighter a destroyer that had laid in wait for him immediately fired him upon.

The lower part of his bridge structure and a large part of his camouflage got hit, as did his for'ard 105mm gun turret. There was another hit into his for'ard cargo deck, before Meir got his A turret to return fire. With its first salvo, a big hole was punched into the destroyer's bridge superstructure. Then as his ship manoeuvred round went down the side of the warship, both of his aft turrets also became engaged, and blasted all the warships guns right off their mountings. This warship wasn't done for just yet, as he was forced to dodge a spread of torpedoes they fired back at him. He returned the favour and despatched the ship to the bottom of the ocean within seconds of his torpedoes hitting it.

Whilst all this was going on, the gassy smoke and exploding ships were adding to the confusion as Meir found yet another warship attacking him, a shell exploded onto his after cargo hatch and another one blasted his lifeboats into matchwood.

This was what Meir had yearned for all these years, a decent scrap in and amongst the British Navy. But he was able to dish out more than he received even though he was outnumbered.

Meir turned onto his new attacker and shot most of its bridge, masts and other parts of the superstructure off with his 150mm A turret. At that short a distance, the 150mm calibre was able to pack enough power to grace even a 300mm gun.

Meir decided that this ship was to be beaten mercilessly and turned into a sieve from all of his guns as he had no torpedoes left. Finally, when he watched it start to sink slowly under the waves, he turned away from the action and sailed at full speed away from the decimated convoy. He was pursued by one of the earlier attackers who had somehow managed to recover enough to re-engage him, but his guns kept it at bay until he managed to outrun it.

The Black Rose

* * *

It took a few hours for his ship to disappear over the horizon from that scene of carnage, and seemingly to be lost in the otherwise empty ocean.

It was several hours later and without any trace of a pursuer, before Meir decided that it was safe to sneak back into his little bolthole to lick his wounds and prepare for another patrol.

As they arrived alongside, everybody on shore was surprised at the damage the ship had received, which the ship repair team needed to sort out.

"Captain. Your damage is limited mostly to the upper deck for'ard, apart from the hole in the side and the passenger saloon. But nothin I can't fix." Emst said after his detailed inspection.

"Thanks Richard. Get it sorted and maybe provide me with extra armour plating around the bridge and gunnery, while you're at it." Meir said quietly as he turned to his other officers.

"Guns! Get my wounded over to the sickbay and have a carpenter make decent coffins for our dead crewmen. We expended most of our ammunition and lost a lot of our Jezebel equipment, so I want my ship fully re-fuelled, re-stored, mended, and with a full crew in four days."

"Aye aye captain." Came the responses.

Meir went into his office and saw Schenk at his desk.

"Victor. Those warships had those funny looking discs on top of their bridges. It must be that gadget Kaufman was telling us about, they seem to be onto us straight away."

"It also means that we can run but cannot hide now, unless we get lost in a convoy or something." Schenk added.

"We had better watch our movements in and out of here, or at least have the radio monitored and a coast watcher system set up before we do anything. Tell Guns and Brantz to organise it as of today."

The Black Rose

Their conversation was interrupted by Brantz who came in to the office telling Meir that he had just intercepted an important signal and showed it to him, who read it out for Schenks benefit.

"It's from the British C-in-C in Cape town to all Southern Atlantic units: *Unidentified hostile ship confirmed as a 'Q' ship operating within 30 degrees Lat and Long of this base. Heavily armed and using chemical weapons. If found, report, shadow and wait for support.*"

"It looks like Jezebel is going to be more necessary for us to survive in their back yard then, captain." Schenk said stoically.

"Not only that captain. When you were out on patrol, we monitored several army signals coming from the south of us. It appears there are some large troop movements coming our way, although approx 200 kilometres to the east of us." Brantz said quietly.

"We'll have to turn chameleon for a while. Send for the other officers would you Brantz, we need to hold a war conference." Meir said at length as he crumpled up the offending signal.

Meir stood sipping his lemonade as the officers filed into his room. When all had arrived, he commenced his discussion.

"We will have to play mouse with our British neighbours, which means that from now on, apart from the U-boats who can enter this base unseen, any ship entering or leaving will do so, only when the coast is clear." Meir stated, then went on to discuss certain aspects of base defence and other items such as communications and ship repairs, before he let his officers offer alternatives or opinions.

"We are in an area with lots of sand, which gets blown seaward in frequent sandstorms.

"We also have a very strong coastal current running south to north. It means that we could leave during one of these sand storms and float along with the current, so as not to let off smoke." Voss observed, and agreed by the others.

Meir reminded them about this new weapon that can seem to detect metal up to at least 5,000 metres, but did not know of its real capability, unless they captured one to find out.

"What if we coat the ship in wood, or at least have big sections covered in it so that whatever it is they look at would be blurred." Flens ventured.

"Just like the whip aerials on board the ship, maybe if we coat the metal in rubber, that should do it. At least try to cover as much metal as possible." Brantz added.

"It appears that we've decided to try and disguise ourselves and at the same time try to hide from this awesome weapon whilst on base. Make no bones about it gentlemen, those warships knew exactly where I was at all times. It was only my sheer speed that got me away, which means that unless the *Cove* can have its engines to go just as fast, it will be doomed if caught." Meir stated, then went on to discuss new tactics to be adopted in the light of their last encounter, before concluding the meeting and for everybody to get organised for their next patrol.

Chapter XIX
Weaving

Meir decided that the gloves were now off, and the time had come to play for real against his enemies. He had his ship returned as much as possible, to its former glory as the *Schlezwig*, with large sections of it covered in wood panelling as it used to look when it was first launched, and as much latex rubber painted on the other metal bits as possible. He also had the *Cove* done up in the same manner, but it would have a different role to play than previously undertaken.

It would be the supply vessel for Meir, and meet him at whatever R/V point given as required. Meir's patrols would now be independent again so his ship was loaded with as much supplies as he could carry without detriment to his engines' speed capability, as this was his ultimate survival weapon.

His contingency plans drawn up earlier were adapted so that if the base was captured, or being destroyed, Brantz was to send a special coded signal to Meir, which meant that he really was on his own. Or vice versa, if the ship was captured or destroyed, the Base personnel would have to sort their own destiny out, which also would apply to the Amazon Base.

It was a very sombre day as Meir left his desert base for he knew and felt that it would be his last departure from it. The officers he left behind waved to him as the ship slipped out of its haven and into the wide Atlantic to make its' way over to the South American sub continent.

"OOW! Your course instructions are on the chart. Set patrol routine, speed 18 knots. I'm going below." Meir ordered as the ship left the base way behind and disappearing over the horizon.

The ship sailed peacefully on its long loop across the Atlantic, with Meir and Klinshoff taking their daily sun and star fixes to plot their course across it.

The Black Rose

* * *

The crew enjoyed a very relaxed time and it seemed to them as if they were the only ship afloat in the whole world, as there was no hint or sight of any others anywhere around them. Meir was transiting a large area with no sea-lanes, like a no mans land at sea.

During that time, as Meir had lost several of his original crew who were killed in the passenger lounge during their last patrol, he allowed some of the captured sailors to take part in the normal sea duties thus to get them integrated into his way of doing things.

The pilot discovered much to his delight, that the prisoner Trewarthy was a fisherman too and also spoke Gaelic. They were getting inseparable even when the pilot took over the helm at action station drills.

On the fourth day an excited lookout reported their first smoke sighting, then another one behind that, and they waited eagerly for their captain to order action stations again.

Meir came onto the bridge and looked through his binoculars to see these smoke signals turning into ships. He saw further smoke plumes further away on each side of the reported 2 and realised that these were warships of the British Navy coming towards him.

"Port 10. Steer 270. Make speed 10 knots. OOW! Hands to action stations. They haven't seen or detected us yet, so tell the engine room to stop making smoke." He ordered swiftly as he sent the ship into instant activity.

"Ship at action stations." Flens reported dutifully.

"Very good 5th Mate. Tell the minelayers to set a depth of 3 metres and roll off 10 mines in a string of 1000 metres per mine when done."

Meir kept looking at these ships getting ever closer, and noticed that it was only at 6 kilometres distance between them

The Black Rose

before a destroyer altered course to come and look him over.

"Did you see that 5th? They saw us but didn't alter course until the 6 kilometre range. They must have been relying on that radar thing to investigate us now, this late on." Meir observed.

Flens looked at the rapidly advancing destroyer and at the other one further back.

"This one is a Tribal class destroyer, the big one is a 310mm Colony class cruiser, and by the look of it, it's the *Tasmania*. The other two out on the flanks must be her destroyer escorts too." Flens reported as he confirmed the sightings from the ship recognition book he held in his hands.

As the warship approached her large signal lamp was flashing at them, and the signalman read out what was said.

"Tell them we're a private company survey ship out of Durban, bound for Rio de Janeiro. Also warn him of the sight of several U-boats on a surface transit going south, some four hours steaming away." Meir said calmly.

The signalman sent the reply and after reading a further message back, Meir was happy to see the vessel turn away, obviously satisfied with things.

"Phew. That was a fuckin' close thing captain!"

"Aye indeed pilot. But we're not out of the woods yet as we've got two more over the horizon coming our way." Meir said slowly as he pointed out the fresh smoke signs ahead of them.

Meir let the cruiser and its two forward screening destroyers almost disappear over the horizon before he ordered a further course change and at full speed.

"No sense tempting fate again is there 5th Mate?" Meir said happily.

"Secure from action stations. Set patrol routine. OOW alter back to our base course and set speed at 15 knots again." Meir ordered as he went over to Klinshoff at the chart table.

"Those must have come from Tristan de Cunha, and the same ones that we pinched their oil from."

"Let's hope so, as I don't fancy mixing it with that class of cruiser. Her guns look as if it could." Klinshoff said but his voice was lost in the wailing sound and a loud whoosh as a tall column of water appeared ahead of them.

"Where the fuckin' hell did that come from." the pilot said in astonishment as another whoosh followed by another tall column of water appeared on their starboard bow.

Meir ran out onto the bridge wing and saw a flash coming from way behind them.

"It must be the cruiser. The others have only got 105mm guns which have a much shorter range." Meir said calmly as he scanned the horizon to see the two back marker destroyers with their funnels belching out black smoke and coming full speed towards him.

"OOW, hands to action stations. Navigator, start your plot again."

Soon the ship was being drenched with water as even the oncoming destroyers shells were hitting the water in near misses all around them.

"Rear 150mm turret to engage the furthest one, the 105 the closest one. Get your range accurate on first shot. Tell the engine room to start making smoke.

"Mortars to lay a pattern of smoke 1kilometre either side of us. Fire when target in range. Full ahead together, speed 35 knots. Pilot, you are to port then starboard your helm every 1 minute, I want to create a smoke screen wide enough to hide behind." Meir ordered smoothly.

He had his ship weave from side to side and in doing so dodge the heavy shells the cruiser was firing at them.

Meir had drawn up several variations of this tactic and rehearsed enough times with his little toy ships, it was the time for him to find out if they worked for real.

The Black Rose

"Signalman, keep a close eye on those destroyers, let me know when they start coming into the smoke. 5th Mate, Have the mortars lob a few gas canisters in 5 minutes. The British will think its just more smoke until it's too late. Have another pattern of mines dropped off but in 500 metre intervals." Meir ordered swiftly as he kept watching the pursuing destroyers and the now almost visible cruiser whose main guns were flashing away, sending death and destruction his way.

"Both destroyers are now arriving in the smoke." the signalman shouted as the aft gun turrets scored a direct hit on the leading destroyer.

"We've stopped the first one captain. The other one is still coming." The signalman reported excitedly.

"Fire canisters. Stop together. Starboard 20. These will come straight through on my base course line, but despite those new fangled things, they are firing at the place they expect me to be in on my zigzag courses. Navigator, I want a course that will take me behind Tristan de Cunha, see to it."

Meir had his stopwatch in his hand and was making a count down when a shell hit the starboard bridge wing killing the signalman and the two lookouts next to him.

"Pilot. Full astern together, and put your helm hard to starboard. We'll catch that one from the side, as it's coming out of the smoke. 5th Mate, tell all weapons to stand by for a full broadside. Range will be 2 kilometres." Meir had his ship almost stop and facing side on to the oncoming destroyer.

As the destroyer came rapidly out of the smoke, Meir unleashed his broadside, which hit it so hard it was blown right out of the water before vanishing under the waves.

He was able to turn his ship around and get back to full speed again before the other two destroyers came onto the scene, followed closely behind by the cruiser.

Meir managed to distance himself from the smoky area and decided to try and outrun them, so he piled on the smoke again

The Black Rose

and went full speed onto the course that would take him around the volcanic island still some hours steaming away.

He had mines catapulted some distance each side of him and astern of him as he went. It was only a short time into this new tactic when one of the destroyers ran into one of them with a spectacular fountain of water as its bows got blown off.

The smoke was keeping the cruiser gunners guessing, and got further and further behind. Meir was winning his race slowly and steadily as he was outpacing the lumbering cruiser.

He guessed that the destroyer was keeping much closer to the cruiser as there was no apparent sign from it, nor the shells from its guns.

Meir got his ship around the back of the island and was about to take a new course away from his pursuers, when a destroyer appeared out of nowhere and right in front of them barely 3 kilometres away.

"Where the hell did he spring from?" Meir asked tersely as he ordered a broadside.

The destroyer beat them to the trigger and the empty torpedo cases on the for'ard cargo deck and the superstructure just below the bridge were blasted away in their opening salvo. The destroyer staggered under the heavier hammers of Meir's 150mm guns and capsized as the torpedoes ripped into its side as it tried to turn away.

Meir was dazed by the blast, and cut with bits of wood and steel, but Flens and the pilot were lying on the deck almost lifeless. He was amazed to find that Trewarthy was handling the ship and steering it away from the sinking destroyer.

"Navigator, get these men off the bridge and have replacements for them immediately." he said as he pointed to the dead pilot, telegraphs men and lookouts.

"Then see to the damage control team below us."

Meir had his ship steered through the sea of bodies from the

The Black Rose

destroyer, and had his machine gunners strafe them as he passed by. He saw that the cruiser was almost around the back end of, but at the other end of the island as he raced his ship away from the place.

"Steer 175, speed 40 knots. Tell the engine room to make smoke." He ordered as he turned to the gunnery command telephone. He realised that the cruiser would be too slow to come around to chase them, so he had his gunnery teams stand down.

"Fire put out. Bulkheads and deck heads shored up and secured. Five men dead and three wounded. Captain." Klinshoff reported as he came back onto the bridge.

Meir was looking out of the now windowless bridge, feeling the draught pushing him back into his chair.

"Very good Navigator, have the men secure from action stations. Get a team of men up here on the double and have it cleaned up. Get the shipwrights to have this place ship-shape again and have those infernal windows fixed as it's getting rather drafty."

Klinshoff looked around the devastated bridge and at his blood-spattered captain.

"You'd better get below captain and see the M.O." he said softly as he tried to put a bandage over his own wound.

"Thank you for your concern navigator, but get yourself below and send me someone up here to take over as OOW."

Meir watched Trewarthy very closely and realised that whilst he was no replacement for the foulmouthed fisherman, he was showing promise, and one that maybe he would nurture into a full OOW in his own right.

"Trewarthy! Let's hope our dead pilot has taught you something worthwhile. If you behave, I'll teach you how to really handle a ship." Meir said with genuine regard.

Trewarthy just grunted, shrugged his big shoulders and kept himself busy with his duties.

"Lt Mansdorf reporting as OOW captain"

The Black Rose

"Welcome to the bridge. We have a cruiser astern following us, and preventing us turning to our original northerly course. Keep on this one, and at 40 knots for another two hours. I have plotted a new course and speed for you to alter onto when that time comes.

"You will have shipwrights and cleaners on the bridge soon. I'm going below to see to our casualties." Meir ordered slowly, then picked his way through the debris towards the undamaged bridge wing.

Meir arrived to his day cabin to find it was wrecked, with Winkler clearing and cleaning it up.

"I've got most of it in hand now captain. I was in the galley at the time when we got hit. We've lost most of our cooks and stewards, but fortunately there was a chef among the prisoners who's now taking charge of the galley. We've lost a few cabins too so it means that some of the officers will have to share." Winkler reported calmly as he dusted and polished around him.

Meir just stood and watched with total astonishment and fascination at this man doing his job as if nothing had happened.

"It appears that you've met these situations before then steward?"

"Aye captain. I was your father's steward when his ship was shot up pretty badly during the last lot. Just a few licks of paint here and there, and maybe a well darned hole and all will be fine again."

Meir left his steward and went up to his bridge cabin for a rest. Even the Gods needed rest now and then.

By the following morning, the crew had everything repaired almost as good as new, for when Meir arrived back onto the bridge.

"OOW! What's our state?"

"Morning captain. All damage repaired. We've lost the

The Black Rose

cruiser but we seem to be running out of ocean, look!" Klinshoff reported as he pointed to the chart.

"We'll come right around Bouvet Island and head towards that group of islands to the west of it. My Uncle visited Santa Cruz in the Argentine on this ship, only a few years ago. Maybe we'll get to put into harbour for a rest and refuel. R&R if you like.

"Tell the Wireless office to contact Brantz and have the *Becks Cove* to come there and supply us with our tinned fish and the like." Meir said at length as he studied the map.

He re-applied his mind onto the tricky navigational feat he was facing.

The Antarctic Ocean and its pack ice, let alone the massive icebergs were floating towards him.

It was nearly evening time when a lookout reported sight of a fleet of icebergs ahead of them.

"OOW! Have two lookouts put up the for'ard mast. Make a temporary crows nest for them if necessary but get them up sooner than later, and double up the ones on the bridge. I want a reliable helmsman on watch at all times. We can reduce speed to 8 knots now. Tell the engine room they can make smoke now during the night." Meir said quickly as he looked at the giant almost island sized chunks of ice stretched out in front of him.

Meir stayed in his bridge cabin all during the night as each OOW and helmsman came and went, until it was almost light again, before he re-emerged from it with an alarm from one of the lookouts.

"OOW! We've had a successful overnight transit, now all of a sudden we've got a crisis on our hands." He said as he looked out to the place where the new threat came from.

"Helmsman. Starboard 20. Slow astern together. OOW get some men for'ard with fenders over the port bow in case we run out of sea and bump into this pack ice. The lookouts must be asleep or blind!" Meir said in temper.

Meir saw that the ship was not responding quickly enough so ordered full astern both engines so that the ship would back off and away from the ice rather than hitting it.

When the ship was clear of the ice, Meir had it move slowly around the edge of the large ice sheet only to find another one in his way. For several hours, he issued telegraph and steering orders that had the helmsman steer the ship slowly around each hazard until they came to open waters again.

"Midships. Make speed 15 knots. OOW! Get that helmsman relieved and off duty." Meir ordered as Trewarthy nodded gratefully to the person who took over from him.

"Well done Trewarthy. I'll make a sailor out of you yet." Meir said softly, as Trewarthy was almost carried off the bridge because of his exhausted state.

"Navigator! According to my dead reckoning, we're about 500 kilometres to the south of the Falklands and only about 150 kilometres off the Magellan Straits. Lay a course to west of the Falkland Islands so that we transit about 20 kilometres off and up the Argentinian coast. Work out our transit speed to arrive Santa Cruz after dark." Meir asked as he too finally left the bridge.

The ship had a couple of days in the cold waters of the Antarctic and the crew were glad that they were going north into much warmer waters again.

It was making its steady northerly transit up the coast of Argentina when a lookout spotted several columns of smoke ahead of them.

Meir came to the bridge and decided that it was time for action stations. He needed a convoy with a tanker to feed his ever-hungry engines and his ever-emptying fuel tanks.

"Ship at action stations." Mansdorf reported as he donned the gunnery command telephone harness.

Meir looked at the ships starting to appear over the horizon and to his disappointment, it was a whole flotilla of warships.

"We have a squadron of what looks like *DIDO* class cruisers and a *King George V* type of battleship coming our way. Port 20. Slow ahead together. Jezebel routine, but get as many layers of whatever you can find onto the after cargo deck, if we've got to reverse course and make a run for it, it will give us some protection from the incoming shells. Stand by mortar smoke grenades." Meir said tensely as he watched the several large warships coming towards him.

"We're about 20 kilometres ahead of them and to their starboard, but as yet the screen warships haven't seen us.

"If we can sneak past those new fangled weapons of theirs, then we're okay." Meir finished saying just as a lookout reported a cruiser that was probably their scout ship ahead of the screen, was coming full speed towards them and is flashing its signal lamp to them.

"He tells us to heave to, to be searched." The signalman said as he read the signal.

Meir slowed his ship right down for the warship to think he was stopping, before it too slowed right down and stopped.

Meir saw that there was a sea-boat ready to be launched from the ship but no heavy guns pointing towards them.

"Range to target is 2.5 kilometres. Set torpedo depth to 4 metres, so that we can get under her armour belt. Helmsman, turn your helm to starboard and keep the weigh on the ship as it almost stops. I'm going to fire a full broadside into them when we're at 1000 metres." Meir almost whispered to his bridge crew.

"Steady. Full ahead together, Port 20. 3, 2, 1... FIRE." Meir shouted.

The ship keeled right over in its delivery of the broadside as it fought to turn full circle.

The sudden punches of the close range guns and torpedoes were too powerful for the protective armament of the light cruiser, as each shell struck mortal blows to it.

Yet again Meir had another allied warship fighting to stay

The Black Rose

afloat, before it succumbed to its injuries and sank.

Meir was in the races again as the other warships in the screen came chasing after him.

He was able to dodge a few salvoes before the inevitable happened. In one large blast, Meir lost his after 105mm gun turret, and part of his after superstructure above the 150mm turret, as the other cruisers snapped at his heels with their bigger guns.

"Make a 2000 metre smoke screen across the stern. Start dropping mines when the smoke obscures us. String of 10 at 800 metre intervals. Helmsman zigzag 10 degrees off your base course. 3 minutes between alterations." Meir shouted over the howling noise of the incoming shells that were splashing way ahead of them.

"We've got the battleship on our tails too. That was his calling card." Meir said to Mansdorf.

"Helmsman. Every time a salvo lands to our port steer the opposite way and vice versa to starboard. They know we're in front of them, but the smoke is making them blind to shoot accurately."

"Ship coming towards us on our starboard quarter captain, about 7000 metres. She must have the new type of turbines to catch us up so quickly." Klinshoff reported.

Meir looked over to see for himself.

"She's steering a parallel course to us trying to keep us from land. Starboard 10. Tell the engine room to give me as much speed as he can. Take the governors off the engines if necessary, but I need more speed."

Meir had his ship directly in front of the flanker but slowed right down so that it would rush onto his torpedoes.

"Midships your helm. Steer 220. Stand by rear tubes. Fire when angles critical. X turret to engage when target re-emerges again." Meir said swiftly as he saw the bow of the cruiser starting to emerge out of the gassy smoke.

The Black Rose

Two torpedoes sped swiftly to its target and hit with a deafening thump, as the 6inch shells hammered into it at the same time, until it was seen as yet another stricken vessel.

"Full speed. Make revs for 40 knots." he said almost absentmindedly as he smiled with satisfaction that his tactics were working brilliantly and priceless in such a one sided contest.

"Islands ahead of us. It's the gap of the Magellan Straits captain!" Klinshoff said excitedly.

"They won't be able to crowd us now, we've got the central channel covered and they won't enter for fear of us mining it." He added.

"Well done Navigator, that's good thinking. Helmsman! Slow ahead make revs for 10 knots and stand by for a series of steering commands. We're about to dodge a raft of very solid islands ahead of us." Meir said as a shell landed right in front of them, making the ship raise itself out of the water. Meir looked at the bow through his binoculars and saw that his lovely bowsprit was shot clean off and his anchor was now hanging out of its fairing.

"That was the battleships parting shot. It will probably go around Tierra Del Fuego and the Cape Horn to catch us on the other side. We on the other hand will be docking in another place I happen to know." Meir laughed, which eased the tension on the bridge.

After several more hours dodging islands playing mouse to the destroyers that were coming way behind, Meir announced their arrival.

"Helmsman. Port 20. Steer 340. 3rd Mate! Get as much damage cleaned up and or screened with some of our Jezebel skirts. We'll be entering port in about 30 minutes.

Starboard 10. Steer 010. Tell the engine room to keep making smoke for another 5 minutes, the wind will keep it in their faces for a while, and long enough for us to disappear."

The Black Rose

Trewarthy was steering the ship like a racing driver through the chicanes of a racing track as the ship neared its shelter.

"Slow ahead together. Steer 025." Meir ordered as the ship sailed slowly into the sheltered Chilean harbour of Punto Arenas.

"Port 20. Full astern port, half ahead starboard." Meir rattled off his manoeuvring orders as the ship obeyed its master into a strange harbour. The ship appeared almost as if by magic as people stood and gawped at it, making its way along to an empty berth.

"Secure from action stations. Navigator, tell the wireless office to inform the base where we are. I need all supplies as of yesterday." Meir ordered as he donned Feldsbusch's best uniform jacket, hat and left the bridge to meet some aficionados waiting for him on the quay.

Meir stepped ashore to a warm welcome and a battery of photographers, as he introduced himself. He recognized an elderly man with a gold chain around his neck and winked at him as he leaned over and whispered in his ear.

The elderly man just nodded and contained his surprise, and commanded that everybody should now go to the local civic centre.

"Admiral. We saw the large column of smoke several hours ago, but we didn't realise it was coming our way until a fishing boat told us to expect you." The man announced.

Meir was welcomed as a hero and the darling of the people, whereas the nasty British were to stay away and not come near their port.

"As you know we are a neutral country just like Spain, and any merchant ships being harassed by whatever warship, would be welcome to stay as long as they wanted. The warships would have to leave and wait in the stormy icy waters of the Antarctic." the local Naval Liaison Officer announced as he saluted 'Admiral Feldsbusch'.

The Black Rose

* * *

This set the scene for a whole week as the ship was repaired and refuelled. The icing on Meir's cake was when he saw the wonderful sight of the *Becks Cove* come into harbour and tie up alongside the *Schleswig*.

The reunion was a wild party on board, with Meir's secret elderly patron beside him.

"Hans, it's good that you live, but I won't be able to help you much on account of your activities at sea, if the world press is to be believed. Here is my special card I give you in case you need it." he said with a whisper.

"Come with me dear friend. I have a small present for you that I forgot to give last time I came here with Uncle Heinz."

"Ah yes, dear Heinz!" the man said with reverence as he followed Meir up to his bridge cabin.

"Here this for you, happy anniversary dear friend!" Meir announced as he handed the man a small pouch.

"And this is in case you need it later. I've got a lot more secreted in various locations." Meir said as he handed the man one of his special gold bars.

The man opened the soft pouch and tipped out its contents, to find several large precious stones falling into his hand. He looked at it in amazement and then at Meir, as he took the special gold bar in his other hand.

"Hans! This is a Kaisers' wealth you've just handed me. I've never been so rich for such a long time now, I wouldn't know how to begin spending it all." He said in total astonishment. And gasped even more when Meir snapped open the gold bar.

Meir just chuckled and embraced the old man who stood there with a large smile on his face.

"This will buy me a lot of happiness enough to see me to my grave Hans! Thank you!" the man said gratefully, he put it all

The Black Rose

back into their containers again and stuffed them into his large pockets, as they made their way back to the party.

It was another four days before Meir was ready for another crack at the British, when a destroyer came into the harbour and tied up opposite the *Becks Cove*.

Meir saw the ship and because there was no public outburst or accusations coming his way, he deduced that his ship was not seen because the *Becks Cove* was hiding him.

He made emergency arrangements to get undocked and out to sea, whilst the local Naval Office kept the warship tied up alongside and with mountains of red tape to fill in whilst he made his escape.

Meir said goodbye to his old friend and to his old comrades still aboard the *Becks Cove* before he slipped out of harbour under the cover of darkness.

It was 2 weeks of glorious feasting and merriment that had been ruined by a sheer fluke of a chance call by the enemy.

He decided that the only way back to his Amazon base was via the long way round and through the Panama Canal. At least they'd have several days of lovely sunshine and good weather compared with the grumpy Atlantic they were used to.

The Black Rose

Chapter XX
Hands Up

The ship was on its 2nd day out of Punto Arenas, when again a lookout spotted several columns of smoke coming their way. Meir knew the local language and had the wireless office tune into the local radio, and was surprised to learn what those ships were doing coming towards him.

The incessant radio chatter stated it was a large battle fleet of American warships coming south and around the Cape Horn to their Eastern base, instead of going through the Panama Canal. But what he didn't know was that his photograph and that of his ship alongside in Punto Arenas, had been sent to the American Navy. He was identified not as Admiral Feldsbusch whom they captured some months ago in North Africa, but none other than the infamous Captain Hans Otto Von Meir.

Meir had his ship closed up at action stations as the first screen of warships approached. He took no notice of them nor did he take notice of the two cruisers behind that. It was the two biggest battleships he'd ever seen sailing behind them that made him sit up in his seat.

"If you thought the British has the biggest and most powerful fleet in the world. Take a look at that on the horizon." Meir whistled as he pointed ahead of him. Several men trained their glasses at the oncoming armada and started whistle at the size of them even at that distance.

"Aircraft approaching green 20, range approx 20 kilometres," came the signalman's voice.

Meir looked at the light aircraft and smiled.

"It must come from their battle cruisers or there's an aircraft carrier away to port somewhere." Meir answered.

"Okay then gentlemen. Say your prayers now as we'll be too busy later to do so.

The Black Rose

The only thing we can do is fight a rearguard action and head back into the islands again." Meir announced as a twin column of water appeared in front of the ship.

He saw that there were a few smaller ships coming like a pack towards him and fancied that he heard their shout of 'Tally ho' as he turned his ship around and raced full speed away from the pack.

He started to zigzag again and rolled several of the new type of mines in his wake as he laid a wide band of gas and smoke for the unsuspecting destroyers to race into.

His counter-attack or rearguard tactics were perfected during the last attack, so he waited until one of them was far ahead of the others.

He turned his ship around and raced through his smoke and caught the first by torpedoing it as he went close with less than 800 metres between them. He stopped the second one by overwhelming it with his firepower, before he turned around again and went after the warship on his starboard flank. He met it in thick gassy smoke and sank it before he emerged out into the clear blue sky again.

He found that the other screen destroyer was picking up survivors as the slower heavy cruisers started to open fire and bracket him with their salvoes.

"That gentlemen, means, Hands up or you're dead." Meir announced, but ordered more smoke and as much speed as the ship could give. He managed to dodge one set of guns but was hit on for'ard cargo deck where both his gun turrets were turned into twisted metal.

Meir waited until the nearest ship right behind him got as close as he dared before he launched his last stern torpedoes, his last salvo of 150mm shells, and as he sped away again he dropped his last mines.

It seemed ages before Meir's patience was awarded with an

almighty bang and a flash of light coming from the smoky area. He trained his binoculars to the other heavy cruiser and saw that it was zig-zagging thinking there were U-boats after it.

He turned around to look ahead and saw that the *Becks Cove* was steaming directly towards him with its funnel belching out thick black smoke tinged with yellow. It was the mustard gas and Zyklon B that it was sending out into the air and could kill several hundreds in seconds.

"Here comes the cavalry." Meir laughed as he told the signalman to tell it to turn around because of the American battleships *Mississippi* and *Colorado* coming their way.

Before the *Becks Cove* could reply to its friend, it seemed to leap out of the water, disintegrate and disappear as if by magic before Meir's very eyes.

"That was the 480mm guns of a battleship." he said angrily, as he looked up into the sky and saw the small plane circling around him.

"Shoot that fuckin' plane out of the sky. " Meir screamed at Mansdorf, who calmly relayed the order to the bofor guns.

The air around the plane turned black as puffs of shrapnel exploded around it. Meir took great delight in seeing it explode with perhaps a lucky shot and watched the pieces fall out of the sky anyway.

"That's their eyes poked out. Let's get back into harbour before they get another one up to look for us." Meir said sharply, as his ship re-entered the maze of islands and ran for cover again.

He managed to hear several more large bangs and explosions before he re-entered the harbour again. This time there was a destroyer lying across the harbour mouth as if to block his entry.

Meir fired his last forward torpedoes at it and blew the ship in half, before he sliced through the two sinking pieces. This piece of bravado was watched by several hundreds of people

275

The Black Rose

lining the harbour walls and wherever else they could get a view from.

Meir tied his very battered ship neatly alongside where he had it only a few days ago, much to the delight of the locals.

They loved the sight of a David and Goliath fight and always took the underdogs side, Meir's.

It only took a little while before one of the American battle cruisers stopped at the entrance of the harbour to block any further ship movements, especially the *Schlezwig*. And a further hour before an irate American Admiral arrived ashore demanding the local aficionados hand Meir and his ship over to them, else it would be blown to smithereens where it docked.

Meir had sunk or crippled 6 of his enemy warships for the loss of just one of his own, unarmed merchant ship. For that reason, the Americans were baying for his blood.

It was an international law of engagement between opposing factions had prevailed once more, and the battle cruiser was sent packing as violating a neutral country's territorial waters.

Meir was saved yet again by the rules of political protocol of a neutral nation.

Chapter XXI
Faces

Meir saw the crippled cruiser limp away and remembered the faces of his good friends and colleagues on the *Becks Cove*, but he did not have time to mourn the loss of his friends.

He was asked to attend a press conference, which was totally different to the last one. It was hostile and there were several people from the International Red Cross there, accusing him of butchery and other such crimes against humanity.

When the conference was over, the local naval man whom Meir was toasted and revered by, asked him to surrender his ship and for it to be interred for the rest of the war.

Meir in turn, asked for time to bury his dead and have his wounded to be seen to before anything else, which was agreed to. He also had his secret signal sent to Becks Bay and the Amazon Drum, but from the obscure answers received, told him that they too were captured or even destroyed, and that he had lost further good shipmates.

A week later, the local naval officer had the local police chief have Meir arrested on suspicion of murder and gassing innocent fishermen along the coast from the port.

Meir was taken away handcuffed and bundled into a lorry with his other officers and his crew.

Meir was *The Black Rose,* which meant that the ship was no more, and their daring deeds were bound to be told in the tales of local folklore.

For all the combined might of the Allied navies, not one of them was to achieve what a ream of red tape and a local policeman did. By finally catching and locking up the scourge of the Caribbean and the deadliest swashbuckling pirate of the modern world.

Trewarthy and his fellow prisoners were sent to hospital and treated for their wounds before they too were allowed to go free.

The Black Rose

During their stay, they told the judge at Meir's court hearing, all that went on whilst they were in captivity. They said that Meir should not be recognised as a genuine war hero such as Fieldmarshal Rommel, whom even the Allied forces had recognised as a true and gallant foe, but as a war criminal such as Himmler, Goebbels, Dr Mengele and their ilk.

As Trewarthy and the other erstwhile prisoners waited for the war to finish before they could go home, they were shocked to hear from the local radio station that someone had managed to free Meir from his captors and he had been spirited away to somewhere, nobody knew where.

Meir was reported to have escaped, using a large cache of gold he had somehow smuggled off his ship, but was re-apprehended in Valparaiso posing as a South African Sea Captain, several months later.

But even then they could not hold him and he managed to disappear and slip away from his captors yet again, just like he did with his ship at sea; in a cloud of smoke and over the horizon.

As for the ship? She was taken and impounded in Punto Arenas Naval dockyard for the remainder of the war, but was eventually salvaged and put up for auction.

But who would buy such an evil ship that had so much death and innocent blood spilt from its decks?

Trewarthy and some of his prisoner friends vowed to get even with Meir in their own way, if they ever had the chance, and even if it took the rest of their lives to do so.

For it was they that pointed the finger to Mier and his crew when they were being bundled into the back of a truck to be taken away as internee prisoners.

The local radio and a horde of journalists were around to take an abundance of photographs of these men. This was hailed as the second best local news of the world war that was

The Black Rose

raging around these 'neutrals' since the scuttling of a very famous German battleship some years earlier, allthough some several hundreds of miles further north.

But who will find Meir and finally bring him to justice?

The answer to that lies within the pages of '***A Fatal Encounter***'.

The Black Rose

About the Author

Frederick A Read was born in Norwich and raised in Northern Ireland, but has been living in South Wales for over thirty years. His first book – the collection *Moreland & Other Stories* – was received with acclaim throughout the United Kingdom.

He is a retired sub-mariner and ex-lecturer, and is married with two grown-up children.

The Black Rose is a continuation of, yet the prequel, to the epic *Adventures of John Grey* series, which comprises of:

A Fatal Encounter
The Black Rose
The Lost Legion
Fresh Water
Beach Party
Ice Mountains
Perfumed Dragons
The Repulse Bay
Silver Oak leaves
Future Homes

All published by www.guaranteedbooks.co.uk

The Lost Legion is due in November.